The
Wise
Women

ALSO BY GINA SORELL

Mothers and Other Strangers

The Wise Women

A Novel

Gina Sorell

HARPER LARGE PRINT

An Imprint of HarperCollinsPublishers

HarperCollins books may be purchased for educational, business, or sales promotional use. For information, please e-mail the Special Markets Department at SPsales@harpercollins.com.

FIRST HARPER LARGE PRINT EDITION

ISBN: 978-0-06-321168-1

Library of Congress Cataloging-in-Publication Data is available upon request.

22 23 24 25 26 LSC 10 9 8 7 6 5 4 3 2 1

For wise women everywhere.
And for Jeff and Grady, my beloved wise men.

The
Wise
Women

A Wise Woman knows that the biggest investment she can make in her marriage is her husband.

—WENDY WISE

Just make sure your husband isn't a liar.

—CLEMENTINE WISE

Who needs a husband?

—BARB WISE

One

Summer, Queens, New York, 2017

*N*othing says "I do" like real estate. Not diamonds, not a fancy white dress you'll wear only once, not a party that eats up all your savings in a single day. No, nothing says "I want a future with you" like owning a place together, and building your love one square foot at a time. Together a house becomes a home, and with it, the security that comes with knowing that you've invested in one another.

Just make sure you're there on the day the deal is done, or else you might be in for a nasty surprise, and whose fault would that be? Yours, dummy, that's who.

The old house was a sweatbox in the summer, the heat along with Clementine's frustration trapped inside. Clementine was waiting for Steve to get back from one of his endless brainstorming retreats—yet another one for the carbonated vegetable water idea that wouldn't die—so she could ask him why the man he'd promised to call about the ductless air-conditioning on the second floor had never showed up, and what's more, why Steve hadn't answered any of her texts. It was the third time the unit had broken down, and her patience had run out.

Clementine heard the screen door open and walked down the stairs as fast as she could, ready to have it out. But when she looked through the little lace curtain that covered the glass window on the door, she was shocked to see not Steve, but Mr. Gregoris, the house's former owner, standing in the sun and pressing the doorbell that no longer worked.

"Mr. Gregoris," she said, opening the door wide. "How are you? How's life in the Greek islands?"

"Well. Well. Thank you, Miss Clementine," he said as he stepped inside. "We are just back for a visit, my granddaughter's christening."

"Wow, another grandchild. Congratulations." Here it comes, she thought, the talk about children, plural.

"Yes, well you know it's good for kids, to have a sibling."

There it was. She was tired of having to explain that having only one child felt right for her, it's not like they were shoes, you didn't have to have a pair. But she knew he wouldn't let it go unless she gave him an answer he couldn't argue with, so she said, "Ah yes, well we're stopping at one. Better for the environment, carbon footprint and all that. At this rate we're probably gonna run out of water, so . . ."

"Climate change." His tone made it clear he wasn't a believer. But instead of having the same conversation they'd had so many times before, he handed her a small plate of cookies covered in icing sugar. "My wife made these for Jonah. She remembered how much he likes them."

The cookies were indeed a favorite of Jonah's; he'd bought nearly the entire plate of them from Mrs. Gregoris at a Christmas bazaar one year. Clementine knew he'd be thrilled to see them when he got home from YMCA day camp.

"You got the oven on?" Mr. Gregoris asked.

"No. The AC unit is broken." Clementine wondered if that's what he thought she did all day, stood and cooked. "Besides, cooking is Steve's job."

Mr. Gregoris started to frown. "Is he home?"

"No, not yet, soon. Why?" She wondered if he was back to collect something he'd hidden deep in the basement. So far they'd found an old photo album, some war medals belonging to his late relatives, and his grandmother's brooch. Steve had suggested to Mr. Gregoris that maybe a safety-deposit box would be a good idea.

"I should talk to him."

"You can talk to me."

"It's better I talk to your husband, Miss Clementine. It's about money."

She didn't think it was possible, but she felt herself get even hotter. She reminded herself that he wasn't trying to insult her—it was a cultural thing, a generational thing, a mind-numbingly frustrating thing.

He looked around the house and nodded appreciatively. "You've done a very good job keeping the place nice, Miss Clementine."

"Thank you," she said, choosing to rise above her indignation. "I love this house, you know that. And I'm so grateful to be living here." She meant it. In spite of their differences, she liked Mr. Gregoris and often wondered if he regretted the private sale he'd done with her, given he could have gotten so much more for it now. She was sure his greedy breeding children did, even though they'd had no desire to live in the less hip, less cool, family-friendly neighborhood of Sunnyside, Queens, and had settled in Brooklyn (Park Slope, of course) instead. The only thing they wanted from their father was for him to sell the house to someone who would overpay for a chance to do a gut reno on a home in the garden community. But Mr. Gregoris had no interest in having someone gut the first home he'd bought in America, the wedding present he'd given his new bride, Anastasia, who'd joined him five years after they'd gotten engaged in Athens. It was the place where they'd raised two beautiful children into the ungrateful spoiled adults they were today—too spoiled to appreciate the little house with crooked floors and a front hall light that flashed when the doorbell rang, and radiators that sang to one another in the winter, calling *you can do it* to each other from room to room as the house slowly heated up. He'd offered to do a private sale with Clementine and Steve after listening to Clementine talk endlessly about how much she'd love to own a house one day instead of renting the one-bedroom apartment he owned above his store.

For years Clementine had dreamed of being a homeowner, of having enough room for a home office for her fledgling marketing firm On Your Mark, and space for Jonah to grow and play. It had seemed impossible with the way the market was going, house prices rapidly rising, and multiple buyers bidding on places the day they went on sale. Clementine knew enough from her architect sister Barb, and her own work writing copy for a real estate development company, that the city showed no signs of slowing down. If she hadn't jumped at the chance to do a private sale with Mr. Gregoris, her dreams of home ownership might never have become a reality.

The house turned out to be everything Clementine had hoped. It was close enough to her sister Barb in Brooklyn and not too far from her mother in Manhattan. Yes, it was old, and the floors creaked so loudly that it was impossible to be heard if you walked and talked at the same time. But it had good bones and a strong foundation, and was part of the historic Sunnyside Gardens, the first planned urban community in America. Clementine's backyard not only backed on to a gorgeous common space that felt like a magical oasis, but it also had the community's only tree house—a deviation from the current bylaws that her neighbors overlooked, being fond of Jonah and his love of the little treetop home. Besides lending them the balance of the down payment, Barb had designed the tree house in the massive London plane tree to be the coolest any child had ever seen, with a rope swing and ladder that climbed through a series of lookout decks in the lower branches until it finally reached a little wooden house that was high enough to see across the block. It was where Jonah went every day after school and on the weekends, and if he'd been allowed to live there he would have moved right in.

With its beautiful parks, mom-and-pop shops, and terrific public schools, Sunnyside had seen the value of its homes increase at a dizzying rate. For once Clementine had been ahead of the curve; it had taken all of their savings, well, all of her savings if she was being honest, every single dollar she had, and some of Barb's, after Wendy had declined to help with the down payment in favor of her retirement portfolio. The fact that Clementine couldn't do it entirely on her own would only have given Steve more ammunition to say no, so she never told him. He'd been so against the idea, still in business school, and talking about using their money for his new start-up. But knowing that he didn't really have a say because he wasn't contributing financially, he'd had no choice but to go along. And in an effort to soothe his ego, Clementine recalled the words of her mother Wendy, the famed advice columnist of *Wise Words: It's okay to be the breadwinner as long as your husband thinks he's the bread baker*, and told Steve she thought it would be best if he handled the money from now on. "You've always been better with numbers than I have, and we'll need your business sense for a private sale." They'd invest in his business next time. This time they were doing what was best for Jonah.

Having more space, and not being on top of each other all the time, actually helped their marriage at first. With Jonah being in school they'd work in separate parts of the house, and meet in the kitchen for lunch or on the back deck, and talk about what they were doing. Occasionally, they'd even share a beer, and Clementine would listen as Steve told her about his idea to reinvent the whole sparkling water space, his excitement and desire for her to share in it, reminiscent of when they first met. He cared about what she thought of his ideas and wanted her to believe in them as much as he did, and she loved how much her opinion mattered. Sometimes, if Steve was having a particularly great day and she could spare the time, they'd sneak upstairs after lunch and make love, and afterward they'd lie together naked and Clementine would talk about all the things she wanted to do to the house when they could afford it, while Steve twirled his fingers through her long brown curls. For the first few months, she was almost giddy at the fact that she'd been able to pull it off and would often wander from room to room and marvel at her good fortune.

They had moved just in time for Jonah to start kindergarten at PS 150, the elementary school with Mr. Nettler, the fantastic kindergarten teacher she'd been told would be perfect for Jonah—the one his preschool teacher said "got" kids with different learning styles or exceptional abilities. Jonah's interest in things, be they dinosaurs, sharks, or understanding the meaning of a turn of phrase, could border on obsessive. Empathetic and deeply thoughtful, he was prone to perseverating over the tiniest of problems. He didn't like surprises, or too much noise, or people who didn't play by the rules. Clementine understood from speaking with a child therapist that not only was Jonah exceptionally bright with a big beautiful heart, but that he also had anxiety, and she did her best to help him manage it. But that was easier to do at home than it was in a classroom of six-year-olds.

So, when Jonah had some trouble fitting into first grade with the other kids, the school responded by suggesting he participate in a new pilot program they were starting in the fall that would be taught by Mr. Nettler. It was for exceptionally bright kids like Jonah, who they felt might benefit from a smaller classroom and student-led project-based learning. The school already had a gifted program and an arts program, and Clementine was hopeful that this new program would take hold and be just what Jonah needed, unlike Steve, who thought that she worried too much and that Jonah would be fine, wherever he went. Clementine didn't want "fine" for Jonah, she wanted the best.

"Miss Clementine . . . ," Mr. Gregoris said, interrupting her thoughts and motioning for her to sit while he slowly lowered himself into one of the chairs at the old pine table she'd painted bright white and yellow. "Is everything okay, with you and Mr. Steve? He and you, you're still together, yes?"

She was so startled by his question that she answered.

"Yes, yes, of course." It was hard to believe sometimes, but they were. "I mean we have our issues."

Those issues included Steve's decision not to send out résumés when he graduated from business school a year ago, in favor of chasing the dream of having his own start-up, a chase that often took him away from home to meet with investors and potential partners, leaving the burden of their mortgage and never-ending list of renovations, like new wiring and a new roof, on her. When Steve decided to go back to school, placing the financial load on her, she told herself that it was just until he graduated and was able to get a real job at a big company. Steve used to tease her that corporate language was her aphrodisiac. Salary, performance bonuses, health benefits, he'd whisper in her ear as they made love, his breath hot on her neck as they pushed their bodies closer together, until every grievance and resentment that she'd harbored melted away. And just as they were about to climax, he'd say, don't forget my big . . . pension . . . plan, and they'd laugh. Business school had taken two years. Two years of late nights and solo parenting, of thrift store outfits for her and hand-me-downs for Jonah, birthday parties held for free in Sunnyside Gardens Park, with homemade gifts, budget one-pot meals, and living off of her earnings, all while waiting for Steve to graduate, and now that he had, she was still waiting.

She wasn't about to say any of this to Mr. Gregoris, it wasn't any of his business. But there was something about the way he looked at her now, his eyes wide and sad, and how his hands gently patted hers as he waited for her to continue.

"Mr. Gregoris, is everything okay? Why do you want to see Steve? You can tell me. Please, tell me."

He reached up to the crucifix that always hung around his neck, held it, and took a deep breath. "Because his rent check bounced. Three months now, and my kids tell me that I should say no more chances and tell you to leave."

Clementine's ears were still replaying the word: *rent.* Rent check-what-check-who-was-renting-what? This house? He must be kidding. She owned this house. Why would she rent a house she owned?

Mr. Gregoris leaned back in his chair. Turns out she'd said all those things out loud.

"Miss Clementine?" asked Mr. Gregoris.

"I'm sorry, I don't understand," she said. It dawned on her that maybe he was confused—he was older now. She put her hand on top of his and spoke gently. "Mr. Gregoris, we used to rent the apartment above your store, but then we moved to this house and bought it from you. Remember?" She waited for him to catch up, but he looked at her like she was the one who wasn't making any sense.

"Ms. Clementine, I offered, but you didn't buy. Mr. Steve said you were going to keep renting because of his new business."

"What? No, we did a private sale, and you and Steve agreed to the price. I saw the paperwork, and I gave him the money for the down payment and he paid you . . . and the bank . . . and our mortgage . . . Oh my God, please tell me he . . ."

Panic was rising hard and fast in her body. She didn't need him to answer; it was all right there on his face. She could hear herself hyperventilating as Mr. Gregoris rushed to the kitchen to get her a glass of water.

No, Steve hadn't given him all her money. But how and why, and God it was hot, and the heat was wrapping around her and squeezing her tightly. And the next thing she knew the door was opening and Steve was walking in all tanned and relaxed and talking.

"Hey, babe, I know you're pissed, but there was no cell reception where we were. We can all go out to dinner tonight, my treat, and—"

Clementine watched his mouth flap open and his face turn white at the sight of Mr. Gregoris, who was shaking his head and cursing under his breath. Clementine bolted from her chair with her fists balled, but she got so dizzy from her sudden burst of energy that she tripped over her own feet and hit the floor. Shit. She hoped she didn't crack her head, she hoped it was all just a big misunderstanding; she hoped that she'd wake up and the house would be cool and Steve and Jonah would be there and everything would be all right. But as the room got dark and everything got quiet, the words of her mother rang in her ears.

Hope is what people who can't face reality do.

• • •

The first thing that Clementine noticed when she came to was the small pouch of belly protruding above her jean shorts. It had never returned to its prepregnancy shape after Jonah was born.

"Jonah," she whispered as she tugged her T-shirt down. What was she going to tell her son if they had to move? She waited for her eyes to focus and took a deep breath before sitting up slowly. She propped her back against the staircase, eyes settling on Steve, who was talking on the phone while staring out the window.

"Oh my God, she's all right, Barb," he said, turning around to face Clementine.

"Jonah . . ."

"Oh shit, Barb, we're not going to make it on time, can you pick up Jonah? Thanks." He walked over to her. "Don't worry, Barb's getting him," he said. "I was so worried, I didn't want to leave you. You really scared me." He held a bottle of water to her mouth and helped her take a sip. "Here, this will help."

Clementine gagged at the taste.

"Too much kale, I know. We haven't quite figured out the flavor balance yet. Not enough lemon, right?" Clementine's anger must have shown, because he waved the question away. "It's not important right now."

Clementine shook her head and started to stand. "How long was I out?"

"A few minutes."

"Mr. Gregoris still here?"

"No, I told him that I'd call him later to let him know how you were doing. How are you feeling?"

Clementine was relieved that he finally thought to ask but hesitated to respond, knowing the moment she did, he'd make a mental check mark and the conversation would turn back to him. She wondered how many people he'd texted in the time that she'd been out, to co-opt her experience as if it were his own. He was never going to change. She saw that so clearly now. *God, I should fall down and hit my head more often,* she thought.

"Why'd you do it?" she asked.

He shook his head in that way of his that said he had no idea what she was getting at and even if he did, it wasn't his fault. "Do what?"

"You know exactly what I'm talking about. Why did you betray me?" She walked over to the little wooden rocker by the window that she used to read to Jonah in, and calmly sat down.

"Look, Clementine, I don't know what Gregoris told you, but I really don't want to fight right now. I just had a great weekend, a real life-changing weekend. We've pulled the lid back on this whole vegetable water thing in such a major way, you have no idea, and I was excited to share that with you."

"I should've fainted at a better time?"

"No, no, of course not, that's not what I meant."

"Did you mean to steal from me?"

Steve looked at her stunned. He knelt before her, placing his hands on her shoulders. "I didn't steal, Clementine, I borrowed. I was going to pay you back. I *am* going to pay you back. It's all going to be worth it, because AquaVeg is going to be huge."

He leaned in and kissed her on the mouth, and when he pulled back, Clementine understood that he'd already crafted the story of his underdog success, and that her sacrifices were in no way a part of it. There was no apology coming, just as there'd be no thank-you. She sized him up, his wild eyes, the forced smile that dared her to call him out, and all the anger drained from her as her brain calmly told her what she needed to do next.

"Pack your things."

"Excuse me?"

"No. I won't. Not anymore. I've been making excuses for you long enough. Unless you can stand there and tell me that you didn't lie to me every day for *two years* by letting me believe that this house was ours, that you didn't risk everything we have, everything we've built, to fund AquaVeg—which is a terrible fucking name, by the way—then you should leave."

Steve's face reddened as he stood. "You'll thank me

when we're able to buy a house three times the price of this shithole."

Shithole. The house she loved, the house she'd worked so hard to get, their home, wasn't good enough for Steve? "Come on, you didn't do this for us. You did this for yourself. You've always thought of yourself first, and I've always gone along with it. Putting you through school, working double duty until you graduated, saying yes to every shitty job . . . no wonder you don't respect me enough to be honest."

"Of course I respect you."

"No, you don't. You don't cheat and lie to someone you respect, Steve. And if I trick myself into believing you really did this for us, then I don't deserve to be respected."

"I'm sorry you feel that way."

"That's not the same as sorry." She stood, picked up his overnight bag from where he'd dropped it at the front door, and put it on the porch. "I'll tell Jonah I got the dates wrong, and that you're not back for a few more days. You should go before he gets home."

"You're serious? You do understand what you're doing, right? You're breaking up our family."

Clementine opened her mouth to respond and then shut it. Normally she'd take the bait, tell Steve those words were pretty rich coming from him, but looking at him now, she knew that there was no point. Family wasn't just three people living under the same roof. It wasn't sporadic sex after months of sharing a platonic bed; it was putting each other first. It was putting *Jonah* first because more than anything, you wanted your child to have the best life possible.

She rubbed the back of her head and exhaled deeply. She'd imagined the end of their relationship many times, all the smart and enlightened things she'd say, and how amazing she'd look while doing it: her biceps glistening as she tossed her freshly blown-out hair over her shoulder then run toward the beach, its waves of victory crashing on the shore her anthem of freedom, never mind that she didn't have a personal trainer, run, or live anywhere near the ocean. None of those daydreams were anything like this moment, where she lifted her tank top to wipe the sweat off her forehead and caught Steve's grimace at the sight of her exposed stomach flab. Too angry to be hurt in that moment, she took her time lowering her shirt and then glanced at her watch.

"Tick-tock."

"Wow," he replied, dragging the word out. He picked up his bag, slung it over his shoulder, and turned to face her, anger twisting his features into disgust. "You're not the same person I married, you know that?"

"No, I'm not. But you are. You're exactly the same, and you're never going to change. That's why I have to," she said, and closed the door.

Two

Relationship problems, they're not just for
straight people.
— WENDY WISE, "WISE WORDS"

"Grab us a couple of those sweet blueberry pierogies too, kiddo, we can have them on the drive home," Barb told Jonah, handing him a fifty-dollar bill as she stepped away from the take-out counter at Tony's Pizza & Pierogies, to continue her call with Clementine. "You can tell me more when I get there," she said, and hung up.

She looked back at Jonah, standing on his toes to pay Tony, the owner, and felt her heart break. Poor kid had no idea what was going on, not that it mattered. When Barb was only ten, her and Clementine's own father had been sick for months before he died, and knowing he was ill hadn't made losing him any easier. Nor had seeing Wendy fight with her new husband prepared Barb for their bitter divorce and her mother's return to work, which made Barb, at age twelve, Clementine's main caregiver.

"That's some appetite you got there, Jonah," Tony said as he passed him two boxes of pizza and a container of sweet pierogies. "You must have a hollow leg."

"It's not just for me, Tony," Jonah said seriously. "It's for Aunt B and my mom. Besides, if I had a hollow leg, it wouldn't get full from eating, because food goes into your stomach."

"You're telling me!" Tony said and slapped his. "It's a good thing I've only got one."

"All humans have only one. Unlike cows, who have four, even though they only eat grass." For a moment they were all quiet until Tony laughed.

"You're a smart kid, you know that? Here, on the house," he said as he handed Jonah a bottle of Italian soda.

"Thanks, Tony," Barb said as she grabbed their food and headed out to the car with Jonah.

"I have your change," Jonah said, after slurping his soda, and held out a fistful of bills and coins.

"You know what, keep it—you can buy yourself something after camp tomorrow."

"Are you getting me tomorrow too?" Jonah asked, getting into the backseat and buckling up.

"If I'm lucky," Barb said.

She was already planning how she could move the next day's afternoon meeting on the likely chance that Clementine needed her to get Jonah. Or maybe she could get his bus to drop him off at her office. Either way, she knew it was better for Jonah to know. He'd already had one unplanned pickup. "I'd say it's a fifty-fifty chance, does that work for you?"

"That works," he answered.

She'd figure it out, she always did.

● ● ●

That night, as they ate pizza, Barb watched her sister pretend that Steve was still on a business trip. She felt like she was going to explode. She didn't know how Clementine could do it, act as if Steve hadn't just completely torpedoed her life, but at the same time she admired her for it. She remembered their own mother's oversharing with her about the reality of their financial situation when divorcing Ed, and how uncomfortable it made her.

"What a fucker," she said as soon as they finally had the living room to themselves again.

"Shhhhh," Clementine said, waving her hands at Barb as she snuck down the stairs in some carefully choreographed zigzag pattern that she said generated the least amount of noise. "He just fell asleep."

"Fucker," Barb repeated in an exaggerated whisper, offering up a huge glass of lemonade. Clementine gratefully took it as the two of them walked outside to the little deck overlooking the backyard that opened up onto the communal garden, Betsy on their heels. Settling into the old porch swing, they sipped their drinks.

"Wow. This isn't any ordinary lemonade," Clementine said.

"This isn't any ordinary day," Barb replied, the taste of vodka smoothing out her edges. She clinked her glass with Clementine's and took a big drink. "I never liked him, you know. So full of himself, so convinced that he was the smartest person in the room."

"Barb, don't. Too soon."

"Too late. I should've said something earlier. You just seemed so . . . settled."

She could never quite believe how quickly her sister had gotten together with Steve. Clementine had just started college and the next thing she was phoning Barb to tell her that she'd moved in with her boyfriend and was just so glad to have that whole part of her life settled. *Settled*—the word had never sat well with her.

"He always liked you, you know," Clementine said.

"He was scared of me, it's not the same thing. Look, I'm sorry you're hurting, but not that he's gone. Because he was a spoiled selfish prick and because he hurt you, and lied to you, and stole all your money." *Or my money,* she thought.

"AquaVeg . . ."

"Stupid fucking name."

"That's what I said." Laughter bubbled up in Clementine that quickly turned to tears. She heaved her body against Barb's side. "What have I done?"

The right thing, Barb thought. *The scary thing. What you should have done ages ago, and then maybe you wouldn't be in this mess.* "You stood up for yourself."

"But I'm not sure who I am without Steve," Clementine said, wiping her eyes with the back of her hand. "And he called this house a shithole."

"That's the least of his crimes."

"Not liking this house isn't exactly a crime."

"No, but theft and fraud are. You should call the police."

Clementine sat up straight. "Barb, I—gave him control of the money. He was the one who did the deal for the house, or so I thought, and I've let him handle all our finances ever since."

Barb took a deep breath, the way she always did when she was deciding whether or not to tell her sister exactly how she felt.

"What?" Clementine asked, getting defensive. "I thought it would make things better."

Barb held her tongue as Clementine looked away, her eyes refilling with tears when she spotted the little vegetable patch squeezed into the corner of the yard; it was unlikely Clementine would still be in the house when it came time to harvest the vegetables.

"It's all the money I had, Barb, and I thought it was growing. The house has practically doubled in value since we bought it. Or since I thought we had. Now I don't know if I'm even going to be able to come up with first and last month's rent on a new place, let alone pay you back."

Barb wanted to tell her sister that it was okay, that she didn't have to pay her back, but the truth was she needed the $150,000 she'd loaned her, and had just been waiting for property values to go up a little further before suggesting that Clementine take out a loan against the house and repay her. Barb had overextended herself with a side project renovating a couple of brownstones in her Brooklyn neighborhood. She shouldn't have taken it on, but for a moment she had thought that it could satisfy an itch she had long ignored, the chance to do something more sustainable, turning the beautiful buildings back into gorgeous triplexes, rather than let a single family or power couple merge the two homes into one giant mansion. The problem was that it was easier to just gut them and sell them as one enormous home. The day she'd put her firm's sign outside the brownstones, she was approached by several wealthy couples who expressed interest in purchasing them as a single-family home, and just like that she'd let her restoration project become another gut reno. It had taken all of her extra resources, and had turned into a major headache when she discovered that her neighbor had done a shitty renovation and routed all his plumbing and electrical services through their shared wall, taking up space that didn't belong to him and sealing it back up in a way that wasn't up to fire code. She'd threatened to sue if he didn't fix the issues and he'd called her bluff, landing them both in small claims court. Now she was behind schedule and carrying a mortgage on the two extra properties, her own home, and Jill's gym, all while trying to pay the exorbitant legal fees.

She took in Clementine's fine-boned features, so much like their mother's, whereas she was all her father—her face wide and strong—and bit her tongue. Looking at her sister's big hazel eyes rimmed in red, and her forehead creased with worry, she knew she couldn't tell her any of this, so instead she said, "You don't have a secret bank account? Or an old wallet stuffed with money tucked away in your closet just in case?"

"No, do you?"

"No. I should though. Jill does, she just doesn't think I know about it."

"That doesn't surprise me. No offense."

Barb wasn't offended. It wasn't that Jill loved her for her money, but Barb knew that Jill's love never would have found its way to Barb if Barb hadn't been rich.

"Did you learn nothing from Wendy?" Barb said. "A *Wise Woman* always has to have her own money."

"I had my own money!"

"But you gave it all to your deadbeat husband, so it doesn't really count. And all for what? So he could feel good about himself."

"I thought it would help our relationship," Clementine said sheepishly.

"How?"

"You know . . . *It's okay to be the breadwinner as long as your husband feels like he's the bread baker.*"

"Don't tell me that's a quote from Wendy."

"It is."

"Are you kidding me? You asked her?"

"Not exactly, I wrote to her. It was a while ago."

"Goddamn it, Clementine. Again?"

When they were kids, Barb discovered that Clementine had been writing in to their mother's column under a pseudonym. Wendy was not around enough, and it seemed to Clementine that the best way to get her mother's attention was to send her a letter seeking advice. After all, Wendy always had time for the women who sent her their problems, writing all of them back whether their questions were going to be published or not. She would share their stories with Barb and Clementine at the dinner table, as if regaling them with tales of her best friends. Sheila from Nebraska was frustrated that her husband wouldn't alternate family Christmases with his parents and hers, and wondered if she should just host two? *The best gift she could give herself was a happy husband, so surely it was worth it!* Diane from Oregon wondered if she was being foolish asking her fiancé to wait while she was a summer associate at a law firm across the country? *She wasn't, but she needed to be realistic, no man would wait forever!*

And then there had been the teenaged Tangerine, whose problems seemed to be remarkably like Clementine's. If no one asked her to the semiformal was it okay to ask a boy herself? *Only as a last resort. Better to have a friend tell the boy that you'll say yes, so he'll feel like he made the first move!* Tangerine wanted to leave New York City and go far away for college, but her mother wanted her to stay. What should she do? *New York City is the greatest city in the world, why leave?* It didn't take a genius to figure out that Tangerine was Clementine, and the first time Barb heard her mother say the name out loud, she nearly choked on her dinner. Surely Wendy would realize the painfully obvious, but all she would say was how wonderful it was that young women were reading the magazine and seeking her advice too.

"You should have been telling him to get a fucking job or get out," Barb said.

"I'm sorry, okay, I'm sorry," Clementine said a little too loudly, catching sight of her neighbor next door coming out of the little garden shed he used as an art studio. She gave a small friendly wave as if it to say "All good here, just talking," and lowered her voice. "I'll find a way to pay you back."

"It's not just the money. You did everything for him and he still did this to you and Jonah. What does that say for the rest of us who aren't even half as nice? What kind of payback will we get?"

"Barb, what's going on?" Clementine asked.

"Nothing, I'm just tired."

"Work?"

"Yeah, work . . . home . . . it's a lot right now, but I can handle it."

"Is everything okay with you and Jill?" Clementine asked, turning her body in the swing to face Barb.

"I don't know. We're still having some problems." Not that she or her girlfriend had admitted it to each other.

"What kind of problems?"

"Relationship problems. They're not just for straight couples," Barb said. "It's like Wendy used to say to me: 'In every relationship someone wears the pants—don't think that by dating a woman you can avoid that.'"

"Wow. More 'Wise Words.' Seems like we can't escape them."

Unlike her sister, Barb had never found any comfort in her mother's advice. If anything she felt excluded, as it was for a different kind of woman. Wendy's Wise Woman was hetero, old-fashioned, and placed way too much importance on what the man in her life wanted. Ironic, given how good Wendy was at putting herself first.

"Why is that?" Clementine mused.

"It's because our relationships are in trouble and she was the patron saint of failed marriages," Barb said.

"That's not fair."

"Didn't you ever read *Marry Wisely* and *Wise Wife*?"

"You forgot *Wise Up*," Clementine said.

"No, I didn't," Barb replied. One of the reasons that Barb could never forget her mother's advice was that she sometimes secretly read her old books, not for help, but to feel superior, to use it as a barometer of what not to do. She found it infuriating how Wendy, with all her fame and success, could still give advice to women about making sure that they put their husband's needs first, or at the very least, make them think that they were. Why couldn't a woman just own her success, ask for what she wanted, and be upfront about her needs? Why did she have to pretend to be less than, to make someone else feel better about themselves, in the hopes of then getting what she really wanted? It was so manipulative, and Barb had never been good at playing games. If she liked someone, they knew it, and if she wanted to have sex with them, she said so.

"I prefer to think of her as the patron saint of second chances," Clem said. "Sounds better."

"Sounds like Wendy. Careful."

"What?" Clementine asked, avoiding eye contact with Barb and draining the remains of her vodka lemonade.

"You know what. She's part of the reason you're in this mess, with her old-fashioned ideas about women and relationships, which I don't know if you've noticed, don't apply to her. So, *please*, do not go asking her for advice on how to get out of it, *Tangerine*."

"I won't," Clementine said, staring ahead.

Barb gave a little shudder. "Good. Because you know she has a habit of turning up at times like this. Whenever we talk too much about her she appears. It's like she senses it."

"Relax. She's doing some book club event at a resort in Boca, remember?"

"Oh." Now that Clem mentioned it, her mother had sent a message a couple weeks ago saying she was going on an extended tour. Clementine was better at staying in touch with Wendy, calling her every few weeks and making an effort to try and see her monthly, whereas Barb was content to save her visits for holidays and occasions like Jonah's birthday. Still, whenever Wendy left town, she made sure they knew where she'd be and what she was doing, which Clementine always said comforted her but made Barb feel like her mother was showing off. "She still dating that guy?"

Clem smiled. "Harvey?"

Barb rolled her eyes, remembering the one occasion they'd met for dinner in Manhattan for Wendy's birthday and Harvey had fawned over Wendy, offering to switch seats so she had a better view, ordering for her, and cautioning her about using too much salt. He'd begun every sentence with a gravelly voiced "we," as if they were one unit, and not two independent grown-ups.

"Poor guy, he'll never last. He should run while he still has the chance," Barb said.

Harvey was definitely too nice for Wendy. Her mother liked a challenge, men with careers who would see her as an equal but still shower her with admiration and take care of her. Wendy had never brought men home after the divorce, but she'd go out to dinner or the theater and let her dates pick her up at the door. The nice ones, the ones who were really interested in conversing with the girls, happy to wait while Wendy finished getting ready, those guys never lasted. According to Wendy, they were needy and lacked ambition. She wasn't interested in taking care of someone else anymore, she always said, but if there had been someone else around for Wendy to take care of, maybe Wendy would have also been around to take care of *her own children*. "Anyway, we should stop talking about her."

"She's an advice columnist, Barb, not a psychic," Clementine said, chewing her ice and heading back inside.

"She's a meddler," Barb said, following Clementine and accidentally slamming the screen door behind her.

Barb held her breath as they listened for Jonah. For a moment Barb thought she'd gotten lucky, but then she heard the sound of his door opening and his footsteps on the stairs.

"Mom, I heard a door slam. Is everything okay?" Jonah asked, standing in the dark living room in his now too-small pajamas, holding his one-eyed stuffed shark by its tail.

Clementine reached for Jonah and held him close, and looked like she was going to cry again. "Yes, baby, sorry, we were just—"

"We just got carried away, buddy," Barb said, interrupting and taking charge so her sister could keep it together. "I was remembering the time your mom laughed so hard, she pooped her pants. Did I ever tell you that one?"

"For real?"

"For real. Still makes me laugh. Come, I'll tell you all about it while Mom showers and gets ready for bed. She's had a long day. Sound good?"

She took Jonah's hand and walked him back upstairs, looking over her shoulder and winking at Clementine in that way that said *I've got this*, reassuring her sister just like she always had, even if this time she wasn't so sure.

● ● ●

By the time Barb got Jonah to sleep, Clem was out of the shower and dozing off on her bed. Barb had covered her with a blanket, and let herself out, locking the door behind her with the key Clem had given her in case of emergencies.

As she drove back to Brooklyn in her black Range Rover, Barb cursed the fact that she was always the one who made the trek to see Clem. To be fair, only eight miles separated them, but the one-way trip could still take forty minutes in traffic. Recently she'd read an article about a race between five people to see who could get from Brooklyn to Queens faster: a taxi, an Uber, a bike, a subway, or a motorized scooter. The motorized scooter won.

More than once she had marveled that the three Wise women had all stayed in New York, given some of their happiest memories had been made in Toronto before their dad had died. After all, they were dual citizens. A Michigan native, Dan had met Montréal-born Wendy when they were undergrads at McGill, and the added bonus of their union was the ability to live and work in both countries. But New York had meant a new life for Wendy after Dan's death, and Manhattan; a fresh start after her divorce from Ed. Wendy had remained in the midtown Manhattan apartment, although she might as well be a world away, given how infrequently they all saw each other. It was just as well, Barb thought as she drove through Greenpoint. If she'd learned anything over the years, it was that Wendy wasn't so good at ordinary life. Making dinner, doing laundry, and showing up for school recitals—those things were too mundane for the fabulous Wendy Wise. But a crisis was exciting; a crisis gave Wendy full permission to swoop in and save the day. But God forbid you didn't take her advice; you'd never hear the end of it.

Which is why she hadn't told her mother that she'd gotten back together with Jill. It wasn't that Barb couldn't use some mothering right now, it was that her own mother had never really been capable of providing it.

She pulled into her hard-won parking spot in front of her house. The home's exterior, with its multicolored brick and concrete, still looked like the old dye and tool shop it once was, causing people to pass it without a second glance, never knowing the beauty that lay inside. Jill had never understood why Barb had completely remodeled the interior but left the outside as it was, which probably said more about each of them than Barb cared to admit. She turned off the car and thought about the conversation she and Jill had the night before. They'd been talking about getting away in the fall, just the two of them, somewhere where they could reconnect and see each other clearly without the interruptions of daily life. It was their therapist's idea, the one they started seeing when they got back together.

Jill had been stuffing her clean laundry in the top drawer of her dresser, which held a collection of delicate thongs and lacy bra tops all heaped on top of one another like the bargain bin at Victoria's Secret. Although Barb got her own underwear in the mail—a fresh supply of tan cotton practicality ordered twice a year—she loved that Jill was into lingerie, and she knew every piece of overpriced delicately crafted swatch of fabric her girlfriend had. Which was why the single black pair of boy shorts peeking out from the bottom of the pile caught her eye. Size small, with a Calvin Klein waistband, they were the kind of underwear that women with slim hips and flat stomachs wore: sexy, a little masculine, and definitely not Jill's. Barb had watched as Jill, in the middle of a sentence, tucked them into the palm of her hand and to the back of the drawer out of sight.

And that's when it had all come back. All the pain and uncertainty Barb had felt since the worst Christmas she could ever remember.

It was the year before, after all their guests had left their holiday party and Barb had poured champagne because it seemed they both had something important to say, one of those no-you-go-first moments. She'd insisted that Jill be the first one to talk, and as she heard Jill say that maybe they should see other people while still seeing each other, she was thankful that she hadn't been first, the diamond engagement ring in its white silk pouch in her pocket suddenly awkward and hostile, its beauty tarnished by her own stupidity. How foolish to think that a bigger commitment was what Jill needed instead of a better and younger body to have sex with.

Barb drank her glass of champagne—pink Veuve Clicquot bought because the color reminded Jill of the cotton candy that she loved but never allowed herself to eat—while Jill poured out the monologue it was painfully clear she'd practiced. About how much she loved Barb and didn't want to lose her, but she was just so much younger and not ready to slow down, and it was only sex anyway and it wouldn't mean anything or change anything and in fact it might even be the thing that allowed them to stay together in the long run, which she really wanted, but lately it felt like they were two roommates, and she wasn't going to say anything because she didn't want to ruin their Christmas, but the lie was killing her and that's when she realized that maybe an open relationship was the answer for them as it was for their friends Denise and Karen.

And as she finished this long breathless emotional confession, wracked by ugly sobs, Barb understood that it wasn't just her desire for an open relationship that Jill was confessing, but the fact that she had cheated with Karen, as in Karen and Denise. Karen, whose name used to always go first when they said it, but now went second, as if doing so stressed just how unimportant she was. This person, this mutual friend of theirs, that Jill had fucked. A fact that Jill, when pressed, didn't deny.

"Could you please say something instead of just staring at me like that?" Jill had said, and in a voice so quiet she hardly knew to be hers Barb had replied, "Okay. I'll be back in an hour, and when I return, I want your slutty little ass and your pathetic possessions out of my sight."

That winter had been a blur of drinking with old friends, drinking with new friends she made at bars, and drinking by herself. Occasionally someone would mention Jill's name, as in Jill didn't know how good she had it, Jill would be sorry, Jill couldn't see a good thing when it was right in front of her, but these words, recited by younger more desperate versions of Jill as she left their beds after sex, did little to comfort her. Barb wasn't an idiot. She was easily the richest of her friends, often picking up the tab and fine with it. If she were being honest, she liked the power it gave her. Maybe if her mother had *had* more power early on, she wouldn't have decided the best way to fix things after their father died was to remarry so quickly it gave them no time to mourn. Because of that, Barb vowed she would never rely on anyone financially. And she hadn't.

She and Jill were different in every way imaginable, something the two of them had celebrated at first, Jill the fire to Barb's water, the spontaneity to her stability, the passion to her purpose. Barb used to joke that she made the money and Jill made the fun. An oversimplification, but true. But it was more than that—Jill was one of the first people that Barb had met who wanted to take care of her. She liked to cook for Barb, even though Barb preferred takeout and dining in restaurants (it's healthier), she encouraged her to exercise, even if she hated it (your body won't take care of itself), made her take time off work (you need to recharge), and planned romantic getaways (it's important to shake things up).

It was more than anyone had ever done for her,

and Barb had wanted to do something for Jill, seeing something more behind her carefully curated looks and tight little gym body. She wanted to help her. Jill's parents had kicked her out of the house when she came out on the eve of her prom, and they hadn't spoken to her since. It was the opposite of what Wendy had done, celebrating Barb "claiming her sexuality" at sixteen by throwing her an embarrassing party where she asked all her own lesbian friends to stand in a circle and tell the group the best things about loving women.

Barb knew that she had so much, and she wanted to give and share it all with Jill, who'd been grateful, taking Barb's advice and support and eventually money for her own gym. But gratitude wasn't the same as love.

There were calls and letters and a late-night knock on her door, and in a moment of weakness Barb had called Wendy and told her the whole thing. Having been on the receiving end of a cheating husband, Wendy told Barb to stay strong and ignore Jill. "A Wise Woman knows, if you let her get away with cheating once, she'll cheat again. And when she does, you'll have no one to blame but yourself."

In February Barb posted a bright orange FOR SALE sign on the door of Jill's gym. She saw no reason to back Jill's business if they weren't together. And then two weeks later, after Barb had a few drinks at a Valentine's

Day party held by mutual friends, Jill showed up looking gorgeous with feathered wings hooked around her
shoulders and wearing a little pink dress so tight it
looked like it was painted on, a dress that made Barb's
whole body pulse with heat. And after flirting with
everyone who stopped to fawn over her, her hands
sliding on their arms as they did, her breasts pressed
up against them as they talked, she caught Barb's eye,
aimed her arrow and pretended to shoot. "Gotcha," she
mouthed from across the room, and when Barb didn't
flinch or look away, Jill crossed the room and kissed
Barb fully on the mouth before pulling her into a bathroom where they screwed like it was the first and last
time. After that night, Barb took down the FOR SALE
sign and Jill never suggested opening up their relationship to others again.

For the first month the sex was hotter than ever,
but as it cooled, the monotony and reality of their old
routines, the frustration at their power imbalance, and
the restlessness that made Jill vibrate on high and put
Barb on alert returned.

Barb had told Jill that she was going to stay overnight at Clementine's, partly in the hopes that when
she returned she might find some evidence that would
take away this uncertainty, but as she walked inside,
she didn't know what exactly she was hoping to find:

lingerie strewn across the floor? Jill in the midst of a passionate affair? Instead, the apartment seemed all but empty—at least until she heard the sound of the shower and saw the path of wet footsteps that meant Jill had already leaped out to grab the exfoliating face wash and shaving cream she always forgot.

It had always amazed Barb that Jill could be such a slob, given that she spent so much time taking care of her body, meticulously grooming and buffing her skin until it was so smooth and bald it reminded Barb of the belly of a hairless cat. But today this carelessness could work in Barb's favor if it meant finding the answer to her suspicions, once and for all.

Keeping an ear out for the sound of the water turning off, Barb carefully pulled out Jill's dresser drawer and had just begun searching for the underwear she had seen the night before when she found something else. A lanyard with a badge that had Jill's name on it and an ID number, like the kind you'd wear at a conference. Barb turned it over, the words *Daring in Daytona!* staring back at her. She searched her mental calendar for any conversation they might have had where Jill mentioned Florida, but there was nothing. Had she been? Was she going? They'd been apart only two weekends in the last few months. Did Jill sneak off to Daytona on one of them?

She heard the shower door click open just in time to close the drawer and dart toward her closet at the end of the bed.

"Whoa," Jill said. "You startled me, I thought you were staying at your sister's."

"I was going to, but my meeting got moved to the morning and I didn't have a change of clothes," Barb replied. She decided not to tell Jill about Clementine and Steve just yet. She knew that talking about other people's relationship problems often led back to examining one's own, and after everything she'd just been through with Clementine, she didn't have the energy. She opened the closet to grab her pajamas, and turned her back to Jill to undress for bed.

Jill let out a wolf whistle. "You know, all your hard work is paying off," she said.

"I bet you say that to all your clients. Keeps them coming back and paying the big bucks." She ran her hands through her hair, damp at the roots, and cursed the perimenopausal flashes she'd begun to have lately. She hadn't told Jill about them yet, these hormonal announcements that broadcast the end of her fertility, which she'd never cared about, and the fact that she was officially getting old, which she did. She didn't need Jill to start fussing over her and giving her supplements to ease her symptoms. The whole idea made her cringe.

"You're not a client. Don't be mean, I'm trying to pay you a compliment."

Jill wrapped her arms around Barb, who stiffened as she kissed her suddenly sweaty neck. "Babe, you okay? You're sweating."

"I'm just hot, it was a long drive and I still need to prep for my meeting."

"Is this the one with Dominic?"

"Yeah," Barb said, pulling on a clean T-shirt. Dominic Provato was Barb's old friend from the Rhode Island School of Design, and the developer of the last two buildings she'd designed. Jill gently reached around her and held her close. She both loved and hated that Jill was paying attention to her, but she didn't want to feel close to her, not after seeing the little black shorts and the badge in her drawer.

"It's going to be okay. You have every right to ask for more money for this new project. You're the best in the business, and he knows it. You practically made him. Don't worry."

"I do worry," Barb said, turning around and holding Jill's hands. Worry that you're cheating on me again, worry that my mother was right and I have no one to blame but myself. Barb should just ask her, admit that she snooped. But she realized that what she was really hoping to find out was that Jill *hadn't* cheated on her. If she asked, and she had, then what? She took in Jill's still-young body, with parts that were still where she wanted them to be. Barb's body had never looked like Jill's, young or old, but still there was no denying that over ten years separated them. Before the affair, and before perimenopause, their age difference hadn't bothered her. But now everything was shifting, with sudden hormonal changes that showed up like unannounced houseguests, overstaying their welcome, ruining her sleep, and causing an all-consuming rage that grabbed Barb so tightly she wanted to smash everything in sight.

"I know you worry, but everything's going to be okay," Jill said.

"Is it? Are we going to be okay?"

"Now you're just starting to get morose," Jill said, avoiding the question. She kissed Barb tenderly. "Tomorrow you'll close a big deal, and when you get home, we'll celebrate. I'll even cook. Or better yet, I won't. We can get takeout and watch Netflix, and whatever it is we eat, we won't count it. Call it an extra cheat day."

Barb nodded as she slid under the covers, wondering just how many cheat days Jill had allowed herself lately.

Three

There's a fine line between meddling and mothering. A Wise Woman knows that it's every mother's right to cross it.
—WENDY WISE, "WISE WORDS"

Thousands of miles away in Boca Raton, in a gated community for active senior citizens, Wendy Wise's eye started to twitch in the middle of a self-guided meditation class. She'd had a hard enough time concentrating in the sun-drenched yoga studio as it was, surrounded by all the old people among whom she clearly did not number. Sitting on a folded Turkish towel, her back straight, neck long, forehead immovable in a way she hoped conveyed serenity rather than the effects of regular Botox, she placed her hand gently on her eye and tried to listen to her intuition.

The instructor had told them to *sit in their truth*, but the truth was that the man on her left had fallen asleep again, his mouth wide open in a snore, and he

was making it difficult for her to concentrate on anything other than wanting him to shut the hell up. But
Wendy wasn't here to judge—she was here to listen to
her own needs, because after decades of listening to the
needs of others, it was time to focus on herself. This is
what her third husband, Harvey, who sat on the mat
on the other side of her, mildly humming with each
exhale, had said when she'd come home from a meeting at the magazine and started whipping paperweights
from her desk against the wall. Her editor had told
her that they were no longer going to need her "Wise
Words" column for their print circulation, although she
was welcome to keep writing it, for free, for their online
publication.

Gently pressing her fingertips to her twitching eyelid,
she tried to decipher its Morse code. Something was up,
and it wasn't just the ire she felt at this pointless charade
at anger management. She had every right to be angry,
tossed aside after years of helping women around the
world. Her advice had not always, if ever, been politi-
cally correct, but she thought it had been timely and
effective and hugely popular for years, and hadn't that
been the point?

She should have known she was finished when her
editor had brought on that stupid consultant with her
data analytics on millennials and their views on rela-

tionships. The woman had determined that Wendy's column was not only dated, but also exclusionary, catering solely to women of a certain demographic. She'd spent twenty minutes looking up what each of the things she'd been accused of in that email meant, feeling stupid, angry, and old. She couldn't help it that she had grown up in a different era, one where only women wore skirts and men wore pants. It wasn't like she was against progress, she was just trying to keep up. And until that email she'd thought that she'd been doing a pretty good job. It hurt that someone born with the rights her generation had won said she wasn't a feminist. Maybe she was not feminist enough for today's standards, but surely she wasn't the only one.

"For God's sake, shut up!" she hissed at the man snoring next to her, drawing disapproving looks from both Harvey and the instructor. The latter was sitting at the front of the class, running a wooden baton across the edges of a prayer bowl and filling the room with a high-pitched hum that made Wendy want to scream.

Hadn't she done the best that she could? Three marriages and two children later, she thought so. Her daughters! That must be it—they needed her. There were a few things Wendy hadn't told her daughters yet, starting with her having actually married Harvey and ending with her being fired and moving to a retirement community in Florida. As she thought of them, her other eye began to twitch in confirmation. First there was that weird call from Steve a few weeks ago about an "exciting new investment opportunity," then Barb had rushed her off the phone just when she asked her if she had started dating again, and just last night she had missed a call from Clementine, who oddly hadn't left a voice mail. Something was up. They needed her and she needed to be needed, and what was wrong with that? Nothing, that's what. She would go to them, like any good mother would, and because, well, she could now. It wasn't as if she was needed at work or anywhere else. Besides, it would also give her a chance to check in on her apartment after her not-exactly-kosher subletter had left.

Wendy unfolded her legs from their Half Lotus pose, her knees protesting as she did, and willed herself to standing, one calcium-deficient joint at a time. Then she tucked her meditation pillow under her arm and headed for the exit at the back of the room, ignoring the sound of her instructor clearing her voice in an attempt to get her attention. *Oh for crying out loud,* thought Wendy, *suck a lozenge.*

"Wendy, where are you going?" asked Harvey, trying to catch up. "We're not finished yet. There's still the group relaxation and the lavender oil."

The lavender oil was Harvey's favorite part: a little oily x placed on each person's third eye when they all lay in Savasana—as if the meditation had somehow been too taxing and they needed a rest before getting up and moving on to their next leisure activity. Wendy thought the scent of the oil mixed with the instructor's favored sandalwood incense and Harvey's Old Spice deodorant made him smell like a roast chicken.

"Harvey, I gotta go, the girls need me," she said, not stopping as she pushed open the doors of the clubhouse and made her way along the crushed-gravel paths that snaked through carefully manicured grounds bursting with hibiscus bushes and palm trees, past the tennis courts, where couples in their white outfits and sun visors bickered about who booked the court first, even though there were lots of courts, and all day long to play on them. "You're retired, for crying out loud," Wendy muttered as she passed. "Where else do you need to be?"

At La Vida Boca, residents could play whenever they wanted and as often as they wanted. This was what Harvey loved about the place—you could golf and play tennis and swim and walk the grounds all day, and at night you could dine on the screened patio of the main restaurant and enjoy specially prepared meals that were low in sodium, fat, and flavor. If you needed someone to tend to your muscles or make your bed or get your medication refilled at the pharmacy, all you had to do was call the front desk and it would be taken care of.

But taking care of people had once been Wendy's job—first her girls, and then hundreds of thousands of women all over the world who looked to her for guidance—at least until she was rendered useless, her days robbed of their routine and purpose, her ambition left to idle. "You can retire now," her editor at the magazine had said brightly, as if Wendy had been asking them when she could. Retire from what? Her job? Her purpose? How was she suddenly supposed to be able to just stop being the person she was? She'd been so angry when the magazine had thrown her a little surprise party at lunch and the staff had dutifully shown up, some of them almost young enough to be her grandchildren. They'd scrolled on their phones while her editor read a list of Wendy's accomplishments over the last forty years. As her name got paired with more famous people and publications—*Vogue, Time* magazine, *Cosmopolitan, Life*—their eyes lifted from their little screens and settled on her with new appreciation, as if seeing her clearly for the first time. "Wow, I had no idea," some of them said to her as they returned to work, never mind that they could've just Googled her, but who wanted to Google the old forgotten woman who sat in the corner with the orchid on her desk and pictures in silver frames and still dressed up for work every day and didn't quite understand how her iPhone worked and had to keep asking the patient intern, Parker, for help.

The timing had been terrible, Harvey himself having just retired from his law firm. A widower with two grown children, Harvey had survived a triple bypass surgery six months before meeting Wendy through a blind date set up by their mutual hairdresser. He'd surprised her a few months into their relationship by asking her to marry him. They'd get to know each other while knowing that they were committed, he reasoned, giving them the added comfort of knowing that no one was going to leave easily. Because it shouldn't be so easy for people to leave, he believed, having stood by his first wife through sickness and health, for richer and poorer, for forty years. He also knew that when you knew, you knew, and he knew that Wendy was the one for him.

Wendy was stunned and flattered that anyone would think of her as both a bride and someone they wanted to spend the rest of what was left of their life with—as if that still mattered, as if there was more from life to be gained once you passed sixty-five, an idea she'd been getting the distinct feeling that the new management at work did not share. She knew it would be impulsive, not something someone her age should do. A Wise Woman would say thank you, she was flattered, but she needed more time to see if this was the real thing. And yet, walking the Chelsea High Line, lit up by the café lights that bubbled over patios onto the New York City streets below, Wendy chose to ignore her own advice and accept Harvey's proposal.

They had been engaged only a few weeks when Wendy was officially put out to pasture by *Women* magazine, now renamed *WMN*, with no vowels, because apparently vowels were old-fashioned and no one had time to sound them out anymore. Harvey had liked the idea of being a stay-at-home husband to a career woman, making dinner or at least plating what he'd had his housekeeper purchase from his favorite fine food shop. He liked to put on an apron, light the candles, and have everything ready when Wendy walked in the door. And even though Wendy wasn't nearly as busy as she let him think she was, she loved the way he told their story to friends, loved how he saw her as confident and successful, loved how he listened to her talk about the letters she received and the advice she'd given. He was a modern man and often joked that he should start his own column so other men could be lucky enough to fall in love all over again at the age of seventy-five.

But with her forced retirement, her confidence had turned to anger, and she became hard to live with. Suddenly she was judgmental of how easily Harvey could while away the day, reading, walking, or meeting friends for lunch to relive the glory days of their careers. She was resentful of the satisfaction he got from knowing he'd done all that he'd set out to. As the newlywed glow rapidly began to fade, the reality that their fast marriage may very well have been a mistake came sharply into focus . . . at least until Harvey came home one afternoon from a day at his health club with a brochure for La Vida Boca, a luxury resort-style retirement facility. Putting a positive spin on things, he reasoned that although their current situation was something neither of them had expected, now they could both retire properly. They needed to embrace the change that had been thrust upon them and make the most of their time. They needed a restart button. And with no reason not to say yes, and knowing that their nascent marriage depended on it, Wendy agreed.

She knew she was lucky. La Vida Boca was about as good as it gets for senior living, better really. All she had to do to be happy was give up her anger about being tossed aside and made to feel old and ridiculous and just *be* old and ridiculous. The problem was that changing locations didn't change the fact that Wendy didn't want more time for golf or yoga or crosswords. It wasn't downtime that fulfilled her, it was purpose.

"Did something happen?" Harvey asked as they arrived at their bungalow.

"That is what I need to find out. I have a feeling, and I always trust my feelings." She left out the part about feeling that her brain was turning to mush in Boca as she placed her thumb on the fingerprint entry, the resort having recently switched over from regular locks and keys. "This way you don't have to worry about losing them," a young woman said at the weekly tenants meeting in a voice normally reserved for infants, which was how she clearly saw them. But Wendy was worried; worried that she was morphing into some kind of helpless, mindless marshmallow. And her skin was so dry from all the sun that it was starting to feel like leather, no matter how much moisturizer she used.

"Why don't you just call the girls and ask them?" Harvey asked, trailing behind her.

"Because then they'll know I'm coming."

Wendy knew that the best way to approach her children was to surprise them. If she caught them with their guard down, they'd have less time to go through

the catalog of trespasses they felt that she'd committed against them and instead meet her in the present,
ready and willing to be mothered. When Jonah was
born, Clementine asked Wendy to call before showing up at the house to visit her grandson, but Wendy
had ignored her request. She believed that any new
mother would appreciate an extra pair of hands showing up out of the blue, and she'd been right. She was
greeted at the front door by an overwhelmed and
grateful Clementine, covered in spit-up and sobbing
from exhaustion. Or when Barb had trouble boosting
morale in her firm's early days, Wendy had stopped by
a morning meeting uninvited, arriving in full cheer-
leader mode armed with bagels and cream cheese to
lead everyone in making a company vision board. She
knew she couldn't turn back time, couldn't suddenly
reappear at the countless dance recitals and holiday
concerts that she'd had to work through when she was
trying to keep a roof over her girls' heads by getting
"Wise Words" off the ground, just as she couldn't ease
the burden that she'd placed on Barb with her absence.
But she hoped that her attention to her children now as
adults might tilt a little more in her favor the scorecard
she knew they kept.

"Well, you can't just jet off every time you think
they need you. They have to understand that it's not as

close as when you lived in New York. It's practically a whole day's travel now."

"They know that," Wendy said defensively, because, well, they didn't know that. She couldn't bear to tell her girls that she'd been put out to pasture and deemed irrelevant. Without the title of Wendy Wise, icon and advice columnist, she would just be Wendy their mother, a role in which she clearly hadn't been nearly as successful. Wendy's daughters had never really forgiven her for marrying Ed so quickly after their father died, and here she'd done the same thing; reached for the nearest lifeboat when her world capsized. This time, however, Wendy knew she couldn't say that she'd done it for them. She'd done it for herself, because she was terrified of being old and alone, her whole professional identity taken from her. It was impossible to admit that she'd married a man her girls had met only once and left her Manhattan apartment for a life of palm trees and planned activities, her secret safe with the doorman at her building, who had promised to alert her on the remote chance that one or both of her daughters happened to drop by. If they knew what she had done, they were likely to worry that she had lost her mind and might never take her advice again.

"I just don't like to see you like this," said Harvey,

carefully slipping off his Birkenstocks to pad across the dusty rose carpet of their rattan-filled condo. "You're all riled up, and I thought we decided that wasn't good for you."

"You decided," Wendy said under her breath as she entered their bedroom with its adjustable bed, opened her closet, and pulled out the overnight bag she kept packed and ready to go. *A Wise Woman is always prepared for spontaneity!* It was something her much younger self had encouraged young newlywed wives to do in preparation for when their hint-dropping about a romantic getaway proved fruitful. Nowadays women didn't need to drop hints about going away, they could just book a trip themselves, but the idea itself was still sound. A woman never knew when she might need to get up and go, and having a bag packed and ready made it that much easier. Besides, it was empowering and kind of sexy, and if Harvey would spend more time thinking about what fired her up rather than cooled her down, he'd notice she was actually flush, her skin hot to the touch despite the climate-controlled coolness of the room, and he'd reach for her and they'd make passionate love, aches, pains, creaky joints and all.

The idea excited her: a quick roll around before she jetted off. She turned to face him, shoulders back, breasts out, her toned body on full display in her yoga wear. "Harvey . . . ," she began, when she noticed that he was staring at her feet.

"I really wish you wouldn't wear your shoes in the house."

"Really? This place is cleaned every damn day, what does it matter?"

"It matters because it's not the first time we've talked about it, which makes me feel like you're not really hearing me, which hurts my feelings."

"Oh for God's sake," said Wendy, the heat draining from her body. "I have to go."

"There's that anger, again," said Harvey, his voice full of disappointment as she grabbed her bag and started to leave.

"Don't worry, Harvey, I'm taking it with me."

"You don't even have a ticket!"

"I'll buy one." She reached into her closet and pulled her iPad off the top shelf, where Harvey had tried to keep it out of her sight, in an effort to stop Wendy from checking in too often on *WMN* and its new advice columnist, who seemed to answer every question with a link to an article written by someone else. *That's not advice!* Wendy had screamed at the screen often enough that Harvey had decided that she needed an iPad intervention.

"Wendy don't. Don't leave like this. You're making a mistake!"

Maybe, thought Wendy, but she'd rather risk being wrong than spend another minute trying to undo who she was.

Four

*S*ometimes *life surprises you. An unexpected gift, a possibility, a door opening to a whole new world, just waiting for you to discover it. Welcome to The Point, in Greenpoint, a unique platinum eco-luxury condominium residence in the middle of the city. With wraparound terraces and a stadium-size year-round green roof, the great outdoors are just steps away for your exclusive enjoyment. The surprise? It's affordable. Starting at $999,000 for a one-bedroom, The Point is the answer to all your real estate desires. Be among the first to register, and receive a Majestic juicer, so you can squeeze the most out of life just like we'll squeeze you into less square footage for more money, trading livable space for rarefied air that no one can really own, but*

that at least lets you feel better about mortgaging your-
self to the maximum. Sucker.

Clementine dragged her finger across the trackpad
of her laptop, highlighting the last part and deleting it.
She knew she could never submit the copy she'd written, but it felt good to put it all out there, even it if was
temporary.

She checked her watch and swore to herself. She'd
meant to finish writing this last night, but then she'd
fallen asleep after her shower.

"Two-minute warning, Jonah," Clementine said,
continuing their incremental countdown to go, which
comforted her son. "The Uber is on its way, honey,"
Clementine called up the stairs, and he appeared at the
top, wearing an old Beatles T-shirt Steve had given
him. For years Jonah had been convinced that his
father meant the bugs and not the band when he referred to the group in conversation. She remembered
how she and Steve had tried to hide their amusement
at Jonah's disappointment that his dad wasn't as cool
as he thought. It was too small on him now, the shoulders pinched and the sides snugger than they should've
been.

"Hey, bud, I think it might be time to give that shirt
away."

"No, it's still good. Besides, it's my lucky shirt," Jonah said, trailing his favorite stuffie behind him.

"You sure you want to bring Samuel with you today?" Clementine couldn't help but smile every time she said the stuffed shark's name, which Jonah had specifically chosen to make him seem more approachable. According to her son, the world's fastest sea animal wasn't really interested in attacking humans and usually only did so when mistaking them for other marine life. And of course everyone would be terrified of sharks, Jonah reasoned, with names like Jaws. But Samuel was a nice name. You could even call him "Sammie" for short. It was friendly. It was all in the pitch, Clementine thought.

"I'm sure, Mom. He protects me."

Clementine's pulse quickened, her maternal instincts kicking in. "Do you need protecting at camp, honey?"

"It's good to be prepared. People are still scared of sharks."

Both of these things were true, but still Clementine worried as they walked out the door and were met by Mr. Gregoris standing on the front walk and holding a letter in his hand.

"Clementine, I was just coming to see you. Hello, Jonah."

"Hi, Mr. Gregoris, thank you for the cookies."

"Oh, you're welcome," he said and ruffled Jonah's hair. To Clementine, he asked, "Do you have a minute?"

"I'm sorry, I don't. I'm late for work and need to get Jonah to camp first. Can we talk . . . later?" She looked sideways at Jonah, hoping that Mr. Gregoris would understand her desire to leave him out of the conversation.

"I'm in a bit of a rush myself." He pulled out an envelope from his pocket and played with it nervously. "Maybe I can talk to Mr. Steve? He never called last night."

"He's not back yet, he's on a trip for his new company," Jonah interjected. "But when he gets back, we're all going to go out for burgers and ice cream. A veggie burger for me. I'm not eating cows right now. But I am still drinking milk," he said, this last point clearly troubling him, and the older man gently placed his hand on Jonah's shoulder like he understood his dilemma.

"It's okay," Mr. Gregoris told him.

"Yes, Steve needed to stay a little longer, but he'll be back soon. Would you like me to give that to him?" Clementine asked, trying to keep her voice sounding normal.

"Please. And sorry, I don't want to have to do this, but . . ."

"Then don't," Clementine said.

"Sorry for what?" Jonah asked, looking between them, as if suddenly realizing something else might be going on.

"For making us late," Clementine said.

"Oh. Don't worry, we won't be late, it's a ten-minute trip and we've got thirteen. Besides we're taking an Uber," said Jonah as a shiny Honda SUV pulled up.

As Jonah walked toward their car, Clementine looked at the letter Mr. Gregoris held and shook her head, tears filling her eyes. "Please. I can figure this out."

"I hope so, I really do. But just in case." He placed the letter in her palm and shook his head. "He should be ashamed of himself," he said.

"Clementine!"

The voice stopped Clementine cold, its friendliness bordering on psychotic. Kimberly. The head of PS 150's Parent Teacher Association and mom to a fellow soon-to-be second grader named Ethan, she was a real estate agent with four kids, two nannies, a housekeeper, a personal trainer, and total lack of awareness of her privilege. Kimberly was always exhausted, always busier than everyone else, always empathizing just long enough to seize the opportunity to talk about herself. Kimberly once told Clementine that they could live anywhere in the city but her husband had been born in Sunnyside, and they liked how this particular neighborhood *kept it real.*

If there was anything that could make this situation worse, this was it.

"Sorry, I'm not interrupting, am I?" Kimberly said, looking back and forth between them before sticking out her hand. "Kimberly Henderson, Sunnyside's number one Realtor for the last five years in a row, servicing Queens and Brooklyn, the better boroughs," she said all in one breath, now pulling out a card and handing it to Mr. Gregoris.

"Long name," Mr. Gregoris muttered, but he pocketed the card. "Have Mr. Steve call me," he said and walked away.

"Do you have a minute?" she said.

"I've got to go. I need to get Jonah to camp," she said, then turned her attention to the car and was horrified to see that Ethan had climbed in next to Jonah in the backseat. While Jonah counted Kimberly's son as a friend, Clementine wasn't convinced that a friend was someone who routinely teased you to the point of tears, or created impossible tests of friendship just so they could exclude you when you failed, and then welcome you back after you passed a series of challenges. At best, Ethan was a bully masquerading as a frenemy.

"This won't take long, I'm collecting signatures for

my petition." She handed Clementine a form and a pen to sign and waited.

"What's it for?"

"I'm looking to change the school rules for school zoning."

"What?"

"It's a huge problem. I have clients who want to buy in the area, but they're not guaranteed to get their kids into the school, because it's too full. Now you tell me, why should some renter be able to move into the neighborhood for kindergarten and then once their kid is enrolled, go and live somewhere cheaper, while the rest of us *homeowners* pay higher housing prices and property taxes to be here? Priority should be given to people like us, who actually own in the area, not for people who take advantage of the system and then move away."

"But those are the rules," Clementine said, her voice going up.

"Rules can be changed, if enough of us demand it," she said, tapping the form for Clementine to sign.

"Mom! We have to leave now, or we're going to be late," Jonah shouted from the car.

"I'm sorry I can't right now, we're late, but I'll call you," Clementine said, passing the form back.

"Ethan, get out of there," Kimberly said.

Clementine rushed to the car and saw Ethan give

Jonah a little punch before exiting. She fought the urge to say something to Kimberly, who in the past had waved off all behavior as "kids being kids" rather than kids being playground tyrants.

"That boy needs to keep his hands to himself," Clementine said, sitting in the backseat next to Jonah. She waited for him to say something, and when he didn't, she brushed his hair away from his forehead and asked gently, "Everything okay, honey?"

"Mom, it's fine, we were just joking around," Jonah said, hugging Samuel tightly.

"Well, I'm glad you won't have to deal with him next year." Clementine looked back through the rear-view window to see Kimberly knocking on the door of her neighbor, clipboard in hand, and tried not to panic. A petition? Kimberly was always petitioning for something: a better playground, pizza lunch once a week, a huge donation of new books to the library. She was relentless and had a way of wearing people down until they eventually just agreed with her to make her stop asking. When it was good for all the kids in the school, Clementine didn't mind, but this was different. This worried her. If she could just read the letter, she'd know just how worried she needed to be right now, but it would have to wait until she was alone.

"You have a very nice car," Jonah said to the driver

as he buckled himself in. He ran his hand along the soft leather seats of the car's lemon-scented interior, and nodded his head to the pop song that was playing on the radio.

"Thank you."

"Much cleaner than mine."

"You have a car?" the driver asked, talking loudly over the music and its pulsing dance beat.

"Not me, my parents," Jonah said in a way that indicated that this should be obvious. "My dad calls it the family car, even though he's the only one who drives it."

Clementine felt her cheeks flush as she caught sight of the young Uber driver smiling at her in the rearview mirror.

"You don't drive?" the driver asked her.

"It's just . . . could you please turn the music down? I can't hear myself think." She cringed as she said it, hating how old it made her sound. She continued, turning to Jonah, "It's just that your dad normally does all the driving."

"But why don't you know *how* to drive?" Jonah asked.

"Because I've always lived in the city. I either just walked everywhere or took the subway, so I never learned."

"You never even took lessons?"

"No, and then I met your dad and he liked to do all the driving so I just let him." *And that's been the problem all along. That's why I'm now in this terrible mess, Jonah. Because I gave all my power away to make someone else feel good about himself.* She looked at the letter, wondering how much time she had left in the house, and stuffed it in her purse.

Jonah was watching her, silent, a furrowed line between his brows.

"Besides, sweetie, I prefer to take public transit. It's better for the environment."

"This isn't public, Mom."

"Well *this*," Clementine said, putting extra cheer in her voice, "is because we're running a bit late and I don't want you to miss any of the fun at camp today."

"Have you ever been to camp?"

"No, I went to Camp Wendy, where we ripped the subscription inserts out of all her magazines or weeded the garden." Clementine had longed to go to camp, originally just to get away from the sadness that had followed her mom around after her dad died. In those early days, Wendy had wandered around their new stepdad's house in a fog, doing her best to hold it together, which often meant depositing her and Barb somewhere with orders to carry out some mundane chore so she could lie down. And then after the divorce from Ed and the move to the city, there was no extra money and no garden, so Clementine and Barb would have to entertain themselves and make their own fun at the park or the library.

"Then how do you know it's fun?" Jonah said.

"Up here at the left?" the Uber driver asked.

"Yes," she replied. "Jonah, is something going on at camp that you're not telling me?" She knew that she couldn't fight every battle for her son, that all she could do was ask and hope that he would tell her.

"It's fine, Mom. This is it. This is the entrance. Mom, there's Seth."

Jonah adored Seth, the elementary school teacher who also ran the Long Island City YMCA Summer Camp and had become a fast friend of Jonah's, thanks to their mutual adoration of sharks, and only-child status. It helped that Seth was a patient listener who took all of Jonah's musings seriously.

Jonah called out the window to get Seth's attention and waved the shark back and forth, and for a moment Clementine thought she saw some of the older boys snicker, but then it looked like they might be laughing at something else. Surely they were. They probably weren't even in Jonah's group.

"Wait, give me a kiss, kiddo. And have a great day, okay?"

"Okay," he said, as if seriously considering the magnitude of this task.

"I love you, Jonah." She took his face in her hands and gently kissed the crease between his eyebrows.

"I know."

"I mean it."

"I knoooow. Can I please go now?" He opened the door without waiting for an answer, his face brightening at the sight of Seth waving him over.

"Hey, Clementine!" Seth called.

Clementine waved back and then turned to Jonah. "I'll see you back here at the end of the day."

"Got it!" Jonah yelled over his shoulder.

She watched as Seth took the shark and cuddled it like a baby, making Jonah laugh. She could take worrying about how Jonah was adjusting to camp off the table for the moment and let another worry take its place: the contents of the letter in her bag.

"Next stop, North Sixth Street, right?" the driver asked, checking the ride details on his phone.

"Please."

She reached into her purse and pulled out the envelope. She tore it open, her eyes skimming past the apologies for having to do this, past the kind words for how much he knew Clementine and Jonah loved the house, past the middle where he expressed shock and anger about how this could've happened, to the end where she knew the bad news was waiting: that he had no choice, that his children insisted, that he needed to fully retire, and that this was their official two-month notice and that the house would be listed in two weeks—meaning that Clementine would need to find a place. Finding a place to rent before September wasn't going to be easy, given the low vacancy rate and skyrocketing rental prices. She might have to move out of Sunnyside, she knew, but the idea of uprooting Jonah made her sick.

The year had been hard enough, with Steve spending so much time away trying to get AquaVeg off the ground, never mind that she'd now have to tell Jonah that she and Steve were taking time apart. Moving would only make things worse for him. He loved the neighborhood and his tree house, and the friends he'd finally made who lived across the garden, and playing bocce ball in the summer once a week with the old folks in Sunnyside Gardens Park, and the owner of the convenience store, who always took the time to listen to him and let him take a free saltwater taffy. It wasn't easy for him to get comfortable, but he'd worked so hard, and had done it. They could walk to his school in fifteen minutes, and Clementine could get to work in thirty. It was important that she keep her commute manageable, especially if she was going to be the one doing all the drop-offs and pickups, without a car. She thought about the school's pilot program, and how Jonah was actually looking forward to it. But if they had to move out of the area, and Kimberly got her way, then what?

She rolled down the window for some air, her head buzzing, and clutched Mr. Gregoris's letter, her fingers turning white and her mind racing. She needed to come up with a plan to keep him from selling, or to sell to her privately, for real this time. Even if she could find the money, a cash sale would be out of the question now; she'd need a mortgage, and who knew if she'd even qualify? If she could find a way to finance finishing the basement to rent out, then maybe she could offset the mortgage, or even let out an extra room for an exchange student. That might get her an extra fifteen hundred a month. It could work out, it had to work out, she told herself over and over. But would it? She just needed Mr. Gregoris to give her a chance to sort things out. But he'd given her a chance once before, because she'd promised to take care of the house he loved, and she'd blown it. He didn't have to do it again.

"Here you go," the driver said, pulling up outside of Pinnacle's offices, the marketing firm owned by Barb's good friend Rishi. She exited the car, and marched into the building all flustered and blotchy, the shock of air-conditioning making the hairs on her arm stand up. She stood still for a moment and closed her eyes, the cool air calming her down. She could fix this. She was a grown-up, a mother, and a breadwinner; she would find out where the money went and tell Steve to get it back. But first she needed to make her deadline. The last thing she needed was to lose a job that Barb had gotten for her.

Five

Every woman makes compromises.
A Wise Woman makes deals.
—WENDY WISE, *WISE UP*

"Isn't there something else?" Barb asked, standing in the dimly lit hallway outside the ladies' room of Hook & Crook, Greenpoint's latest bistro. She pressed her free hand to her ear to drown out the music blaring from the bathroom every time the door opened. It was a restroom, for crying out loud, not a nightclub.

She'd excused herself to take the call, leaving Dominic alone at their table nursing his Al Capone, all of the restaurant's cocktails having been named after Prohibition-era gangsters.

"We don't have any more copy to write beyond the initial marketing campaign. She's done a great job, but after this, I don't have anything else for her."

"What about sales? I know that you still need someone there." Barb heard the long pause on the other end of the phone. She hated to put Rishi in the position of having to give her sister another job, especially one that she wasn't actually qualified for, but Clem had Jonah to take care of, and who knew what her legal fees would look like with the divorce and everything else. Barb had recommended Rishi to Dominic years earlier, and her endorsement had translated into two huge jobs for Rishi's firm and garnered him a lot of positive attention. If ever there was a time to call in a favor, this was it. "She's having trouble with Steve and could really use another gig. It's a lot to ask, but I think she'd be great."

"What about Dominic?"

"I'm meeting with him right now. I can't really say anything yet, but it's about his next project and putting the team together." And if you help me, I'll help you. She didn't need to say it, Rishi knew.

"That's great." His tone shifted from burdened to helpful. "I'll give it a try. But if there's any pushback . . ."

"Of course—you have to do what's best. Thanks. Now I better go, before Dominic decides he's waited too long and makes me pay for lunch."

● ● ●

As Barb walked back to their table Dominic was swirling the ice in his glass, frowning with his whole face. She knew that look well enough to know that whatever he wanted wasn't good. The head of one of the biggest real estate development firms in Brooklyn, Dominic was a friend from RISD who'd taken over his ailing father's family business shortly after graduating. At first no one took him seriously, given that he'd spent little more than a few summers in his father's offices. It hardly seemed a natural fit, and many wondered if Dominic Senior, known for his relentless work ethic and tenacity, had gone soft and sentimental by handing over the reins to his son rather than letting his power-hungry partners buy him out. Some of the other architects had refused to deal with Dominic Jr., overquoting him when they did, trying to send the message that he didn't know what he was doing and should let his dad's colleagues step in. Step aside, sit down, wait your turn—it's exactly what Barb had heard over and over as one of the few women bidding on big condo developments. This was a man's job. Or in Dominic's case, an old man's job, something the two of them had bitched about at the dive bar that had once occupied the building where they now ate overpriced lunch.

"Sorry about that. Client emergency. Residential. You know how they are." She slid onto the leather seat of the semicircle booth that faced out onto the restaurant; all stripped wood and wrought iron with worn mercury glass panels along the wall reflecting the light from the Edison bulbs that hung on cables from the ceiling. It was a look she was tired of.

"I didn't think you had time for that anymore."

"I take on the odd commission, just for fun. Now where were we?"

"What I was trying to say was, it's not that I don't think you're worth it. It's just that the margins are even tighter on this one, so I was hoping that you could scale back your fee a bit."

"I see," Barb said, stabbing at her panko-battered fish sandwich wrapped in edible rice paper that had been printed with squid ink to look like newsprint. With its artisanal cocktails and fancy fish and chips, the restaurant had become a hub for those who worked on this strip of Greenpoint where Barb had planted her offices fifteen years ago, before anyone thought to look at the area twice. Back when warehouses and knitting factories lined the waterfront, and people who'd left Manhattan were already starting to feel squeezed out of neighborhoods like Williamsburg. Barb had loved the grittier feel of the area, with its Polish restaurants, bodegas, and views of Manhattan across the water. Her first big expense had been redoing the entrance to her building, installing a double-wide iron-and-glass door with her firm's name—*Mission Statement*—etched in Lotte. She'd chosen the female-designed font with its clear lines and strong lettering out of solidarity with her own underrepresentation in her field. MISSION STATEMENT: one word on each door, the first etched in glass, the second colored in copper leafing. One half of her firm would be dedicated to architecture, the other to interior design.

"Dominic, your margins are tighter because it's your third building in an area that has become more expensive due to the popularity of your first two—which I designed for you. So please don't punish me for being good at my job." She took a big sip of her nonalcoholic ginger beer—alcohol was making her sweat more these days—and winced. She wanted a real drink.

"Whoa, nobody's punishing anyone. That's not what this is about. And of course I remember. I remember that we took a chance on each other when no one else would, and look at us now."

He held open his hands, inviting her to check him out. His Patek Philippe watch peeked out from under the cuffs of his custom shirt. She did a quick calculation in her head: his Tom Ford blazer, AG jeans, Prada shoes, and Louis Vuitton messenger bag easily added up to another ten thousand. Altogether he was wearing over a hundred thousand dollars in upgrades, as developers liked to say, while sitting before her and asking her for a break.

"We've come a long way from two-dollar beers and warm tequila shots," he continued. "Can't say I miss those days."

But Barb did. She missed being able to wander along the sidewalk without bumping into people, the warehouses that doubled as artist studios, the empty sections of waterfront where she could walk alone, before she and Dominic and a host of other developers built them up. There were times she'd go into a restaurant and she'd be the only one there apart from the owners, and be able to sit and eat and talk to them for hours. Back then Barb was an outsider, a woman in a man's world who thought she knew better. Everywhere felt so crowded now, so overpriced, so precious, people were getting less of everything, and expected to pay more, and it was completely unsustainable. *Sustainable.* There was that word again, popping into her head like that nagging feeling you get when you run into an old friend that you promise to make plans with but never call.

After finishing her architecture degree, Barb had traveled across Canada and the United States with the goal of visiting and studying as many cities as she could. While her friends got entry-level jobs in big firms, she'd lived out of a remodeled van. Losing her father young had taught her to embrace life as it came and welcome the experiences of the moment, knowing that the ones we love don't stay just because we want them to—some actual wise words that her mother had given her soon after her dad died.

Her dad would've been proud of her now. As he'd told her once while sitting on the living room rug after dinner, building rainbow-colored LEGO towers, he'd wanted to be an architect when he was little. When she asked him what made him change his mind, he said that he'd gotten offered a good job right after school, but that he thought that one day, maybe when Barb and Clementine were older, he'd go back to school and give it a try. Barb remembered the smell of his after-shave, like fresh-cut grass, as she wrapped her arms around his neck and told him that if he waited, they could go together. "Sounds like a plan, B.B.," he'd said, laughing as he pulled her in for a hug. B.B., short for Barbara. She still missed hearing him say it.

Eventually she'd returned to New York, choosing Williamsburg in Brooklyn to call home. She was hungry to shape the city in ways that engaged people with their public spaces, rehabbing old forgotten corners into hidden treasures until she'd unwittingly become part of the gentrification wave herself, and had moved to

Greenpoint, where it felt like she was dangerously close to repeating the same cycle all over again.

She watched Dominic raise his glass to the waitress to get another, his self-satisfaction big enough for the two of them.

"I can't," Barb said when he turned back to look at her. It was too much; this overpriced restaurant, Jill, Rishi, Clementine. She'd given to everyone, a personal ATM who spat out fifties and picked up the tabs and paid the bills of all those around her. She'd overextended herself, lending money to Clementine, letting Jill redo the gym again, purchasing and renovating the brownstones, floating Rishi when his clients were late to pay, even though she herself was owed hundreds of thousands of dollars in receivables from her own clients. For the first time since she opened her doors, Barb was in danger of having to close them. She needed to do this next project with Dominic, whether she felt like designing another slick, overpriced lifestyle residence on the water or not, and she needed to do it for her full fee.

"Barb, try to understand, the city's killing us with new taxes and fees every year, and that community space we agreed to isn't helping my profit margins."

It had been Barb's idea to turn the main floor of The Point into an art space with a rotating studio residency where artists would work and agree to have their studios open to the public two days a week. They'd share the large main floor with a high-end commissary that would host a monthly cooking school for at-risk youth who would sell the food they made to local residents, with all proceeds going back into youth job training. It had been nearly impossible to pull off, and Barb had devoted hundreds of unpaid hours to making it a reality, proud that she'd actually found a way to do good while still doing good business. Her determination to prove that it was possible for the old and new to coexist and still turn a profit was as much about appeasing her increasingly guilty conscience about gentrifying the neighborhood, as it was about appeasing the people who already lived there.

"The kitchen and art space were the only way to get the neighborhood to approve of the building," Barb reminded him.

"I didn't need their approval. You wanted that. And you got it, but now I want something."

"I understand, and I know that you're just trying to do what's best for your business, so I trust that you'll know I'm just trying to do what's best for mine. I won't scale back my fee, because I should've increased it, given how quickly the units we designed in your last building sold. But if that isn't enough for you, then I have no doubt that there is some younger, hipper, less-accomplished firm that would be happy to take your business and blow past your deadlines, and file your permits incorrectly, and hand you off to some associate, and the next write-up you receive in the paper can be about how you cut corners on this one and it shows. And when that happens it won't be my name on the building, it'll be yours."

Dominic put his drink down, the look on his face revealing that he'd clearly never expected her to say no. "I can't believe that you're taking this so personally. It's just business, Barb. You know as well as I do how expensive it's gotten to build in this city. It's not like it was. Nothing is. I had to buy out all my dad's old partners after he died, I've got hundreds of people depending on me, two kids in private school and on hockey teams." He ran his fingers through his hair and leaned forward, pleading, "I'm bleeding money."

"You should never have taught them to skate," Barb said, softening slightly as Dominic slumped forward and folded his hands under his chin. He still looked too young to be a father of teenagers, though she knew he wasn't. It was a sign that she was getting older, that she was sure all of them still looked as young as they once did, something a glance in the mirror quickly proved to be untrue.

"Tell me about it," Dominic said, looking down at his plate. "All I'm saying is that you're not the only one getting squeezed. I'm getting undercut by other developers who are willing to pay their people less and put up shitty condos all over the city that are going to start falling apart in five or ten years."

Condo Catastrophe. It's what they both called it, seeing the tall glass buildings that now littered the waterfront, facing Manhattan, each one fighting for its own little scrap of sky before another one was erected in its face. Barb didn't know what was worse, the glass behemoths or the tall narrow buildings that were squeezed in between older brownstones. The cranes that Barb used to love seeing, signs that the city was doing well, now seemed like little black-and-orange vultures picking away at the remaining land until there was nothing left.

"I'll think about it," Barb said, a wave of sadness washing over her. Hormones? Nostalgia? She wasn't sure.

"And there's something else . . . I'd like to use someone other than Rishi for the sales team. He's a great guy and he's done terrific work for us in the past, but I think we could use some fresh faces."

"Jesus, this isn't a lunch, it's a revolt against age and loyalty," Barb said, her emotional tide gathering.

If Rishi didn't get the contract then there was no way that he'd be able to help Clementine. Was it so impossible for her to rely on someone else for a change? After everything she and Dominic had been through to get to where they were, she couldn't believe that he wanted to rock the boat now. She waved to the waitress and pointed at Dominic's drink, requesting one for herself. She was sweating already; she might as well have the alcohol. She needed it.

"Come on, it isn't like that," said Dominic, looking around uncomfortably.

"Oh no? *Fresh* isn't just one of those words that you throw around a lot when what you really mean to say is *young*?"

"I'm just trying to shake things up."

"You do know that surrounding yourself with young people doesn't actually make you young again, right? That's not how it works." She took the drink from the waitress, who appeared and left as quickly as she could, and took a large gulp.

"What's going on with you? Why are you taking this all so personally?"

"Because you've made it personal. Because if something is good, you should be grateful instead of looking for ways to fuck things up just because you're bored. We all get old, we all get tired, we all think woulda coulda shoulda about the choices we made, but sometimes you just have to know that things are actually fine and maybe you don't need to screw it all up just to find out how good you really had it!"

Dominic leaned back and looked at Barb for what felt like a long time before he said anything. "Everything okay at home? With you and Jill?"

Barb wiped her forehead with her napkin and lied. "I'm not talking about me. It's Clementine."

She felt bad the moment she said it. Dominic had always had a thing for her younger sister, ever since the first time he'd met her. But even then Barb had known that there was no way that Dominic would ever settle down with a girl who wasn't connected to him in some way, a friend of a friend who had an aunt that was a distant relative who came from the same town in Italy as his mother. He had one of those massive Italian families that came with a ton of unspoken expectations, a family that seemed to spend every weekend together either at a communion, christening, wedding, or funeral. Her sister was just starting to find her feet, and Barb had wanted to protect her. She didn't want her settling for the first guy who came along. Didn't want her believing Wendy's bullshit that what every woman needs is a good husband, except of course Wendy herself, who liked to say that she'd already had two, and now needed to focus on her career. But then her sister met Steve, and what Barb wanted for Clementine didn't really matter. And even after all these years, every time they'd get together, Dominic would make sure to ask after Clementine and Barb would feel guilty, as if maybe she'd read the situation wrong.

As if on cue, Dominic leaned forward, his hand reaching out to touch the end of Barb's fingertips. "Clementine? Is she okay?"

"Yeah, it's just . . . her copy-writing gig with Rishi is done, but she just separated from Steve and could use more work, so he was going to give her a chance at sales, seeing as she knows the buildings so well." The moment she saw Dominic's eyes widen at the mention of Clementine's split with Steve, she knew her sister's job would be safe. It was what she'd wanted, but it still felt dirty.

"That's great. About working with Rishi, I mean. I loved the copy, I just needed something new for the sales, and this is new. Clementine's great with people," he said, his face lighting up. "I'm sure she'll kill it."

"Look, I don't want it to affect your decision. I just know you've always thought highly of her."

"I do. But I'm a businessman. I said I wanted something fresh, and this is fresh. A new face, a new voice, it might be just what Rishi needs. We should at least give it a chance."

We.

"Okay, but if it doesn't work, move on. Try someone else. I appreciate you giving Rishi another chance, but you don't owe me anything." *Not anymore,* she thought, *now that I owe you for helping me bail out my sister and my friend, again.*

"Of course." He looked at her and waited, his hand on the check.

"And . . . I'll figure something out, about my fee," she said. "See if I can't cut back somewhere."

"Terrific, that's all I'm asking," Dominic said, pulling out his black American Express while Barb finished her drink, hoping it would wash away the bitter taste of compromise.

Six

Every woman knows age is just a number.
A Wise Woman just knows it's best to keep
that number to herself.
—WENDY WISE, *WISE UP*

The couple sitting on the plane next to Wendy was celebrating. She knew it the moment she saw them board, breathless with a happiness that spilled out in the form of wide-eyed smiles and friendly exchanges with everyone around them. Wendy remembered what it was like to feel as if you were the first person to discover love, and in spite of a death, a divorce, and a sudden third marriage, she still loved it. These two were wearing matching athletic jackets with LOVERS embroidered over their hearts, and they both wore sunglasses—his over his eyes, hers strategically holding back a mane of perfect blond beach waves. The flight attendant came by with two little bottles of champagne and congratulations. Engaged. The ring and the way the woman looked at it said it all, and Wendy felt the familiar lump in her throat that she got when she saw couples about to get married. It always made her think of her first husband, Dan.

She'd wanted to go to Manhattan for their honeymoon, but he'd talked her out of it—why did she want to go to another city and in the middle of winter? Not when they could lie on the beach in their swimsuits all day and make love under the stars at night, which they did. It had been a wonderful honeymoon except for Wendy's daily guilt that she wasn't enjoying it more, secretly wishing that she could be visiting all the places that had captured her imagination in *Sex and the Single Girl*: Central Park, Grand Central Station, Madison Avenue, and the Hearst Building, which published all the magazines that she read with reverence. She'd hidden her disappointment from Dan, reminding herself how lucky she was and that he needed this break, that he'd been working so hard, and that he promised her they'd go to New York City for their first anniversary. *A Wise Woman knows that when you put your husband first, you put yourself first,* she'd written in the monthly free column she'd just started penning for *The Boardwalk,* a local paper dedicated to the happenings of her Beaches neighborhood in Toronto. Happy husbands make happy marriages, and happy marriages make happy wives.

But instead of champagne a year later atop of the Empire State Building, they marked the day with sparkling apple cider, Wendy already seven months pregnant, her doctors insisting that she couldn't travel. They'd go when baby Barb, already named for Dan's late grandmother, was older. And just when Barb was entering school, along came Clementine, this time named for Wendy's late grandmother from Montréal, Clémentine, and everyone knew that New York was no place for children, so Wendy just pushed it out of her mind, this idea of a different life as something other than a stay-at-home mom. Besides, there would come a time, surely, when the girls were in school and Dan wouldn't be working so hard and she'd be able to get back to her own writing, which unfortunately hadn't expanded much since her daughters were born.

It almost felt bad to admit it, but collecting her mail from the post office had been her favorite part of the week. She'd drop the girls off at school around the corner from her house, hit the post office, and then grab a cheese danish from the bakery next door. Once at home she'd make herself a big mug of instant coffee and spread the envelopes out on the dining room table, amazed that she got to spend the whole day with people who were welcoming her into their lives with highly personal stories. Even though the paper featured only two readers in print, Wendy responded to every person who wrote in, until she had created a loyal following of readers who lobbied *The Boardwalk* into giving her a weekly column. More women reading the paper was a good thing, her bosses reasoned. Women were the shoppers, and more women meant more advertisers and more revenue for the paper, which meant that Wendy moved from the back of the paper to a new section called Lifestyle, her column appearing there on the first page every week. Soon, she needed a shopping bag to bring home her mail every day.

It was the month before their tenth anniversary when Dan surprised her with plane tickets to New York. "Better late than never!" he said, and they'd stayed up all night after the girls had gone to sleep, the two of them in their pajamas like kids at a slumber party, planning the trip they'd never take. The bad headaches that she'd attributed to the stress of his job only got worse, and her days became a blur of doctor visits and babysitters and making coffee for the revolving door of visitors who showed up with casseroles after his diagnosis and good wishes and stories of friends and relatives who'd beaten cancer against the odds, stories that over time she'd tune out, already resenting the happy endings she knew theirs wouldn't have.

When Dan was in the hospital that last time, a tangle of wires connecting him to machines that monitored his vitals, he wished her a happy anniversary and told her that they were almost there, that he could see the Statue of Liberty peeking through the clouds, and boy, did it feel good up here.

She now turned to look out her window at the quilt of white clouds next to the plane, and wondered if she really would see him, free from pain and floating beside her. She imagined he would stretch his arms out wide, make his way over to her and knock on the window, smiling that big full-gummed grin of his.

Six months after Dan was diagnosed, Wendy became a widow. Nine months after, she became a bride for the second time, her husband's boss, Ed, having come from the head office in New York with an offer of marriage. She and Dan had hosted Ed a number of times at their little home when he visited and more than once she'd tagged along to a company dinner with Dan at Ed's insistence, happy to get dressed up and have a meal out that someone else was paying for. But as attentive and generous as Ed had been to her, she'd been shocked by his offer and the international move to Long Island it would entail. Still, she'd accepted, feeling maybe it was Dan's way of sending her a message, that Manhattan was still in her sights. Either way, it was the best option she had.

Now as Wendy turned away from the airplane window and picked a magazine from the stack she'd placed in the pocket of the seat in front of her, she ran her hand over the glossy cover, remembering how much joy these frothy publications used to give her. Pages and pages just for her, full of recipes she would never cook, fashions she'd never wear, and profiles of quasi-fascinating people she'd forget the moment she finished them. But it was the advice columns Wendy had always loved the most, the articles about women and how they felt and what they wanted.

It was after she married Ed, and had resurrected her little column, that she was given the opportunity to interview for the advice columnist of a new national magazine called *Women*. Ed was away on business and she'd called to give him the good news, good news being something that had been in short supply lately. They'd been having trouble, more often and for longer, but she knew that a lot of it was her: her unhappiness at being left behind, her desire to grow past her little column in the local paper. And if she were honest, she knew that her heart had never fully healed after Dan's death. She'd done what she thought was the right thing for her girls. Ed was a decent man but a lazy one, excited about the idea of getting a beautiful wife with the instant family to fill his big Long Island house.

But as soon as Ed answered the phone she'd heard the sound of a giggle in the background followed by a shush. She wouldn't tell him, knowing that the happiness she'd hoped to find wouldn't include him. Four years in and countless women later, Ed had made it clear that he believed he'd done Wendy a favor by marrying her and providing for her girls, giving him a pass on actually being a decent husband and stepfather.

The next day, after leaving the girls with a sitter, Wendy had taken the Long Island Railroad to midtown Manhattan for her interview. The interview lasted all of twenty minutes, the magazine's editor telling her that they were willing to give her a try, but that keeping her on would really depend on the numbers and reader feedback. It was the beginning of a new chapter, and Wendy could feel it. If she made it work, there could be a full-time job with benefits and maybe even spin-off books and touring. But first she'd have to prove herself, on her own.

Seeing as she was technically a freelancer, they wouldn't be able to give her an office, which meant that she'd have to work from home and drop off her column once a week, which suited her just fine. She didn't want them to know that she lived on Long Island, or that she was a widow on her way to becoming a divorcée with two little girls who needed to be taken care of; a woman with nothing but questions about her own future. That wasn't what they wanted to hear, and it wasn't why readers wrote to Wendy Wise. They wrote for the wise words that she doled out with confidence, giving it to them straight, whether it was easy to hear or not. That was the Wendy she needed to be for her daughters, she'd told herself right after they moved into their boxy Midtown postdivorce apartment that she'd bought with the money from her settlement. That was the Wendy she needed to be right now.

"Bon voyage!" the woman seated next to her said aloud, snapping another picture and typing on her phone. She looked up, and seeing Wendy crying, asked if she was okay.

"Yes, no. I mean, I'll be fine. It's just, you know . . . life." It was a very un-Wendy answer, but it was all she could muster.

To her surprise, it seemed to strike a chord.

"Life. I get it. I really do," the young woman said. She nodded seriously, and then leaned into Wendy and whispered, "It can be a lot sometimes."

"Congratulations," Wendy said, changing the subject, or continuing it, she wasn't sure.

"Thank you, I still can't believe it," the young woman replied, staring at the ring that was sparkling like a miner's light on her finger.

"It's beautiful," Wendy said. She would've said it even if it wasn't, because that's what every bride-to-be wanted to hear, even the ones who said they didn't want a ring. That was a sentiment she'd never understood. She knew the arguments that said it was a sign of belonging to some man—or some woman, she corrected herself—but that wasn't how she saw it. There was only one time in the average couple's life where a person could say: you know what, I want a big piece of jewelry that doesn't do anything other than sparkle back at me. That rock that will likely be the biggest expense we have outside of a house or a car. A piece of rock that in rougher times will remind me of a day when it was all about celebrating how much we loved one another, not bills or loans, or colic and sleepless nights and arguing about whose work takes priority, or whether staying at home should even be considered work, or what was fair and who was getting the better end of the deal. All that would be followed too soon by cancer, regret, and mourning for what you wouldn't get to argue about, the bickering suddenly so pointless, the

THE WISE WOMEN • 101

longing for all the things you would not get to share and witness together an agony. That overvalued piece of jewelry would be the one thing left when it was all over.

"I was afraid it was too big, you know," the young woman said, leaning into Wendy conspiratorially. "But the woman at the store told me to go as big as I could, because there are no guarantees in a marriage, except that the bride gets to keep the ring!"

She placed her hand in front of her open mouth in a semblance of shock, or what shock would look like in a selfie. Then she laughed at the look of actual shock on Wendy's face and affectionately squeezed Wendy's arm, as if they were old friends.

"Heading home or visiting?"

"I'm going to see my daughters," Wendy said, unsure how to answer. "And you?"

"We have some meetings in New York, and then we're flying on to Turks and Caicos for my conference. I just want to lie out in the sun and recharge. Then I can focus on my engagement party and wedding. I have a wonderful wedding planner, but still, it's so stressful, all that organizing and fittings and deciding who is going to sit where and the locations for night-before dinners and bridal showers. Just as soon as my conference is over, we're going to have all our friends join us for our Jack and Jill party. I'm so lucky, my fiancé's my manager, so he gets that I'm always working. But that's just the way it is. Love your work, love your life." Monologue over, she leaned over to plant a kiss on her fiancé, who was poring over a pile of papers in front of him and didn't look up. She turned back to Wendy and asked, "Have you ever been?"

"To Turks and Caicos? No. But I'd like to," she said, not really meaning it. The idea of any more forced relaxation made her start to itch.

"Oh, then you should follow me, I'm going to document the whole thing on Instagram for my followers. It'll be just like being there." She squeezed Wendy's arm again and smiled wide.

"I don't have—"

"LoveIt. That's my handle. It works for everything, fashion, food, travel, my wedding, all areas of my life. It's perfect as I expand my brand, which is why I won't be changing my last name when we get married." She waited as Wendy just stared at her blankly. "Love. I'm Samantha Love." She pointed to the front of her jacket. "Lovers, get it?" She waited for Wendy, who shook her head. "You haven't heard of me?"

"I don't have Instagram," Wendy apologized, offering up her phone as some sort of evidence.

Samantha took Wendy's phone and examined it.

"You don't have Wi-Fi either, but don't worry, you can piggyback on mine." She typed in a series of numbers, then found the Instagram app and installed it. "This is exactly what Todd and I were just talking about, how to reach the older generation. Now, what do you want your handle to be?"

"My handle? Oh you mean my name," Wendy said, the terminology coming back to her from one of the many tech boot camp sessions her intern Parker had held for her at the magazine. "Uh, let's go with Wendy. Wendy's Wise Words . . . that used to be the name of my advice column," she said as Samantha typed.

"You're kidding me. You're Wendy Wise?" Samantha said, her jaw dropping.

"Yes," Wendy said, sitting taller, Samantha's recognition warming her to the core. While Wendy might not know who Samantha was, young and shiny, crafting her lightbox legacy faster than Wendy could fathom, Samantha knew her. That was the power of the written word on the page, she thought, suddenly hopeful that there might still be a place for her. Online articles came and went, but print transcended trends and generations. That was what she had been trying to tell her editors when they'd put her out to pasture.

"This is amazing. Synchronicity! Stuff like this always happens to me," Samantha said, and handed

Wendy back her phone. She reached into a mono-grammed Louis Vuitton bag with a pink and white stripe to pull out Wendy's books. "You were my something old," she said, passing the books to Wendy. "You know, something old, something new, something blue. My best friend gave them to me when I got engaged, and I love them. They're so retro, but in the best way," she said earnestly. "Please, you've got to sign them for me." She handed Wendy a rose gold pen.

Something old. Wendy took the pen and leaned her face close enough to the book that she hoped Samantha wouldn't see her humiliation. "Of course," she said, quickly scrawling her name with a little x and o, then handing the books back.

Samantha clutched the slim little hardcovers to her chest. "Amazing, thank you." She grabbed her phone, leaned into Wendy, and took a photo of them both before Wendy knew it. "Smile!"

"Oh, I wasn't . . . ," Wendy said, running her hands through her hair.

"Don't worry, I'll make sure you look great," she said, her fingers already adjusting the picture. A moment later there was Wendy's stunned face, smoother, softer, with sparkles in the background and a shade of pink lipstick she liked but wasn't actually wearing. The hashtags read #somethingold #somethingnew #livinglegend #WendyWise #WiseWords #youneverknow #synchronicity.

"The something new is what I'm hoping to find at my Movers and Makers conference, and the something blue," she said, pulling her blond hair back to reveal beautiful aquamarine and diamond earrings, "I bought myself."

Samantha whipped out her phone again and grabbed another shot.

"Oh wow, another one, okay," Wendy said, flustered.

"You should write another book," she said, as if it was as easy to do as snapping pictures. As if Wendy were an author in a romantic comedy sitting down at her desk facing the ocean, a cup of coffee at her side, with a fresh piece of paper to feed into her typewriter. Not that anyone used typewriters anymore, but they looked better on-screen, and besides she was old—a relic, a typewriter, made sense. Click, click, click, and ta-da! A new book! If only. Good things took time, time was fleeting, and it caught up with everyone in the end, including her agent, who Wendy had only recently discovered had passed away, when Wendy had reached out after the magazine had let her go to see if there was any possibility of a new book contract. But Wendy knew Samantha wouldn't want to hear any of that. So instead she said, "Well, maybe I will."

• • •

Wendy had been standing in a slow-moving taxi line outside the airport for over twenty minutes when she saw her seatmate coming out of the terminal, Todd trailing behind her pushing a cart piled high with luggage.

"Wendy! Need a ride?" Samantha called out just as a Lincoln Navigator pulled up. Wendy, eager to get to her apartment and pull herself together before seeing her daughters the next day, nodded and handed her little carry-on to the driver and hoisted herself up into the backseat next to Samantha.

"Todd's on a call," Samantha said, stating the obvious, while Todd looked back at Wendy puzzledly and then returned to the person on the other end of his wireless earbuds, whom he could not believe had forgotten to tell Sunny that they were going to be late and now he'd have to go to the restaurant right away instead of changing first, and did he really need to do everything himself.

"Where are we taking you?" Samantha asked.

"Midtown, Fiftieth and Lexington."

"You go to Midtown now, you'll never get to Brooklyn by six P.M.," the driver said.

"Really? Can't we just drop her off on our way to our hotel and then go to Brooklyn?" Samantha said.

"Sure, we can do anything, but that's gonna add at least another hour."

"Todd, can't you just text her and tell her we're going to be late?" Samantha said.

"I can't be late for Sunny, how would that look?"

"Like you have other clients to tend to, besides just her," Samantha said, throwing her hands up in the air.

"She's not just another client," Todd replied, turning back to face Samantha. "She's a new one, and an important one at that."

Wendy watched as Samantha's cheeks turned pink.

"I can just get out and walk back to the taxi stand," Wendy said, looking over her shoulder as the car sped up onto the exit ramp.

"That's ridiculous, I'm not dropping you off at the side of the road," Samantha said, glaring at Todd. She took a deep breath and shook it off, her smile returning. "Okay, we'll go meet Sunny right away, which means you'll just have to come and have drinks in Brooklyn with us!" Samantha squeezed Wendy's arm as Todd turned to face forward and continue texting.

"Oh, well okay, I could stay for one drink," Wendy said, taken aback, yet flattered.

It was amazing to see how quickly Samantha could pivot and recover. *Pivot* was one of those terms that *WMN* liked to use, implying quick reflexes, agility, and youth.

Samantha leaned over and whispered like they were two girlfriends and said, "I'd rather talk to you anyway, Wendy. Sunny Day can be a bit too much."

This was a curious description from someone who didn't exactly come in small doses herself. But whoever this Sunny was, Wendy could tell she wasn't just a big client for Todd, but a point of contention in their relationship, and she felt herself feeling a little protective toward Samantha, this woman she barely knew.

"Thank you," Wendy said, squeezing Samantha's arm back. It had been a long time since she had hung out with a girlfriend, or even been seen as one for that matter. A wife, a mother, a grandmother, sure, but a girlfriend, she couldn't remember the last time someone had talked to her like that, and the idea of it sounded more fun than she wanted to let on. "I'd love to, but I really don't want to intrude, so if it's easier, I can get an Uber when we get there."

Samantha turned to face Wendy and said quietly, "'A Wise Woman knows not every fight is worth having, especially if it means your husband looks like the loser.'"

"*Wise Wife*," Wendy said, stunned that Samantha was quoting from her second book.

"Besides it's fate," Samantha said, taking another selfie of them and retouching it. "I was meant to sit next to you on the plane after reading your book, just as you were meant not to get a taxi so we could spend more time together." She leaned forward and kissed Todd on the cheek. "This will be fun! Team Love, let's do this!"

An hour later, Wendy found herself sitting on the edge of her bistro chair trying to ignore the waiter who kept bumping into her every time he rounded the sidewalk on the way back into the restaurant. If she moved forward any farther she'd be sitting on the table, which could barely hold four drinks, a menu, and a mason jar of wildflowers. Wendy had never been much of a drinker and found that the cucumber martini, which she had to admit tasted a lot better than the cucumber water they served in plastic drink dispensers at La Vida Boca, had gone to her head.

"Should we get something to eat?" Sunny Day asked in her thick Australian accent, tossing her sandy blond waves over her shoulder and folding her legs up underneath the bench that ran the length of the restaurant's sidewalk patio. In her distressed jeans and white cotton blouse covered in charm necklaces, Sunny gave off major boho beach babe vibes. She drained her coupe of its bubbly contents and plopped the raspberry garnish into her mouth. Sunny was mostly sober, she'd told Wendy after she'd ordered her drink, but alcohol wasn't one of her triggers. Pot, pills, cocaine, emotionally damaged men, online shopping, casual sex? Those were all off-limits. Those were problems she wished she could've written to Wendy about back in the day. The day in question, Wendy guessed, being not all that far back.

Samantha spoke before Todd could. "Actually, I promised Wendy we'd get her back to the city, seeing as we practically kidnapped her here."

"Oh I could just . . . ," said Wendy, motioning to go.

"And . . ." Samantha pressed on, "we also have dinner reservations at Lola's. Todd made them ages ago," she said, snuggling into the crook of his armpit, "and you know how hard it is to get into that place."

"Oh you'll love it. It's ah-mazing," Sunny said, separating the word into two. "I know Lola, she's a dear, dear friend of mine. I was with her the night she decided to open it, you know. Actually, we were sitting right here, at this exact table, and Lola was obsessing about everything we ordered and what she loved and what she would've done differently and the next thing you know we're talking to the owner of the restaurant, who just happens to be from the same town in Australia as me, and they are totally hitting it off 'cause Lola spent her summers bumming around Bondi Beach. Two bottles of champagne later, I just said, 'Girl, you are the greatest cook I know and Jace, you are the greatest restaurateur I know, and if you two don't just get it on and open your own damn place I don't know what I'm gonna do.'"

"You're kidding, that's ah-mazing," Todd said. "I just love those connections. I mean when you know, you know." He paused for a moment and looked at Samantha, who visibly brightened under his gaze, and Wendy breathed a sigh of relief for her new friend.

"I mean as a manager, I totally get that," he said and turned back to Sunny.

"Right?" Sunny replied. "Totally."

"Eight o'clock," Samantha said, a little too loudly. "Our reservation is for eight."

"That's way too early for New York. This isn't L.A. You can actually get a dinner reservation after nine. Tell you what, I'll just call and get you a later time," Sunny said, not waiting for an answer as she picked up her cell phone, flipped through her contacts, and pressed call. "It's no problem, really."

"Thanks, babe," Todd said, turning to Samantha and kissing her on the cheek, although Wendy hadn't actually heard her agree to the change in plans, or that she'd even been asked for that matter. But she could see it wouldn't make a difference now anyway. Sunny had a way of taking command of the situation and pulling everyone into her orbit, and it was clear to Wendy that Todd was enjoying being in it. She waited until Todd looked away and then whispered under her breath, "Better to give a little to get a lot, then give nothing and get nothing."

Samantha met Wendy's eyes and nodded, and then turned to Todd and said brightly, "You're welcome, babe. Team Love, right?"

"Right," Todd answered.

"The thing is," Sunny said, directing the attention back to her, "people think that I'm just some freak talent. . . ."

"Well, you are," Todd said, lifting his glass to Sunny in a toast.

"Well, I am," Sunny replied and shrugged, as if to say and what can I do about it? "But what people forget is that I'm not just some former child pop star, I'm also really fucking smart. Like, not book smart, but intuitive smart. Like Wends here, I get things and people, and they listen to me, you know?"

"Sure," Wendy answered, because until an hour ago she'd never even heard of Sunny Day. But apparently an hour was more than enough for Sunny to be drawing comparisons to Wendy and shortening her name.

"I mean what I say, and I obvi say what I mean. Like we all make mistakes, but we're not defined by them, which is what I'm going to show everyone. This freak is back, bitches."

"Totes back," Todd said, all of a sudden sounding a decade and a dozen I.Q. points lower.

"I mean, look at you." Sunny turned and faced Samantha. "A goddamn gorgeous lip balm mogul right over here, Samantha Love!" She said it loud enough to get the attention of the other diners and pointed to Samantha until a few people snapped her photo. It was the first time since they'd been here that Sunny had really included Samantha in the conversation, and Wendy noticed it had occurred just when Samantha's focus on her was starting to wane.

"Thanks, Sunny," Samantha muttered and refilled her glass with champagne, emptying the bottle.

"Whoa! Easy, babe," Todd said, taking her full glass and swapping it with his nearly empty one.

"And that's what I want," Sunny pressed on, pointing to Samantha. "For people to know that I'm not just a talented singer-songwriter, I'm not just another pretty face, I'm a fucking businesswoman with my own damn brand."

"And they will. You know they will."

"I know you'll make it happen," Sunny said to Todd.

"Of course, but as you know, it's all about timing," Todd replied, picking up the menu, as if it were suddenly interesting.

"You're so lucky," Sunny said to Samantha, reaching across the table and placing one hand on top of hers. "You got one of the good ones. Smart and handsome and nice. I mean, it's almost too much!"

As Todd beamed at Samantha and replaced Sunny's hand with his own, Wendy felt her whole body exhale. It was time to go. Sunny was happy, Todd's ego was stroked, Samantha was glowing, and Wendy was tipsy. There was still so much she had to sort out before she saw her girls, whether or not to tell them she'd been let go before they noticed her missing column and the fact that she had secretly married Harvey were near the top of the list, just below finding out what was really going on in their lives. She grabbed her purse and stood, ready to end their gathering on a high note, and Samantha joined her, arms reaching out for a hug goodbye.

"No, I'm the lucky one. I mean, look at me, in the company of not one but two . . . uh three," he said, as if only just remembering that Wendy was there, "incredible women." Then he looked at Samantha. "Babe, are you taking Wendy home?"

"No, I thought we were—" Samantha started.

"It's fine. I get it, you're exhausted, and you haven't stopped working for months. Why don't you go back to the hotel after you drop Wendy off and get some rest, so you're fresh for our meetings tomorrow?" He stood and wrapped his arms around her waist and pulled her in close. "Sunny and I still have a few business things to go over, but I won't be long."

Wendy saw the look on Samantha's face as she registered that she was being dismissed and the quick decision she made to take control.

"Thanks for understanding, babe," she said and placed both hands on his chest. She turned to Sunny and rolled her eyes. "I mean Palm Beach last night, New York tonight, Turks and Caicos tomorrow . . . this girl needs her beauty rest!"

Wendy was in awe of the way Samantha made it clear to anyone watching that this was her decision, her man, and she was the one in control. Samantha turned back and said flirtatiously, "Don't be too late," and then kissed Todd as Sunny yelled, "Oh my God, get a room! True love, right there people, literally."

And the next thing Wendy knew she was back in the Lincoln Navigator on her way to Manhattan, watching Samantha chow down a protein bar she'd found at the bottom of her purse and sip from a small bottle of champagne that she'd taken from the tiny car fridge.

"It's just business, I know. I get it," she said, her bravado discarded now that it was just the two of them. "But it doesn't help that Sunny's younger, richer, thinner, and more famous than me. You know?"

Wendy did know. She knew exactly what it was like to be traded in for a newer model. She also knew what it was like to have a husband who placed his ambitions over your own. But she didn't really know what Samantha and Todd's relationship was like behind closed doors, so even though everything she'd witnessed so far led her to believe that things were not as rosy as Samantha's Instagram made it out to be, she chose her words carefully.

"But you're his *fiancée*. Sunny is just his client."

"I was just his client too once. Back then, I could text him and in seconds he'd text me back, now I have to wait until he's already dealt with everyone else."

"That must be hard," Wendy said, raising her eyebrows as Samantha drained the minibottle of Veuve Cliquot and reached for another.

"It is, especially when things are so critical." She paused for a moment. "I haven't told anyone this, but I feel like I can trust you. I mean, after all, you're Wendy

Wise, people have been trusting you with their problems forever."

"Well, technically, only four decades."

"A *lifetime*."

"Okay," Wendy said, choosing to ignore the fact that Samantha thought forty years was a lifetime, and therefore she was actually having this conversation with her from beyond the grave.

"The thing is, I've done well with my lip balms. Really well. But the clock is ticking. Every day there's some new young Insta star hawking her own essential oil line, or face cream, and if I don't find a way to expand my own brand, I'm in trouble. Already Sundance told me that they didn't have space for me in their gift bags at their film festival this year. Please, how much space does lip balm take up?"

"Not a lot."

"*Not a lot*. Thank you. At least we have our wedding."

Samantha told Wendy how she had already secured a young reality TV show designer who'd agreed to do all her outfits at cost for publicity, and the *People* magazine exclusive that Todd had gotten right after Sunny Day promised to sing at their reception. The plan was to get everybody to either donate or trade their services in exchange for publicity, and Wendy was genuinely impressed by what a good businesswoman Samantha Love was. She'd made a product everyone could use, turned her name into an ideology, and created a successful brand. It was not unlike what Wendy herself had done.

But unlike Wendy, Samantha wasn't going to let herself be pushed aside just because there was someone younger nipping at her heels. Listening to her made Wendy wonder if maybe she had gone too quietly from the magazine. It wasn't that Samantha would be immune to any of the challenges that Wendy had experienced, but she seemed determined to get out in front of them before they could take her down. Wendy had to admit it was awe inspiring.

"I know I should be happy, but I just can't shake this feeling. Tingles. It's a feeling I get when things are either really right or really wrong. It's probably nothing," Samantha said.

As the car pulled up in front of her building, Wendy thought of how listening to her intuition that morning had led her to get on a plane to see her girls, a decision she knew in her bones was the right one. So when Samantha leaned forward to give her a hug goodbye, she found herself saying, "Listen to that feeling, Samantha. It's your inner truth teller and it's trying to tell you something." She didn't add, Whether you want to hear it or not.

Seven

*N*othing is more romantic than buying your first place together. Now you can commit yourselves to home ownership and take your love to the next level, high above the city, by saying "I do" to The Point. Although given that a million dollars won't even get you your own storage locker, laundry, or bike rack, we probably should have called it, What's the Point?

Clementine checked the clock on the wall of her little all-white office at Pinnacle. She knew Rishi had given her this copy-writing job as a favor to Barb, and she'd be sorry when it was over. It had started out as just a few days a week, paying for Jonah's extracurricular activities, summer camp, and a new laptop, but it had grown into a full-time gig that she relied on. She'd taken it while Steve was still in business school, the break from hustling for clients and the attractive monthly retainer that made it possible to afford health insurance on the exchange for her family, too good to ignore. While she missed the idea of being her own boss, she loved that she was responsible only for writing copy and that it was someone else's job to get the clients, manage them, and handle all the paperwork. She'd always known this gig would end, but the timing couldn't be worse.

"Oh my darlin', oh my darlin', oh my darlin', Clementine, we need the copy now more than ever, oh my darlin', Clementine."

Clementine sighed loudly enough for Rishi to hear her as he rounded the corner.

"Never gets old," he said, bringing in more than a splash of color in his bright blue suit and silver sneakers.

"You sure about that?"

"Ouch, someone's in a mood."

"Sorry. It's just . . ." *My husband has stolen all my money and I'm going to be evicted and I think my kid might be getting bullied at camp.* "Do we really have to call these million-dollar shoe boxes 'affordable'?"

"These shoe boxes have built-ins, Carrera marble islands, and heated floors. Heated. Floors." He said it like it was a miracle of science rather than an upgrade whose necessity could be avoided by just wearing socks.

"Yes, yes, I get it. They are state-of-the-art shoe

boxes. But still, a million bucks for seven hundred square feet? In what universe is that affordable? And, you know, the point on the top of the building looks kind of phallic, so maybe we don't need it in every picture." She pointed at the glossy flyer that boasted glorious full-color artist renderings of the high-end places that were being snapped up by young professionals who didn't have the need for garages, second bedrooms, or nearby schools, and who were eager to get a piece of the real estate market before it eluded them any further. Many of them had already lived in far more expensive cities and were able to reassure themselves that they were still getting more for their money than if they owned in Paris, London, or Tokyo.

"Technically they're nine hundred ninety-nine thousand. Not *quite* a million."

"Not *quite* affordable."

Rishi opened his mouth to speak when the alarm on his smart watch beeped. He smoothed the front of his jacket and ran his fingers through his silver hair, which always made Clementine think of a meringue, curving upward and folding over at the peak. "Shake time. Follow me."

Clementine grabbed her empty thermos and followed Rishi down the hall, past the floor-to-ceiling posters of every successful Pinnacle campaign, to the reception area, where he was met with his liquid lunch order, delivered by a flirtatious twenty-something guy whose blond hair was swept into a perfect messy bun at his neck.

"Nice bike," Rishi said, pointing to the collapsible bike the delivery guy easily carried under one arm, showing off his biceps. "I've been thinking of getting one of those myself." Out of the corner of her eye Clementine saw Rishi puff out his chest and stand a little taller. She slunk over to the office's coffee station, where she refilled her thermos and pocketed a handful of the artisan granola bars that she knew Jonah liked.

"Oh, you'll love it," the delivery guy said. "Best investment I ever made. Completely revolutionized my life. I'm so much faster on this one. I was literally dying riding around on that other thing."

Clementine was tired of hearing proclamations like that after writing them all day: best ever, revolutionized, ultimate. No, she wanted to say, no—a bicycle is not the best thing ever. Having her son was the best thing ever, falling in love was the best thing ever, going to bed at night knowing that the ones you cared about were safe and healthy and happy was the best thing ever. Owning the roof over your head, something she believed she'd accomplished until yesterday, was the best thing ever. And how was this guy's life completely revolutionized? He was still doing the same thing he'd been doing with his old bike, delivering overpriced juices to men and women who wanted to believe that sipping the drinks would somehow make them look like the guy who delivered them. The rest was hyperbole and empty promises and Clementine had had enough of both.

"Shit," Clementine said as she splashed coffee on her hand.

"Careful, that stuff will like, *literally* kill you," the delivery guy said.

"No, it won't."

"What with all the caffeine and toxins, yeah, it will."

"You know what will kill you, Goldilocks? Riding a bike without a helmet because you don't want to mess up your hair. That will *literally* kill you. Giving unsolicited advice to someone you don't know about their beverage of choice, that just kind of makes *me* want to kill you. But not like, *literally.*" She exhaled loudly and shook her head.

Clementine looked at Rishi, whose eyes were so wide, his eyebrows were practically in his hairline. "Clementine, could you wait for me in my office?"

"Sure."

Clementine knew she had it coming. She slunk down the hall and made herself as comfortable as she could in a strange modern plastic guest chair shaped like a hand, feeling like it was gripping her in an awkward hug. After a few moments of whispered apologies right outside the office, Rishi entered.

"Goldilocks?" he said.

"I didn't know his name."

"Oh well, good guess then." Rishi shook his red drink and took a swig before continuing.

"I'm sorry. I'm having a shitty day."

Rishi raised his eyebrow again and took another sip, leaving a red beet mustache on his upper lip.

"Fine. Shitty week, month, summer. Steve and I are having problems."

"I'm sorry to hear that," he said.

"Yeah, well, he was *literally,* a liar." Clementine smiled, but she was the only one.

"You know what your problem is, Clementine? You have a real disdain for what you do and what we're all about as a company."

"Whoa, Rishi, I'm sorry. I'll apologize to that guy next time I see him."

"It's not that. I've been meaning to say something for a while."

No, please don't do this, she thought, *not now. I can't afford to lose this job.* "Rishi—" she started, but he held up his hand.

"Now, I'm not saying that I don't understand your attitude. Because I do. I get how frustrating it can be to spend all day coming up with more ways to say the same thing, all while knowing that someone younger than you by at least a decade is going to buy one of these apartments that you could never afford yourself."

Clementine felt her face get hot. "Wow. Okay . . ."

"And I know that working here isn't your first choice. But the problem isn't that *we* are making over-priced shoe boxes and that people are lining up to buy them, the problem is that *you* haven't found a way to see yourself as part of this transaction. You're on the outside looking in, and as long as you stay there, you're only going to get angrier and angrier."

"Rishi, please my contract's almost up, just let me finish it, Jonah and I are barely scraping by," she blurted out, tears threatening to spill down on her face.

"What? No, oh no," Rishi said softly, and passed Clementine a Kleenex from the box on his desk. "I'm not trying to fire you. What I was going to say was that I think you'd view this whole thing a lot differently if you had something to gain. Then you'd want these places to sell."

"I don't understand."

"I'm saying, get off the sidelines and come in."

Clementine stared at him blankly.

"I'm trying to ask if you want to train to be one of our on-site sales reps. Once I sign off on this last round of copy, I won't have anything else for you until I get another account. Seeing you already know everything about the properties from having written all of our marketing materials, you'll know what to say. And this way you'd get a commission on top of an hourly rate."

"Are you serious?"

"Well, now that I know that you're having issues with Steve, and not waging a one-woman war against cute bikers and their hipster hairstyles, then yes, I'm being serious. Like I said, you know everything there is to say about these places and how to say it. You're smart, I like you, and in light of your current situation, I believe you'll be extra motivated."

"I don't know what to say. *Thank you.*" She stood and shook Rishi's extended hand.

"It took me a long time, Clementine, to learn that if I can't have all their money, at least I can take some of it. One *affordable* eco-luxury property at a time."

● ● ●

At 3:30 P.M. Clementine raced down the stairs of the subway, desperate to catch the train before the doors closed. She was cutting it close, but she should still be able to make it in time to pick up Jonah. Maybe things were looking up.

"Excuse me," she said, pushing a young man wearing headphones farther inside the car, carving out just enough room to squeeze through before the doors shut behind her.

The air was hot and full and she suddenly wished she had brought a personal fan like a few of the other riders. She jostled her way toward the center, eyeing the last palm-size piece of real estate on the metal pole, and pulled her shirtsleeve down over her hand, using it as a shield before she held on. Her legs were tired from sitting all day, which of course only made her want to sit more, but there were no seats left. Sales rep. She hadn't seen that coming, but she was grateful, and Rishi was right, she was extra motivated.

She was starting to craft a sales pitch for The Point in her head when the lights went out.

"Ladies and gentlemen, we're experiencing a service issue up ahead and the G train will be temporarily delayed until we can address the situation. We apologize for the inconvenience and hope to resume service shortly."

A collective groan traveled through the subway car. When wasn't there an issue with the G train? "Shit,"

Clementine muttered. She should've left earlier, but she'd wanted to finish the brochure she was working on early as a way of thanking Rishi. If the train didn't get going soon, she was going to be late for pickup.

The lights flickered on and the voice returned. "Ladies and gentlemen, once again we're sorry for the delay. Maintenance has arrived and we're busy addressing the situation."

"It's a jumper," an old woman next to Clementine said, then pursed her bright red lips tightly.

Clementine winced. "How do you know?"

"I ride this train every day in summer to escape my apartment. No air-conditioning. You'd be surprised how many people jump."

"I'd no idea."

"You're not the only one. Train full of people all rushing to get somewhere, pissed about being delayed, and some poor asshole is sauce on the track."

"I just don't want to be late to pick up my kid," Clementine said, feeling sheepish.

The woman shook her head sympathetically. "No, you can't be late for a kid. Whole city of pervs out there."

Jesus, thought Clementine, stepping away from the woman, who continued talking as if she were still standing right next to her. At moments like this she missed working from home, even though Steve liked to use the fact that she did against her. "There's a whole world out there that you know nothing about, Clementine!" Steve had shouted once when she'd pushed back on the commercial viability of one of his ideas, doubting the size of the market for caffeine-enriched licorice.

"I do happen to know that there's a coffee shop on every block, Steve."

"Yeah, and if you went to any of them, you'd see how impatient people are waiting in line. Who wouldn't want a caffeinated candy?"

Before she could point out that caffeinated candies already existed, he'd spat out, "You should try getting out more before you give your opinions." He'd said the last word as if the idea of her having any opinions was strange and ridiculous, and she couldn't quite blame him; it had been a long time since she'd used her gift for language to do anything but form a chorus that supported and embraced every idea he had. As Clementine continued to avoid eye contact with the older woman, who was still talking about pervs, she decided that she actually hadn't missed all that much working from home.

"Ladies and gentlemen, we're back, thank you for your patience."

Clementine checked her watch, and panicked. She still had three more stops.

When her train finally arrived at the station, she bolted out the doors and took the stairs two at a time, running the last few blocks, her heart racing. Weighed down by her heavy canvas tote bag, and jogging like a three-legged cart, she came up to the YMCA, but there was no sign of Jonah or his group anywhere in sight. Her heart pounded as she ran around the building toward the playground.

"Jonah! Jonah!" she screamed at the top of her lungs, trying to push one terrible thought after another out of the way. "Jonah!"

"Mom, I'm over here!"

Clementine spun around to see Jonah swinging from the monkey bars, Seth by his side.

"I'm so sorry I'm late, there was a problem on the train . . . I ran here as fast as I could."

"It's okay, Mom. Seth waited with me."

"Hey, Clementine," Seth said, smiling as he walked toward her and out of earshot of Jonah. "Jonah was really upset. He was worried that maybe you mixed up something on your calendar again?"

Steve. The lie she'd told Jonah about why his dad didn't come home yesterday was paying her back tenfold. "No, I would never forget about him," she said, her voice breaking.

"Of course not, that's what I told him," Seth replied, placing his hand on her shoulder. "Look, I was happy to stay behind with him 'cause I know he can get really anxious, but if you're gonna be past four, you need to call. . . ."

"I know, but there was no service on the subway. . . ."

"I get it, I do. But if I'm not at drop-off, they have to take him back inside and he'll stay in the admin office until you get there. And I don't think he'd like that." He grabbed his backpack and took out his clipboard that had the sign-out sheet on it, and pulled a pen from behind his ear.

"No, you're right, he wouldn't."

"It's okay, I was a sensitive kid too, and I think I turned out all right." He smiled at Clementine, blinking his big brown eyes with enviously long lashes in an exaggerated way that made her think of a llama. She noticed the fine lines around his eyes and the gray in his close-cropped beard, and for the first time realized that they were probably the same age, although you'd never know it, considering how much energy he had.

Clementine took the pen and signed Jonah out. "Yes," she said. "Yes, you did. I'll be sure to make arrangements so this doesn't happen again."

"Did you want me to put Steve on the pickup list? I don't have him here."

"No." It came out more forcefully than she meant it to, and Seth seemed to catch it. The last thing she wanted was to ask Steve for anything. "I just, well, he's away on business right now and even when he's here, his schedule is—"

"Seth, watch this!" Jonah shouted as he swung himself around the bars and flipped to his feet.

"Careful!" Clementine called, the muscles in her groin retracting out of fear of something going wrong. It was her body's automatic reflex whenever she saw Jonah doing anything physically daring, as if she could inhale him back inside for safekeeping.

"Nice landing. Way to bend the knees. Gotta protect them, right?" Seth said.

"Right. They gotta last." Jonah's face glowed as he climbed the bars again.

Seth smiled, gave him a thumbs-up, and turned to Clementine. "He's such a great kid."

"I think so too," she said and paused for a moment. "Can I ask you something?"

"Sure," Seth replied, looking her in the eye.

"Don't you ever want to take a break from hanging out with kids all day? I thought one of the perks of being a teacher was getting summers off."

Seth laughed. "It seems weird, I know, but I actually love hanging out with kids. Probably because I still feel like a kid myself, or act like one if you ask my ex-wife."

"I'm sorry."

"What? No, it's okay. We're great friends. Truth is we got married and had kids when we were practically kids ourselves, which on the one hand was great, because now they're almost grown up and I'm still young enough to play tennis and basketball with them. But on the other hand, it kind of sucks, because I'm wiser and more patient and would probably be a way better parent now."

"I see," Clementine said. She had no trouble believing he was a great dad at any age.

"Besides, I'm too young to retire and I've got two college tuitions to contribute to. Hence the summer job."

"Well, we're glad you have to work the summer."

"Me too," Seth said, his face breaking into a smile, and for a moment, it felt like maybe there was something more that he was going to say, but then he shook it off and continued. "Okay, well, you let me know if you need us to change anything, add him to the after-hours program or something. I get it, I was raised by a single mom too."

"I'm not actually—"

"Dude, now that your mom's here, I gotta motor. See you tomorrow, okay?" As Seth unlocked his bicycle from the fence, Clementine couldn't help but notice the chipped paint and faded stickers and see that it was a heavier, older model. There was nothing trendy or revolutionary about it, but it still worked, and she smiled as he lifted the bike, spun it around with ease, swung his leg over the middle bar, strapped on his helmet, and rode over to Jonah for a final fist bump.

Jonah's face slackened as he watched Seth ride off, and all of Clementine's worries about camp returned.

"Everything okay at camp today, Jonah?"

"Yeah, it was fine," he said, looking at the ground. "When's Dad coming home again?"

"Soon, bud," she said, already dreading the conversation she knew was on the horizon. As they walked back toward the train, Clementine started silently calculating how much money she had left for the week and whether she had enough room left on her credit card to get them to her next paycheck. She stole a sideways glance at Jonah, his gaze downward, his slight shoulders slumped, a night of frozen chicken fingers and sliced carrots followed by a half hour of TV ahead of him.

"Hey, I know it's not planned, but what do you say we grab some burgers and shakes tonight?"

"What? But it isn't even Friday."

"I know. But do you think maybe this week, we could mix it up a little bit, just because?"

"Because why?" He turned to her, his eyes round and worried.

"Because I love you," she said, smiling wide in the hopes of erasing the concern she saw on his face. "Because you're my favorite person in the whole wide world. Because it's summer. Because life's too short to say no to milkshakes."

"With whipped cream!" Jonah said, jumping up and down. "And no sharing!"

"Who's living large now?" Clementine laughed, her heart ready to burst at the smile that spread across Jonah's face, and without asking if she could, and knowing he was too big to do so, she scooped him up in a hug and held him to her tightly. As he wrapped his legs around her waist, she felt her tired back falter, as if it could give out at any second, but there was no way she was letting go.

Eight

We're never given more than we can handle.
And a Wise Woman can handle a lot.
—WENDY WISE, "WISE WORDS"

Barb was sitting in her therapist's office, on the same side of the loveseat she'd chosen on her first visit and not varied from since. The cushion next to her, where Jill usually sat, was glaringly empty. Her girlfriend had canceled last minute, saying that she had double-booked and was so sorry, and by then Barb had already pulled her water bottle from her bag, and unwrapped the cream cheese bagel that she'd bought for lunch. She'd been unable to pack everything up in time to escape before Dr. Carroll saw her and welcomed her in for a private session.

"How old were you when she said you could handle a lot?" Dr. Carroll asked as she sat in her huge high-backed chair. Barb's therapist was like a painting that could talk. Nothing in her face gave away how she felt, and nothing moved, except her mouth. She could be older than Barb, or younger—it was impossible to tell. The closest thing to judgment that Dr. Carroll exhibited was a quiet clicking of her tongue against her teeth.

"Twelve. *Handle*. What bullshit. More like, here Barb—you deal with it."

Barb's mother wasn't a regular topic of conversation these days, although Dr. Carroll was no stranger to Barb's issues with Wendy, having been her therapist before she and Jill started going as a couple.

Click—the tongue against the teeth. Barb heard it.

"Tell me about it," Dr. Carroll said.

Barb shifted uncomfortably in her seat and pulled her shirt from her body so she could use it to fan herself. She checked the little clocks on either side of the couch, relieved to see that their time was nearly up. She'd told her shrink about Dominic, and about Clementine and Steve, and had nearly gotten through a session without mentioning her mother, but she had wrecked it by quoting her.

"She'd gone to her office Christmas party and had left me alone to deal with Clementine, who was sick."

"Did she know she was sick?" Dr. Carroll said, leaning forward.

"Of course she knew, but she was all dressed up and ready to go, so she said it was nothing that a cup of warm milk and a good night's sleep wouldn't cure. She told us that she wouldn't be late and that if we needed anything to call Mrs. Abrams, the old woman who lived in the apartment next door."

Barb grabbed a handful of tissues and wiped the back of her neck. She couldn't believe that with everything happening in her life she was back talking about her mother. *It's always about you, Wendy, isn't it?*

"And what happened?"

What happened was that Wendy was really, really late, and wasn't yet home when Clementine got sick in her sleep, bolting upright and vomiting all over her bed. Barb had run to the living room and dialed Mrs. Abrams's number, but no one picked up—her mother hadn't checked to see if their neighbor was actually in town for the holidays. She knew the number of her mother's office, but when she called it, no one answered. She tried the concierge, but they had gone home for the night. She was terrified and needed someone to tell her what to do, so she picked up the phone and dialed zero.

"Hello, Operator."

"I need help," Barb shouted into the receiver. "My sister's sick."

hang up and call 911."

"No, I need help now. She has a fever and is throwing up and I'm supposed to take care of her."

"How old are you, honey?" the operator asked.

"Twelve, and my sister is seven. And my mom's not home."

After a long exhale, the woman told her to get a thermometer, how long to put it in her sister's mouth, and asked what the temperature was. It was a fever, but not too high—maybe from the flu or food poisoning. She told her to run a lukewarm bath and to give Clementine ginger ale and saltine crackers afterward to see if she could keep them down. She asked for Barb's number and called her back every ten minutes to see if she was okay, and when Barb took Clementine's temperature again, the fever had broken, and her sister was resting peacefully in their mother's clean bed.

But when the operator called back the next time, saying she'd like to send the police by just to make sure that everything was all right, Barb had blurted out that she didn't need to and lied that her mother had gotten home before hanging up.

"So not only were you taking care of Clementine, you were taking care of your mother as well? You must have been very scared."

Scared was an understatement. She'd been terrified.

She'd slept next to Clementine with one eye open, making sure her little sister was okay. But all she said was, "Actually, I was grateful."

"Grateful?" Dr. Carroll asked.

"Yes, because I knew that when Wendy left us again, we'd be okay. I could handle it. Just like she said."

"So you expected her to leave you again."

"Yes, because that's what she does."

"And what about you?"

"What about me?"

"Is being left something that you expect? Is that what you're waiting for Jill to do?"

Barb opened her mouth and closed it again. Why was this suddenly all her fault? What had she done, except take care of everyone?

"Why would I be expecting that?" She could hear how it sounded: defensive and irritated, both of which she was.

"Because it's what the people you're close to have done. Your father, Wendy, Jill."

"First of all, my father didn't leave, he died. And I'm the one who kicked Jill out."

"And your mother?" Dr. Carroll said, just before the gentle chime of the bell that announced the end of their session rang out. Barb stood and clapped her hands together.

"Well, time's up. To be continued, Doc."

"Barb, did your mother ever tell you why she was so late that evening?" Dr. Carroll said, walking Barb to the door.

Barb stopped, the image of a forlorn Wendy taking off her party dress in the dark and slipping into bed where both girls lay suddenly swimming up into her mind. That night her mother had reached her arms out across both of them and whispered that she was so sorry, and that she loved them more than anything.

"No. I never asked," Barb replied.

"Huh. Interesting," Dr. Carroll said, clicking her tongue against her teeth as Barb left her office.

"*Interesting*," Barb muttered as she made her way out onto the street, irritated by the comment. She'd been seeing Dr. Carroll long enough to know that what she really meant was: "And why not? What are you avoiding? How can you expect an answer if you're not prepared to ask the question?" She'd been avoiding asking Jill what was going on because she was afraid that Jill would admit that she was cheating on her again, and maybe some part of her expected her to. God knows she wasn't exactly easy to live with, she was moody at the best of times, and even more so lately, thanks to her hormones and all the stress she was having at work. But what was she afraid her mother would say, if she would even remember her whereabouts on a random night in the 1980s?

Barb's eyes started to well up as she thought about how scared she'd been, waiting for Wendy to come home, and how in spite of all her anger she'd been so relieved to feel her mother's arms wrap around her, and then cursed herself for being sentimental. "Stupid hormones," she said, walking out onto the street. Hadn't she just told Clementine not to dwell on Wendy?

Still, she couldn't get her mother out of her head. And the more she thought about Wendy, the more she thought about the last time they had really talked. It was after Jill cheated, and Wendy had been so mad at Jill, so protective on Barb's behalf, going on and on about what a catch Barb was and how she deserved to be treated better. Hearing her mother so aggrieved for her, before diving into all the things she had never really liked about Jill, had caught her off guard, and had made her actually feel . . . mothered. Barb took a deep breath and sighed slowly. Okay, she should call her mother, just to tell her that everything was fine—just to prove Dr. Carroll wrong, that she wasn't actually avoiding anything.

Barb called Wendy's cell phone but it went straight to voice mail. *Oh well, I tried,* she thought and was about to start the car, when she remembered the number her mother had left her for the Florida resort she was visiting for some book event, in case of an emergency. And while this wasn't actually an emergency, now that Wendy was on her mind, Barb decided to fish the number out of her inbox and try her there.

"La Vida Boca, how can I help you?"

"I'm looking for Wendy Wise, she's an author speaking at your—"

"One moment please," the receptionist said, cutting Barb off and placing her on hold. Barb listened to the sounds of Frank Sinatra before a click said someone had come back on the line.

"Are you ready to speak about your anger now?" a man's voice said.

"Excuse me?"

"Who's this?" the man asked.

"It's Barb, I'm Wendy's daughter . . . Harvey? I didn't know you were going to this event with Wendy," Barb said, surprised that things had gotten so serious that they were traveling together now.

"What event? There are so many here."

"What? Wait a minute, is Wendy there?"

"She just left! One minute she's here, the next she's gone!" Harvey said, his voice breaking with emotion.

"I thought moving to Boca was a good idea, I love living here, but your mother . . ."

"Oh, I see," Barb said, putting it together. Somewhere along the way, Wendy and Harvey must've ended things and then hooked up again during Wendy's book event in Boca. "Yeah, long-distance relationships never work, in my experience. I'm sorry we won't get to know you better," Barb lied. "But I do wish you well. Take care," she said, hanging up the phone before he could say anything else.

Barb took a deep breath, the familiar feeling of disappointment rising in her as it had so many times when she'd hoped Wendy would be there and she wasn't. She shook her head ruefully. What did she expect? Some things never change.

Nine

A Wise Woman knows you're not just choosing a husband, you're choosing a life.
—WENDY WISE, *MARRY WISELY*

"I don't think you're being fair," said Steve.

Clementine shifted in her seat, unsticking her legs from the faux rattan café chair and draining the last of her iced tea from her glass. This lunch meeting, at a restaurant near her office, had been Steve's idea, a chance to plead his case once more, but somewhere between "Imagine how I felt" and "I didn't have any choice" she interrupted Steve to tell him that she thought they should skip the separation part and go straight to the divorce.

"I told you that I was going to pay us back and I meant it. I don't understand why you aren't giving me a chance."

There were lots of things Clementine didn't understand. Like why, if he had no freaking money, had he ordered a club sandwich with salad and fries and extra avocado, knowing that the avocado alone would add three more dollars to his already seventeen-dollar sandwich, while she had ordered the chilled cucumber soup because it was the cheapest thing on the menu. Because he expected her to pay, that's why.

Clementine studied Steve. He was dressed in the young man's uniform he'd adopted shortly after Jonah was born: Converse runners, skinny jeans, and vintage superhero T-shirts, as if by insisting that he was young and fresh, others would think so too. She knew his furrowed brow and sunken shoulders—his victim posture—was to show that her words had physically wounded him. There had been a time when seeing him like this would make her grab his hand and lace her fingers through his, believing that his remorse was real. But time had taught her that if she refused to give in, and waited just long enough, the shoulders would start to work their way back closer to his spine, and Steve would change his tactic and go on the offensive, puffing his chest out.

"So that's it? You're just going to sit there and judge me without a fair trial?" he said, sitting up straight.

And there it was.

"You lied to me for two years, Steve. I thought we owned the house we lived in, for God's sake. I thought we were building equity and a future for Jonah and not subsidizing another one of your stupid start-ups, and you want to talk about fair?"

"Lower your voice, people are starting to stare."

"Let them stare! You think I care about that? I care about the fact that I'm going to be evicted." She pulled the letter from Mr. Gregoris out of her bag and slapped it down on the table in front of him. "And that means uprooting Jonah from his home and his friends in the neighborhood, and maybe even his school."

She watched as Steve skimmed the letter, while taking a bite out of his sandwich, amazed that he had any appetite at a time like this. But that was Steve; no matter what was going on, he remained finely attuned to his own needs. He folded it up and handed it back to Clementine without looking at her. "Don't be so dramatic, he'll be fine."

Fine, Clementine thought bitterly. "We've been through this already," she said, when he finally looked up from his sandwich, "I don't want fine for Jonah, I want what's best for him. And what's best for him is staying where he is, and starting the pilot program at his school in the fall. He doesn't need to be around us fighting."

"So that's it then? I don't know why I'm so surprised, you've always made all the decisions."

"Excuse me? All of the decisions we've made have been about you. What you wanted always came first."

Steve leaned back in his chair and stared at her, as if he couldn't believe what she was saying. "That's how you see it? You're the one who wanted to move in together so quickly, so we did. You're the one who wanted to get married, so we did. I didn't need a piece of paper, that was you. And because it was important to you, we did it."

Clementine's cheeks were stinging hot. Steve was making it sound like she'd pushed him into all of his big life decisions. "I also supported you for two years while you went to business school, Steve. Was that an okay decision to make?"

"You're the one who said I needed to get serious and get a job that actually made money, so I had to go back to school. But then when I actually had an idea that could make money, you insisted that we buy the house."

"The house was a good investment."

"But I wasn't."

Clementine let Steve's statement hang for just a beat too long to deny it, leaving both of them staring at each other uncomfortably.

"I can't believe that you're trying to make out that this is my fault," she said. What else could she say that she hadn't said a million times already? Clementine took a deep breath and spoke evenly. "You should come over tonight, so we can tell Jonah together and you can get your things."

"And where am I supposed to stay? I can only crash with friends for so long."

"I don't know. That can be your decision." She stood to leave.

His face reddened and he tossed his napkin on the table. "Don't do that."

"Do what?"

"Dismiss me. You started doing it ever since Jonah was born, pushing me aside, as if I didn't matter anymore, as if the two of you don't need me."

"That's not true," Clementine said, but her voice betrayed her. How could she explain that she'd actually needed him more after Jonah arrived than before, but that he was unable to do things the way that Jonah needed? Like taking twenty minutes to explain not just that we had to brush our teeth but why, followed by another half an hour researching who invented the toothbrush and how they were made and whether or not other cultures had them and if not why and what did they do, and if they were able to manage, what made it so important to us, and did we really think our ways were better, and if so, what did that say about us?

Clementine knew it could be exhausting, and that it would be so much easier just to say "Because I said so," but that didn't work with their kid. Pulling parental rank only ever resulted in a complete meltdown. She understood Jonah, she recognized so much of herself in him, and was determined to give him all the parental patience and attention she had never received as a child.

Steve found Jonah's ways tiring, which they were, but he told her that he didn't feel the same sense of satisfaction that she did after the end of the day, wrung out and used up, but truly believing that all her efforts were shaping her child. She had needed her husband to be a father more than ever, but he lacked the patience, often snapping at Jonah and being irritable with her.

"I get it, nothing is more important than our son, but I thought that you'd be able to love both of us."

"I did love both of you," Clementine answered quietly, sitting back down. "But I'm only able to parent one of you."

"That's harsh, even for you."

"You betrayed us, Steve."

"I wanted you to believe in me again, the way you used to."

"So you lied to me?"

"You gave me no choice," Steve said as the waitress stopped by and placed their check on the table. And right on cue, Steve reached for his phone and checked its display. "It's about AquaVeg, I have to take it," he said, and then added, when she sighed loudly, "I'll come by tonight."

Clementine picked up the bill from the table and unhooked her purse from the corner of her chair, knocking it over as she did and tripping on its strap to land on the concrete.

"Shit." She stood quickly, wiping the little bits of patio off her scraped knee as the tables nearby turned to stare, then she hurried inside the restaurant to pay.

"Clementine?"

It was Dominic Provato, standing next to a beautiful young woman with long dark hair that cascaded down her back. He excused himself from her and came over to Clementine. He looked as handsome as he had the first time they'd met.

"How are you?" he asked, and Clementine felt her cheeks get hot. It wasn't his looks that she remembered from all those years ago, it was how he focused all his attention on her when he spoke, as if he genuinely cared about what she had to say. His intensity both flattered and unnerved her, and she heard her voice come out higher than usual. "I'm good, yeah, really good," Clementine said.

"You have, uh . . ." He stared at her knee, his hand

reaching for it and then stopped himself, handing her a linen pocket square from his jacket instead.

Clementine looked down and saw the small trickle of blood running down her shin and took the handkerchief. "Thank you," she said, dabbing her knee and tucking the stained cloth in her purse when she was done. "I'll wash it."

"There's no need."

The young woman he was standing with lifted her phone to take a selfie with the restaurant's sign behind her. He ignored her, taking a step forward.

"You okay?" he asked.

"Oh, I just tripped. It's nothing. I was just grabbing lunch with Steve, before heading back to the office—to work for you actually." She pointed toward the water, as if he didn't know where his sales office was, and then lowered her hand, feeling stupid.

"I thought I recognized Steve," Dominic said, looking toward the patio. "That's good, that you're having lunch together. I mean, for Jonah."

Clementine stared at him.

"Barb said something," Dominic offered, clearly flustered at having spoken out of turn.

Her whole face flushed with anger.

"I'm sorry, shouldn't have said anything."

"No, actually, Barb shouldn't have said anything."

She was silent for a moment, wondering how much to tell him. "But, seeing she did . . . Steve and I are separating, because he lied to me and took all my money, which is why I'm going to start selling units in The Point."

"Jesus," Dominic said.

"Look, I have little doubt that there were many better candidates for this job than me, but I promise I'll get up to speed fast. I'm a really hard worker, and given my situation, I'm incredibly motivated. You won't regret it."

"I only have one regret about you, Clementine, and I've got no one but myself to blame for it."

Clementine looked Dominic in the eye and held her breath. After all these years, they'd never spoken about the connection they felt when they'd first met. She'd never seen any upside to doing so. Surely they weren't going to now?

"Mr. Provato, your table's ready," the hostess announced, putting an end to the awkward moment.

"It was nice seeing you, we'll have to catch up soon," he said and touched her arm, his hand resting on her skin for a moment as they briefly held each other's gaze.

As Dominic and his lunch date took their table, Clementine realized that he'd never introduced her, which struck her as odd. Back in her office, Clementine closed the door behind her and leaned against it, letting herself cry openly. Fucking Steve, and his terrible lies and terrible timing. Things were bad enough as they were—the last thing she needed was any awkwardness with Dominic, or for him to feel sorry for her or think she was a screwup, especially now that she was going to be in his sales department. She sat at her desk, blew her nose, and whipped out the little compact that she kept in her side drawer, trying without success to cover the bright red blotches on her cheeks and nose. As she clicked her laptop to life, a warning message popped up in her email.

Spam, she thought, dismissing it at first, but saw it was from her credit card company. Irregular activity, it noted, along with a link that took her to a list of recent transactions. A car rental, a plane ticket, a hotel charge, and a cash advance, all totaling several thousand dollars. Clementine thought she was going to be sick. Clearly Steve's question of what he was going to do if she didn't let him come back home had been rhetorical. His plan B was already in place. She searched the name of the hotel, and the top result was a luxury resort in Turks and Caicos.

"Unbelievable," she said aloud, her whole body shaking with rage as she phoned the number of her credit card company, hurriedly answering the security questions a patient woman named Darnell read off her script on the other end of the call.

"Okay, Ms. Wise, now that we have that out of the way, what is it that I can help you with today?"

"I'd like to report some incorrect charges on my card, please."

"Oh, I'm so sorry to hear that, ma'am. Are you telling me that your card has been stolen? If so, I can connect you with our fraud department."

"Uh, wait, no, it wasn't stolen exactly, it's just that there are some charges on it that I didn't authorize."

"And what charges might those be?"

Clementine read the list aloud, her anger barely concealed as she bit down on each word.

"That's a lot of charges. Do you happen to share this card with anyone else?"

"Well, I . . ."

"Because it says here that a Steve Jenkins also has access to this card."

Then why did you ask me? Clementine thought bitterly, not liking where she thought this was going. "Yes, that's my husband."

"Ma'am, is it possible that your husband simply made these purchases without your knowing?"

"Yes, but that doesn't mean I authorized them."

"I'm sorry to hear that, but it sounds like maybe this is something for the two of you to discuss. I'm afraid unless you're telling me that the card was stolen, there's nothing we can do."

"Damn it," Clementine said, her voice breaking. There was no way she could afford to cover all these expenses. The line was quiet for a moment and then Darnell lowered her voice to a serious whisper.

"Don't tell anyone I told you, but what you need to do is cancel this card right away. The last few charges, like the hotel and the rental car, are pending, which means that a hold on your funds has been made but the charges haven't gone through yet. Do you understand? If you cancel now, they might not, but there's no guarantee. Either way, you're going to have to keep making the minimum payments or you'll wreck your credit score, and trust me, you don't want that."

"Thank you," Clementine said, wishing she could take back her earlier shortness.

"And after you cancel this card, you'll want to check any others you might have."

If only Clementine had other credit cards she could use. "Thank you again. I'm guessing you've been through this before."

"Yes, ma'am," Darnell chirped through the phone,

pleasant and professional, as if a supervisor was nearby. "Is there anything else you need help with?"

Yes, so much, thought Clementine.

"Pick up, pick up, pick up," Clementine muttered into her phone as she raced up the street from the subway on her way back home. The afternoon had been a struggle, trying to concentrate on the final copy changes for the promotional materials that were being set up in the sales office on the main floor. She'd be there soon herself, thanks to Rishi's generous offer, and had done her best to stay focused on the nuances of every headline she wrote. The subtleties of syntax—*Welcome Home,* or *Welcome, home*—were something she normally appreciated, but not today. Today, all she could think about was Steve racking up her credit card. If she canceled it she would have to apply for another one, and who knew when it would come. She needed to keep her credit card with what little room she had left on it.

"Pick up, pick up," she repeated until her call to Steve went to his voice mail again. "Yo, you know what this means? Leave a message and I'll call you back. Or better yet, text me."

She'd already texted him, but he hadn't texted back. She'd ask him when he came over that evening. Give him a chance to explain. What if the tickets were for her? A family trip to try and make things right? Not that she relished the idea of paying for it, but the idea of it was still better than the possibility of her husband racking up debt and leaving the country.

Her phone dinged and she read the message from Barb: *Got Jonah. Ordered takeout. See you soon.* It was followed by one hundred random emojis that Clementine knew were from her son, who'd recently discovered the joy of sending the little picture messages, like a code for Clementine to unlock: thumbs-up, A-OK, shark, shark, big hug, teddy bear, soft-serve ice cream, a truck, sunshine, trees, shark, heart, double heart, and the obligatory poop emoji, all of which Clementine took to mean that everything was good and that Barb had gotten Jonah and Samuel, who was sweet as a teddy bear, and an ice cream from the ice cream truck. The poop was just because he was six. Unlike Clementine, who never let Jonah play with her phone because if anything happened she couldn't afford to replace it, Barb loaded up her phone with all the latest apps and games popular with the first-grade set.

She texted back a heart, thumbs-up, and a hug, and rounded the corner onto one of the prettiest streets in Sunnyside, where multifamily houses were being renovated into single-family homes on corner lots with landscaped gardens.

"Clementine! I was just going to call you," Kimberly said, all made up and wearing a beautiful wrap dress. She was standing next to her assistant Marie, whose arms were full of flower arrangements. "I have another showing, I swear it's nonstop," she said, gesturing to the bouquets, as if Clementine had asked.

"I'm sorry. I know I said I would call, I just haven't had a minute, but I will. I'm running late and need to get home to Jonah. My sister had to pick him up for me."

"This will only take a second," Kimberly said. "Take those inside," she directed Marie, then walked over to Clementine. "I wanted to talk to you about this year's fall fundraiser. We were hoping that you'd be able to do the copy for the posters again."

"Sure," Clementine replied, wondering what the rush was when the fundraiser was still months away. "Can we talk about it when I have more time?"

She started to walk away, but Kimberly reached for her arm.

"The thing is, I'm only in town this week, and I'm slammed with showings and then we're going to the Hamptons. You know the girls really love it out there—they spend the summer riding, and Ethan's going to start this summer too. I'll be back and forth to the city of course, the housing market as hot as it is, but I really don't know when I'll have time to focus on this again."

It was more information than Clementine needed.

"Just email me," Clementine said, walking away only to have Kimberly walk alongside her.

"Well, I was hoping . . ."

"Kimberly, I have to get home *now*."

Kimberly stared at Clementine, her mouth open wide. "Okay. Well, what I was going to say was that the committee is all getting together this Friday at my house before I go. We're going to be barbecuing and the kids will all be there, so you're welcome to bring Jonah. I mean, if you can find the time."

Clementine immediately felt bad, which she knew from experience was what Kimberly wanted. That, and an audience for her stories about how busy her life was, which Clementine could sometimes trick herself into finding amusing, but not today. Today she thought she might just scream, which she dare not do, so instead, she apologized again, when she really had nothing to apologize for.

"That sounds nice, thank you," she said, immediately worrying about Jonah having to play with Ethan. "I'm sorry, I just started a new job and I'm trying to juggle everything while Steve's away, and it isn't easy."

Kimberly immediately brightened. "Oh, tell me about it. Charlie is never around. Never! But I suppose we all have our roles. His is to provide and mine is to nurture, although it's not as if I don't make my own money. But we can't all be multitaskers and I can't expect everyone to take on as much as I do." She was about to continue talking, when Clementine cut her off.

"Okay, see you Friday!" she said, and broke out into a jog up the street.

"Great! And you can sign the petition then!" Kimberly called after her.

"He's not talking to me," Barb said as soon as Clementine got home.

"What? His text said everything was fine," she answered while patting Betsy, who was circling her feet in hopes of going for a walk. "Well, you know, it didn't say, as much as it . . . you know what I mean."

"Yeah, well that was in the presence of ice cream, before we got home. After that he totally shut down. Said he wants to be alone."

She pointed to the tree house out back, where Jonah always went when he was upset. Clementine grabbed a bag of blue corn tortilla chips off the kitchen counter and headed outside. As soon as she poked her head inside the tree house Jonah started talking.

"Are you and Dad getting divorced?" he asked and crossed his arms, denying her entry until he got an answer.

"What makes you ask that?" Clementine said.

"Seth's parents got divorced when he was little. He said they used to argue all the time, but they both really loved him and just decided that they were better off as friends. So he had to live at two houses."

"I see." She offered him the tortilla chips, which he took before reluctantly allowing her to enter. She took in his sloped shoulders and worried brow and gently kissed the top of his chlorine-scented hair. "Well, your dad and I both really love you, you know that," she said, holding his hand and looking him in the eye.

"I know," Jonah said. He opened the bag of chips and started eating. "But you don't argue all the time, just some of the time, about Dad not working enough and you having to make all the money." He rolled his legs in and out, like he always did when he was upset.

A wave of shame came over Clementine. All those whispered conversations in the kitchen, the ones where they tried to keep their voices down, talking unsuccessfully in innuendo and false hypotheticals in an attempt to shield Jonah. She knew he wasn't stupid, but still she'd hoped he hadn't put it all together.

She reached into the bag and ate a chip, buying

herself a moment. "It's not just that, honey, and besides, Dad makes money too, or he will once his company gets going." It was amazing how she could still defend Steve, but she didn't want her son to think less of his father. Then he might think less of himself, and what good would that do? "And sometimes parents go through things and need some time to figure it out on their own."

"So you're separated, like Adrian's parents."

Clementine took a deep breath, reached her arms around Jonah, and pulled him toward her. "Well, not officially, but yeah, I think we're going to try living apart for a while."

"I don't want to live in two houses. I won't be able take care of all my stuffed animals, and I won't know where my things are, and I need to look after Betsy. Dad never walks her and I don't know where he's going to live, and it might be too far from school and then Turner and Adrian won't be able to come over and I won't have playdates, so I have to stay here with you. And I can't leave my tree house. We have to stay right here. Promise me, promise me we'll stay right here."

Clementine gently rocked Jonah side to side to calm him down, the way she always had, willing away whatever ailed him. "I promise, Jonah, I promise. It's going to be okay, we're going to stay right here." She said it even though she didn't know how she was going to be able to make any of it true. "And you know that both Dad and I love you more than anything in the world, and we'll always be a family, even if we aren't all in the same house."

Jonah grabbed her in a hug and squeezed her back tightly.

"I know, that's what Dad said, too." He untangled himself from her and headed toward the stairs. "I'm thirsty," he said, climbing down as Clementine scrambled after him.

"He did? When? Did he call Auntie Barb?" Clementine asked, her heart racing.

Jonah walked into the kitchen and grabbed a juice box from the fridge. "No, this afternoon at camp when he came by to pick me up. But Seth said he couldn't, because he wasn't on the sign-out sheet." He stabbed his straw into the juice box.

Barb looked at Clementine, her eyes wide. "Seth did want me to tell you that he tried to call you," her sister said carefully.

"You should've put him on the sign-out sheet, Mom," Jonah said, between sips. "Dad wanted to take me out for dinner before he left for his next work trip and he couldn't. Seth gave me an extra Popsicle 'cause he felt bad. A red one." He stood as tall as he could, his face defiant. He knew she hated the bulk Popsicles the camp handed out, all full of sugar and food coloring. "The junkiest kind, and I ate it," he added.

Clementine's mind was reeling as Jonah talked. Had Steve just tried to kidnap their son? And what if Seth hadn't been there? It was all she could do to not let on how freaked-out she was.

"I didn't think of it, honey, I'm sorry. Another time. I'll call Dad and set it up, okay?"

"Okay," Jonah said, taking his drink and the bag of tortilla chips with him to the living room. Clementine waited until she heard him turn on the latest recorded episode of *Shark Week* on the Discovery Channel, a highlight of his summer.

Never in a million years did she think that Steve would do something like this, but she never thought that he'd lie about buying their house either.

"Can you believe this?" she asked Barb.

"Which part? That you ran into Dominic after having lunch with Steve, that you don't check your freaking messages, or that Steve tried to kidnap Jonah?"

Clementine fished in her purse for her phone and saw that she had three new voice mails from Seth.

"I didn't see these before. My phone's been acting up." She pulled out a chair and sat down as she listened to Seth's messages. "Shit, shit, shit."

"Why don't we start with your lunch with Steve," Barb said, taking the chair opposite her. "Dominic said you were really frazzled, and you didn't even notice your leg was bleeding. What happened?"

"Why don't we start with the letter?" She reached back into her purse and pulled out the letter from Mr. Gregoris when the doorbell rang.

"That's the takeout," Barb said, putting the letter down. "Hang on."

"Mom! Mom!" Jonah yelled as Betsy started to bark her head off.

"I'm coming!" Clementine answered, grabbing her wallet, but Barb stopped her.

"Oh please, I'll get it."

"I can still buy my own food, Barb," she said, frustrated.

"I doubt that," Barb said as the doorbell rang again.

"Mom!" Jonah yelled, opening the door.

"Jonah, don't open the door, wait for me. You don't know who it is!" Clementine ran to the door as Jonah pulled it open wide.

"It's Grandma!" Jonah yelled, running into Wendy's open arms and holding on.

"Mom?!" Clementine said as Wendy scooped them all in for a group hug. "What's going on, is everything all right?"

"Of course not, that's why I'm here," Wendy said, wrapping her arms tightly around the three of them. "You need me."

Ten

*A Wise Woman knows, everyone can play
the blame game. But nobody ever wins.*
—WENDY WISE, *WISE UP*

For the first time in a long while Clementine agreed with her mother. She did need Wendy. She needed her bold-faced assurances that everything was going to be all right, even if she didn't know what was wrong yet. She needed her tidy summaries and confident announcements telling her what to do. In short, she needed some of Wendy's Wise Words.

"No matter what's going on, we can fix it. We're Wise Women after all," Wendy said, hugging them all a little tighter, and making Barb cringe.

Clementine rested her head on her mother's tanned shoulder, which smelled like coconuts, and started to cry.

"Mom, are you okay?" Jonah asked. He snuggled in closer, wrapped his arms around her waist and placed his head on her belly, his favorite part of her body ever since he was little. It was the one reason Clementine was glad it had never bounced back.

"I'm fine, I'm just so happy to see Grandma."

"When did you get back, Wendy?" Barb asked. She had started calling their mother by her first name when she turned twelve, and had never stopped. Though she tolerated it, Wendy had never really grown to like it.

"Last night. I spent the day in the city. I had some things to take care of at work." She ruffled Jonah's hair. "You know, go away for a week and come back to two weeks of work, it's always the same."

"I'm too young to work," Jonah said.

"True," Wendy replied.

The doorbell rang and Barb jumped to get it. "Food's here, let's eat."

"Barb's right, we can catch up over dinner. After all, everything looks better on a full stomach," she said, before reaching into her big canvas tote bag and taking out a giant shark puzzle for Jonah. "I thought you might like this."

"You thought right," replied Jonah, beaming as he grabbed it from her.

"I'll set us up outside on the grass so Jonah can use the picnic table to get started on the puzzle. That way you girls can catch me up," Wendy said carefully, gathering plates, cutlery, a tablecloth and napkins, her arms full as she walked outside after Jonah, who wanted to know all about her trip to Florida and if she had actually seen any sharks up close, and if so, was she scared.

Barb started unpacking the food, grabbed a beer from the fridge, and took a big gulp. "Two minutes and she's already bossing us around." She held the cold beer to her forehead and closed her eyes.

"She isn't bossing us," Clementine said, taking the bottle from Barb and sipping it. "Give her a break, she just got here and had no idea what was happening."

"And whose fault is that? Hers." She grabbed another beer from the fridge. "I'm warning you, don't let her get involved in this, she's only going to make things worse."

"That's not fair."

"Since when do fair and Wendy have anything to do with one another? I'm telling you right now, she thinks she can just swoop in and try and make it all right in the easiest way she can. Not the best way, the easiest. When we were little it was a present, when we were older it was some glib advice. She doesn't do hard, she doesn't do messy, only pithy answers and a conviction that she alone knows what's best. But God forbid you don't take her advice, then watch out."

Clementine stepped outside with their food while Wendy hung on Jonah's every word as he unwrapped his puzzle and chatted to her nonstop.

"How was Florida? Did the event go well?" Clementine asked, grabbing a plate for Jonah and filling it with flaky spanakopita, pita, hummus, and cucumbers. The smell of garlic and butter was making her hungry. After years of living close to Astoria, the Greek neighborhood of Queens, they rarely ate Greek food anymore, spoiled by the fact that it was always there. The one exception was when Barb came over. According to her there was no decent souvlaki in Brooklyn and after going through all the "trouble" of coming out to see Clementine, she felt she earned it.

"Oh, it was fine," Wendy said, her voice sounding unnaturally breezy as she helped Jonah spread out the puzzle pieces and turned them all picture-side up.

Clementine stopped mid-hummus scoop and looked at her mother. "Fine" was not actually *fine.* Clementine knew how much her mother loved giving her talks and being the center of attention. She'd seen the way she'd light up when people asked her to sign their books or told her stories about how they'd read her column for years. It energized Wendy, giving her a reserve of adoration that she could draw on for months afterward.

"Fine?" she asked.

"It's Boca, what can I say?" Wendy shrugged, not meeting Clementine's eyes.

"I thought you loved Florida," Clementine said, placing the spanakopita directly between Jonah's fingers so he'd remember to eat it.

"I love New York, Harvey loves Florida."

"Who's Harvey?" Jonah asked, taking a bite while he started piecing the edges of the puzzle together.

"Grandma's boyfriend. You haven't met him yet. It's very new."

"Depending on who you're talking to," Barb muttered, and Clementine shot her sister a confused look. She looked at Wendy, who acted as if she hadn't heard.

"Is he coming too?" Jonah asked.

"Not this time. This time I wanted you all to myself." She hugged Jonah. "Now, why don't you get the edges done while I chat with Mom and Auntie Barb for a bit? I want to hear all their news. Sound good?"

"Okay, but you might want to talk fast, since this won't take me long."

"Roger that." Wendy kissed him again, covering his face with kisses until he laughed and wiggled away.

It was another warm night, and the grass felt cool beneath the picnic blanket. Barb finally joined them, and for a moment the three of them just stared at Jonah in happy silence. And then Wendy said, "For crying out loud, something is up with you girls, now will somebody please just tell me what is going on?"

"Don't tell her, it'll only make things worse," Barb said.

"Tell me what?"

"Well . . . ," Clementine began.

Clementine looked at Barb then at her mother and after a moment's hesitation leaned forward and whispered, "Steve and I broke up, he lied . . . about the house, it's not ours. . . ." She felt like she might cry again and looked at Barb, who shook her head. "It turns out the deal to buy the house never happened and Steve took the money for his business. And the mortgage money I've been giving him every month was actually for rent, unbeknownst to me, and now the landlord is evicting us."

"What are you talking about?" Wendy asked.

"He used the money for his carbonated vegetable water start-up, AquaVeg, and when I discovered this, I kicked him out."

Wendy looked back and forth between her daughters, and after a moment she spoke. "I don't believe this." She tore off a piece of pita and ripped it into shreds on her plate. "I could strangle him. What kind of man does that to his wife and child?" she asked.

"He's always been entitled, and too good-looking, as if looks were a hard-won skill that he used for the betterment of others. Ridiculous."

"You left out the part about Steve possibly trying to kidnap Jonah," Barb said, in between bites. "I mean if you're gonna tell her, you might as well tell her every-thing."

"He what?" Wendy asked, her eyes wide.

"I don't know, I mean it isn't like him, but then again he was so angry at me, that maybe he was just trying to punish me."

"Well, you did kick him out," Wendy said.

"What's that supposed to mean?" Barb snapped.

"It means that maybe she's right, he might be trying to get back at her, for what she did."

"So this is her fault?" Barb spat.

"I didn't say that, did I?"

"Not yet."

"Don't fight," Clementine said, checking to make sure that Jonah was occupied with his puzzle. "Please."

"I'm so angry," Wendy spat out.

Clementine exhaled, taking comfort from her mother's anger until she heard what came next.

"How could you have let this happen?"

"There it is," Barb muttered.

"I've told you both a thousand times, a woman

always has to have her own money. You never should have given it all to him. Why on earth would you do something so foolish?"

Barb stopped chewing and turned to Wendy. "She did it to make him feel better about himself, to make him feel like a big man. Isn't that the advice that you would've given her?"

"Never," snapped Wendy. "I would never tell you to do something like that."

"But you wrote it," Clementine said quietly. "*A wise woman knows that the biggest investment she can make in her marriage is her husband.*"

"*Wise Wife,*" Barb added, shoving another piece of pita in her mouth. "And when you wanted to move in with Steve without being engaged . . ."

"*Why buy the cow if you can get the milk for free? To quote Marry Wisely.*" Clementine sighed.

"Oh and don't forget, *It's okay to be the breadwinner as long as your husband feels like the bread baker.*"

"What? That's not from one of *my* books," Wendy said.

Clementine shot Barb a look before her mother could realize that Barb was quoting from advice her mother had written to her alter ego, Tangerine. "Stop it, don't fight," Clementine pleaded and stole a look at Jonah, who was still deeply involved in his puzzle.

"Why didn't you just ask me directly, instead of relying on my books?"

"Maybe because you weren't around," Barb said.

"Well, that didn't take very long," Wendy said, rolling her eyes.

"I wasn't sure how much time we had with you, Wendy. I mean who knows how long you're staying?"

"I just wish you'd told me," Wendy said.

"Would you have told her anything different?" Barb said, her mouth full.

"I might have. You're my daughter," Wendy said. "That's not the same as giving out advice for someone who picks up my book or some stranger who writes in to my column."

"*Living in the gray is asking for trouble, it's important to know right from wrong*," Barb said, destroying the pita as she dipped it into tzatziki.

"Stop twisting my words," Wendy snapped. "This isn't my fault."

"It's never your fault, it's everyone else's. Isn't that right, Wendy?" Barb said.

"You should've just called me, Clementine. I never would've told you to let Steve handle all the money, not when you're the one working so hard to earn it."

"Grandma, come! It's time to do the middle," Jonah called out.

"Coming!" Wendy stood and turned to face Clementine, her cheeks flushed and her voice shaky. "Let me give you some advice now, to your face—if Steve can keep a secret this big for this long, then he's got to have others, and if he was willing to try"— she threw a glance in Jonah's direction—"Then who knows what else he'll do? But I for one am not going to sit around and wait to find out."

"Mom, I'm not asking you to fix things."

"I'm not doing this for you," Wendy said, her voice catching. "I'm doing it for Jonah."

Barb crumpled her napkin and threw it on her plate. "Wendy to the rescue," she said, her face bright red with anger. She stood and exhaled and then called out to Jonah. "Hey, kiddo, I gotta run, but I'll see you soon, okay?"

"Okay!" Jonah yelled and waved as Barb gave him a thumbs-up and headed back inside, Clementine following behind her.

"You're not really going are you?" Clementine asked, stunned.

"You don't need me, Wendy's here," Barb said, grabbing her jacket and walking to the front door.

"Barb, don't do that."

"What? It's true. The second she shows up, you're that same seven-year-old who can't believe her mommy actually came home. Do you have any idea how screwed up that is?"

"I'm just happy she's here. She's our mother."

"When she wants to be."

"Can you please just try?" Clementine pleaded.

"Me? Listen to you, she's the one who gave you the shitty advice and made things worse, and you want me to try? Wow, you sound like Wendy."

"Barb, don't leave like this. It's not fair to make me choose sides."

"The only side I ever wanted you to choose, Clementine, was yours."

"Barb, please . . ."

"Call me when she leaves again. I'm sure it won't be long."

Clementine watched as Barb stomped down the front steps toward her car and drove off.

Eleven

A Wise Woman knows that an angry
woman is never an attractive one.
—WENDY WISE, *WISE WIFE*

Barb leaned on her car horn the first chance she got and swore. The driver in front of her had noticed the green light a second later than Barb had decided was acceptable. It wasn't really the driver that Barb was angry at. It was Wendy and Clementine and Steve and Dominic and Jill and everyone else who just expected her to keep showing up and listening to them and solving their problems only to be pushed aside whenever it suited them, just like Clementine was doing now.

It was fine that Clementine wanted a relationship with Wendy. They'd had different experiences growing up, Barb knew that. For Clementine, Wendy was her exciting professional mom returning from a book tour with gifts and stories, letting them have dessert before dinner, and staying up late to watch movies as a way of making up for missing their recitals and school concerts. She was the fun parent, making Barb the strict parent, the boring parent, never mind that she wasn't actually anyone's parent and could have done with some parenting herself.

She took a deep breath, inhaling and exhaling on a count of four, the way she'd been directed by the woman on the mindfulness meditation app that Jill had installed on her phone, even though all she wanted to do was scream. At least she'd managed to leave without actually having it out with Wendy, or without Jill's name coming up. Wendy would lose it if she knew that Barb and Jill had gotten back together. Barb had sent her girlfriend three texts that night, the others being invitations to meet her at the Y to pick up Jonah and have dinner at Clementine's. Jill texted back that she couldn't, she was training clients and wouldn't be home until later. Because Barb didn't trust her girlfriend lately, she'd lied about her own return time, hoping to catch Jill doing whatever it was she was doing with whoever it was she was doing it with.

When Barb got to her front door, she could hear Jill laughing inside. She took out her keys, remembering what Wendy had said about secrets: where there was one, there were more. Was this another of Jill's? Her mother's proclamation was an earworm that she couldn't get out of her head. She pressed her ear to the wood and listened, waiting for the next time Jill laughed out loud so she could quietly slip her key into the lock and let herself in.

Jill was sitting a half-floor up in their elevated living room, on a low sofa that overlooked a private landscaped garden, and talking to someone on her laptop. As Jill stood, Barb could see that she was wearing only bright-pink running shorts, oversize headphones, and a sports bra, the muscles in her back on full display as she lifted her arms over her head and then brought them down, flexing her biceps for the screen and laughing in response to something the other person must've said. She didn't know that Barb was standing at the front door, exhausted and smelling of garlic and oregano from all the Greek food she'd eaten. Or that Barb now knew that she wasn't in fact running, as she'd indicated in her return text just a few minutes ago.

She tucked herself behind the floating bamboo wall that she'd installed to block the view of the home's interior from the street, leaned her head against the cool exposed-brick wall, and closed her eyes. She was too tired for a fight right now; her mother's arrival had caught her off guard and she'd regressed into a sullen teenager in a matter of moments. Wendy had always been unwavering in her view that her children needed to be accountable for their choices and face their issues head-on. Anything less just meant that the issue would grow until it was ten times the size and had the power to bite you in the ass, or sleep with your friend, or spend all your money, or flirt with a stranger online and lie to you.

Barb took a deep breath and called out, "Honey, I'm home!" and saw Jill pull off her headphones, shut her laptop, and sprint into the kitchen.

"Oh, hey," Jill said. "I just got home myself. Last client canceled, so I went out for a run." She poured herself a big glass of water as Barb walked past her and opened the doors of their liquor cabinet, grabbed a gold-rimmed rocks glass, and mixed herself a large vodka tonic.

She took a lime from the bowl on the kitchen island and rolled it back and forth across the marble before cutting and squeezing it into her drink. "I wish I'd known, I would've swung by the gym and picked you up. You could've joined us for dinner."

"It was last-minute. I actually waited around for half

of the session before my client called," she said, her eyes widening as Barb took a long drink.

"Is that so?" Barb said. The vodka was going straight to her head.

"Are you okay?" Jill asked, turning to face her.

"Sure, why do you ask?"

"Because . . . ," Jill said, looking at Barb's half empty glass.

"You know, my mother always said that in every relationship somebody has to wear the pants and I just realized that I'm always the one wearing them." Barb undid her pants, and let them drop on the porcelain tile floor. She finished her drink and started to make herself another, her face already feeling numb.

"Did something happen at Clementine's?"

"You mean something other than her husband stealing all her money and her losing her house and having to move somewhere new where Jonah will have to try and make friends all over again while worrying about being bullied and ostracized?" Barb left out the part about Steve possibly trying to kidnap Jonah. It was bad enough that Steve had pulled the rug out from underneath Clementine with the house, but showing up out of the blue at Jonah's camp like that? Barb didn't want to believe he was capable of taking his child, but then again she didn't want to believe that Jill was cheating on her. And wasn't that the real problem, that we all chose to believe what we hoped to be true? The truth was, desperate people did desperate things.

"Right, I know that, what I mean is . . ."

"And my mother showing up out of the blue in full Wendy Wise mode ready to solve everything?"

Jill's eyes widened. "Jesus, Wendy's here?"

"That's where your head goes, to Wendy, not Clementine?"

"Of course I'm worried about Clementine," Jill said. "It's just that Wendy stresses you out. And I know she's never really liked me."

"But this isn't about you."

"I know that," Jill said, storming out of their kitchen and into the bedroom.

"Do you?" Barb asked, following her in. "'Cause I'm just wondering why it is that you don't seem all that bothered."

"What do you want from me?" Jill asked, naked now, her hands on her hips. "I think it's terrible what Steve did to her, but it takes two to tango."

"So this is her fault?"

"No, but she has to take some responsibility for it. She can't just expect—"

"What? To trust her partner? Believe that he

wouldn't betray her after everything she's done for him?"

"Why are you yelling?" Jill asked before Barb realized she was.

"I don't know, Jill, why am I? Why don't you tell me, huh? Go on, tell me." Barb stared at Jill, her heart pounding, and for a second their eyes met and Barb thought that she actually might confess about the underwear in her drawer and the Daytona badge, and the person on her laptop, but then Jill lowered her eyes and walked toward Barb seductively.

"Because you're cranky, and a little drunk, and I don't need to listen to this. But I do need a shower, and frankly, so do you, so why don't you stop talking and join me?"

She pressed herself up against Barb and then took her hand and led her into the bathroom and under the hot water. And Barb gave all of her anger and jealousy and resentment over to Jill's touch.

It was just after midnight when Barb woke up, flat on her back, her throat dry and mouth bitter from falling asleep without brushing her teeth. She spotted Jill's earplugs and guessed that she'd been snoring again, a casualty of too much alcohol and not sleeping on her side. It was a moment before she realized that they'd had sex; aggressive, greedy sex that had technically satisfied them both and ended the conversation neither one of them really wanted to have. Not yet, not now, later; only as she got older, "later" seemed to be coming at her faster and faster.

She rose slowly so as not to disturb Jill, picked her clothes off the floor, dressed in the hall, and snuck out onto their landscaped terrace garden. The air had finally cooled down and the city was quiet except for the occasional snippet of a cell phone conversation from the sidewalk below. Barb opened the little shed where the gardener kept his tools and grabbed a cigarette from the pack that she had stashed there a month ago. The gardener was a luxury, but the outdoor space with its bamboo-slatted screens and brick walls covered in creeping vines that sprung from planter boxes full of native grasses and morning glories was one of Barb's favorite things about the house. It was also from the garden that she had the best view of her home. She'd taken her time designing it, using reclaimed and sustainable materials and opening up the space so that it felt larger than it actually was.

Barb lit her cigarette and inhaled deeply. She wasn't really smoking again, so much as smoking sometimes, a secret that until recently she'd felt bad about keeping from Jill. It was stupid, and hardly worth the extra mouthwash and hand soap and dry cleaning needed to keep it a secret. There was something so adolescent about this rebellion that she found herself thinking of Wendy and the first time she caught her smoking.

It was just after Barb's graduation from RISD and Wendy was furious that her older daughter was choosing to travel around the country rather than accept a job offer. Did she have any idea how lucky she was, to get a job right after school? Any idea how hard it was for a woman to have her own career, and yet here it was being handed to her and she was just going to throw it all away? Well, it hadn't been handed to her—she'd graduated top of her class and had earned her offers. And she wasn't throwing it all away, she was throwing it all in. Back then Wendy smoked and Barb had reached into her mother's pack of cigarettes, grabbed one for herself, and lit it dramatically. She was going on the road and there was nothing her mother could do about it.

The sound of young people on the street below just starting their night brought her back. It seemed like a lifetime ago that she had been one of them. If she weren't so angry at her mother right now, Barb would ask her if this is what happened when you got older— that you found yourself returning time and again to your most formative years, the time when you got to focus solely on yourself without sensible qualifiers or reality checks. She'd ask her mother if this was what a midlife crisis looked like, if this was what her own crisis had looked like after her divorce from Ed, when Wendy had thrown herself into her writing and touring, spending more time mothering her fans than her own daughters. She wanted to know if it was really so easy to just pack up and leave everything behind, to forget about the people who depended on you and chase your own happiness.

When Wendy was away, it was easy for Barb to just put her into one of the neatly designed boxes she'd crafted inside herself and close the door. But seeing her mother always opened that door and the others that Barb had forgotten she'd stuffed parts of her childhood into.

She should stop this line of thinking, take two Advil, and go back to bed. Tomorrow she had to visit the new site that Dominic wanted to develop, and Wendy would want to meet and talk because Barb had been too quiet at dinner, then too loud, and Clementine would most likely call her to get Jonah again. Jonah. Her stomach dropped thinking about how hard this was going to be on him, they needed to make sure that he was going to be okay, and then there was Jill . . . who knew what Jill would be doing or who she'd be doing it with. She needed her rest if she was going to be able to deal with any of this like the responsible adult everyone relied on her to be.

"Fuck it," she muttered and stubbed out her cigarette where Jill would find it, then headed out to the last real dive bar on her block.

Twelve

A Wise Woman knows sometimes we
overlook the ones who need us the most.
—WENDY WISE, "WISE WORDS"

"I'm glad you're here, Mom," Clementine said as she dumped a load of clean laundry onto the couch in the living room. They had just gotten Jonah to sleep in Clementine's bed so that Wendy could spend the night in Jonah's. Wendy had gladly accepted the invitation to stay over, rather than make her way back to Manhattan, eager to find out more about what had been going on with Clementine and how she could help. For hours she'd waited for an opening, but the moment dinner ended, there had been playtime and dishes to wash and the next day's lunch to make, and a quick walk around the block for Betsy, and as soon as Jonah sat down to watch his show, Clementine had whipped out her laptop to return work emails and then it was bath time and stories and now laundry to fold.

Wendy was exhausted just watching her daughter move from one task to another, her body in constant motion, and recalled her own days of being alone with her girls, and how overwhelming it was. It had seemed impossible to get anything done when they were around. The day she'd finally gotten her own tiny office at the magazine, she had closed the door behind her and cried tears of relief. The eight-by-ten-foot space with its bright lights, clean desk, and single potted plant was a refuge to her, free from the constant refrain of *are you finished yet?* And toys at her feet, and the basic needs of her children that for some reason never came at the same time, but were called out, one after the other like a musical cannon. Snack, snack, water, water, book, book, play, play, snack, snack, until Wendy was so dizzy she'd send them away to entertain themselves, saying that clever children are never bored, or some other slightly shaming proclamation uttered with no real purpose other than to buy her a moment's peace. But at least her girls had each other, and as overwhelmed as she was, as busy a mother as she remembered herself being, she had to admit it was nothing compared to Clementine.

In Wendy's day it was only the women who didn't work who had time to do laundry more than once a week, tidy up the house every night, run around the backyard, cut sandwiches into shapes, make bedtime snacks, read stories, and sing songs until their children fell asleep, instead of saying good night right after bath time and closing their bedroom door. And now, with computers and emails, people assumed that you were on call all the time, just because there was a signal that could reach you. She had never believed that anyone could work and parent properly, a belief she used to defend her inability to parent better than she did. But as she watched her daughter now, it was with a sense of awe and guilt as Clementine proved her wrong. She was suddenly aware that with the exception of texting Harvey to say that she was all right, she'd done little else but wait around since dinner, so she reached for a pair of Jonah's socks and started folding.

"Well, at least that makes one of you. I wouldn't say that Barb's glad I'm here."

"She's just really stressed right now," Clementine replied, stacking Jonah's little T-shirts one on top of the other. "And I'm to blame for some of that stress. It was her money too."

"What do you mean?"

"For the house," Clementine said slowly, stopping to look at Wendy. "She was the one who loaned me the money when you said you couldn't help."

"I told you all of my money was tied up in my retirement and . . ."

"And if it was really important to me, I'd find a way, I know," Clementine said, repeating her mother's words. "Barb was my way, I couldn't have done it without her." She took the small stack of Jonah's clothes, all of which she'd folded neatly in the time it had taken Wendy to do two pairs of socks, and placed them in the laundry basket.

Wendy's face burned as Clementine finally sat down on the couch, stretched her legs out on the ottoman in front of her and exhaled, her whole body deflating. Once again Barb had stepped in and been there when she couldn't, and for two years neither of them had said anything to her. But why would they? Wendy had always been clear that she expected her girls to be financially independent, because she'd learned the hard way after Dan died how important it was for a woman to have her own money, and it was a lesson she never wanted to forget.

"I didn't know."

"No one did . . . not even Steve," Clementine admitted.

"What?" Wendy said, shocked.

"It's nothing compared to his deceit. I thought I was

being smart, I thought I'd found a way, and we'd all get a home out of it. He couldn't contribute anyway, so I decided not to tell him."

"I see," Wendy said, not sounding very convinced.

"Barb's also the one who got me my new job, *and* she's doing a reno *and* she's bidding on a huge project right now. She's juggling a lot."

Wendy realized that she hadn't been in touch nearly as much as she should've been since her firing.

"You're juggling a lot too," she said, wanting to steer the conversation back to Clementine and her situation. "How did this happen? Surely you must've had some idea."

"Obviously I didn't, or I wouldn't be in this mess."

"Right, well, you're going to need a plan," Wendy said, coming to sit next to her. "Unfortunately something this big isn't going to just work itself out."

She'd expected to find her girls in need of some kind of help when she arrived, but she hadn't expected to find things had gone so horribly off course. She knew that Clementine had been frustrated by Steve's lack of paid work and the amount of time he devoted to his fledgling career as an entrepreneur. Despite the enormous financial burden on her daughter, Wendy was happy that Clementine was fighting for the marriage, for Jonah's sake. She knew how difficult it was to raise a child without a husband and she'd never wanted that for Clementine.

"It *just* happened, Mom. I haven't had time to figure out a plan yet."

"I know and I'm not trying to criticize you, honey, I'm trying to help."

"Who just hands their finances over to their spouse?"

"You were just trying to protect his ego, nothing wrong with that. And I bet it worked."

"For a while . . . but it's also the reason I'm in this mess."

"You're in this mess because Steve's a liar. And that's not your fault, and we're going to get you out of it," she said, and reached for Clementine's hand.

"How?" Clementine asked, her eyes wide and voice hopeful, as if Wendy actually had the answer. And wasn't that what Wendy wanted? For her daughters to trust that she knew best.

"Well, I don't know yet," Wendy replied, trying to sound reassuring, and squeezing Clementine's hand, "but we'll figure it out."

Clementine sat up and leaned her head on Wendy's shoulder. "Oh, Mom, I've made such a mess of things."

"Honey, you were doing what you thought was best for your marriage."

"No," Clementine said quietly, "I was doing what you thought was best for my marriage."

It caught Wendy off guard and she chose her words carefully. "Well, that's how we did it back in my day. The husband controlled the finances."

"But that wasn't how *you* did it," Clementine said and turned to face Wendy. "You divorced Ed and raised us on your own, you never handed over your money to anyone."

"That was different, I had no one to rely on, and besides I had my career."

"I don't rely on Steve and I have a career. I'm the one working and making all the money."

"I know you work hard, but it's not . . . the same."

"Why not?"

Wendy paused. She thought the reason was obvious, but she could tell by the look on Clementine's face that it wasn't. "Because, what you do is more of a job and what I do is more of a *career*, a calling really, it's important to a lot of people. That's why I give so much attention to my work. And you, well, you chose to give that attention to your family instead."

Wendy watched as Clementine's face clouded over.

"Do you think I invested so much in my marriage and family because I had nothing 'important' to do with my life?"

"That's not what I meant. . . ."

"You had a family, you had me and Barb. Are you saying that your work was more important than us?"

"Of course not," Wendy said flustered. "Clearly you're important, I'm here aren't I? And we're going to find Steve and make him come back and make things right."

Clementine stared at Wendy.

"So that's your plan? For me to just forgive Steve and move on?"

"I know it's not going to be easy, but it might be what's best for you and Jonah. It's hard raising a child on your own, trust me."

"You weren't on your own, Mom, Barb helped. She's still helping."

Wendy was silent. None of this had gone the way she'd hoped, and she didn't understand why everything that came out of her mouth sounded different from how she intended it. It was so much easier giving advice to strangers than it was to give it to her daughters, who took everything Wendy said and used it against her.

"You know what's interesting? That everything you've told me to do, you didn't do yourself. But I always thought it was what you *would* do, if things had been different, you know if Dad hadn't died, and if Ed was actually a stand-up guy, but maybe I was wrong.

Maybe it wasn't so much that your advice was good for me, but that it was good *enough* for me. After all, what else have I got going on?"

"Clementine . . . ," Wendy said and reached for her daughter, who stood up and moved out of her way.

"You know what Barb said? That whenever you're around, I turn into the same seven-year-old who is just happy that you came home. And she's right. I do. I am. But I'm not Jonah's age anymore, and if you really want to help me, then maybe it's actually best if you keep your opinions to yourself."

"Honey, please," Wendy said, standing to stop Clementine from leaving.

"I'm tired and I have to go to bed. I'm starting a stupid new job after I get Jonah to camp. I'll see you in the morning."

Wendy watched as Clementine walked up the stairs. The moment she was out of sight, she collapsed onto the sofa. Clementine wasn't wrong. She had given her daughter advice that she herself would have rejected. But wasn't that what a good mother did? Take a clear-eyed look at her children and advise them to do what she believed was best for *them*? Wendy knew that, above everything else, Clementine had always craved stability and security—the stability and security that Wendy hadn't been able to give her. If she could appease Steve and his ego, if she could find a way to make her marriage work, then maybe Clementine could have what Wendy hadn't been able to give her?

Now, sitting in a dark living room in a house her daughter didn't own, Wendy began to doubt herself. Had she laid the burden of making the marriage work solely on Clementine, simply because she was the wife? And wasn't that just the kind of old-fashioned thinking that the magazine had accused her of? Wendy lay down on the couch and found Jonah's stuffed shark Sammie wedged between the cushions and rescued it. Cradling it for comfort, she squeezed her eyes shut and sighed heavily. She'd been right about her daughters needing her, but she'd underestimated how much they'd learned to fill that need with one another a long time ago.

Thirteen

You don't have to be a celebrity to live like one. At The Point, we believe that all our homeowners are stars. Offering a carefully curated selection of high-end finishes, we understand that your home is more than just a luxury condominium; it's a reflection of you, and just how fabulous your life is. Or at least how fabulous it looks to others, which, let's face it, is what you really want, because the alternative, that you're just a regular person, with a regular life, and regular problems that you can't fix with the right light fixture or faucet, is just too damn depressing.

Clementine regarded her reflection in the mirror and frowned. She looked like she was wearing a duvet cover, one that had just emerged from the dryer all tangled and wrinkled and misshapen. She'd felt fashionable and professional when she'd left the house an hour ago after a careful goodbye from Wendy, both of them still tender from their argument the night before. She'd raced to get Jonah to camp, only to miss her train as she checked the recent credit card charges, which included a massage and a meal of over a hundred dollars at the resort. She'd called the hotel, hoping to speak to Steve, but unless she knew the number of the room he was staying in, the front desk wouldn't connect her, let alone confirm that he was even staying there. And even though it made her blood boil to see Steve still using her card, she was glad that she could track his movements. When Clementine's train to work finally arrived, she'd piled onto the un-air-conditioned car where she was just another piece of meat in a human sandwich of angry commuters, and arrived in Greenpoint rumpled and covered in sweat not entirely her own.

Standing now in the women's bathroom of The Point's sales office, Clementine dried the back of her neck with paper towels and tried once more to use her damp fingers as a poor substitute for an iron. It was no use. She twisted her hair up into a knot and brushed on some bright-pink lip gloss before grabbing her binders. It was the best she could do. You didn't need to be a model to sell model suites, right? Then again, maybe you did, she thought as she came face-to-face with a woman holding the identical binders and looking like she had just stepped out of the pages of a fashion magazine. Clementine immediately recognized her as Dominic's lunch date.

"I'm Arianna. You must be Clementine. Follow me."

She led Clementine across the concrete lobby situated on the future site of The Point to the sales offices and model suites that faced the street. On one wall hung large artist renderings of The Point next to plans of the different layouts available. In the middle of the showroom sat staged reproductions of what the units would look like, provided the clients went with all of the upgraded finishes *and* still had money to furnish their apartments at designer stores. It was a tricky distinction; this aspirational lifestyle category appealed to hardworking, upwardly mobile thirty-somethings who molded their lives in the image of their influencers whose homes were regularly featured in shelter magazines. They might never be famous themselves, but that didn't mean they couldn't live like famous people.

Clementine stared at one of the ads she'd written. In it, a man and woman in their early thirties walked arm in arm, she in a camel-colored cashmere coat, he in a dark cable-knit sweater and soft wool cap. Holding their environmentally friendly glass and cork to-go cups of steaming coffee they walked against an autumnal backdrop of red and orange leaves in a park in the middle of a city, with the caption *The Point is . . . to Fall in Love.* Another couple, this time two men in winter coats with groomed silver hair that complemented their snowy surroundings, walked their large black Labradoodle along the waterfront beneath text that read *The Point is . . . to Be Home for the Holidays.* There was one for spring too, and Clementine marveled over the hairstyles of the women sitting on a landscaped terrace: a sleek blond blow-out, a sun-kissed Afro, silky jet-black bob, and soft brown waves, the heads they belonged to all thrown back in laughter as they raised their glasses of rosé over the words *The Point is . . . to Spring into the Weekend.* The photo was saying we all belong here, we celebrate diversity, albeit the kind that applies to under-forty-somethings who are preternaturally gorgeous—not economic diversity, or age, or parents of young children, God forbid. The final poster, with a summer scene, was the largest and was centered on the building of *The Point.* Looming larger than life as slightly out-of-focus people swirled around its base on bikes and frolicked on its rooftop balcony, it beamed as the sun hit its shimmery glass surface, *The Point is . . . Your Home.*

"You haven't done this before," Arianna said matter-of-factly, watching her.

"No. I work with Rishi. I wrote these . . ." She gestured to the posters. "I had my own marketing firm, but . . ." She stopped herself. "I'm trying something new."

"Well, you'll either love it or hate it."

"What about you?"

"It pays the bills for now. You'll get a lot of window-shoppers, but that's okay, because we can shop too," Arianna said.

"Dream, maybe. There's no way I could afford any of these places," Clementine said. She couldn't imagine that they'd be making that much money in commissions, but then again Arianna did look as affluent as the buyers they wanted, which she guessed was the point, pun intended. She'd have to try harder in the wardrobe department tomorrow.

She was about to ask her new colleague how long she'd been doing this when Arianna whipped out her phone and handed it to Clementine. She then flung her arms open wide and stood against the wall with the final image, *Your Home*, just above her.

"Take a few, they're for our Instagram," Arianna said, angling herself perfectly, and Clementine did.

By two o'clock, Clementine had completed only two showings. Though she'd been dreading giving potential buyers the tour, Clementine had found herself increasingly frustrated as Arianna pounced on people the moment they walked in, like a salesgirl in a department store on commission during the holidays. No matter where she positioned herself in the sales office or how quickly she greeted people who entered, Arianna's enthusiasm and well-practiced repertoire of conversation starters—she loved their shoes, had the same handbag, also went to NYU, big fan of dogs, adored the restaurants in the area—hooked everyone. Her ability to find common ground had her making fast friends who gladly gave over their information to the The Point data bank in under a minute before being whisked upstairs to a mock-up of the penthouse suite.

She *did* let Clementine handle a nice young couple with a fussy baby. Clementine suspected they had come in only for some air-conditioned relief, perhaps taking a brief reprieve from their new reality as exhausted parents by playing tourist in someone else's imagined life. A life without bottles and spit-up cloths and unmade beds, and dishes on the counter where they ate, their dining room table now a place to fold endless piles of laundry. Clementine could practically read their minds as they stared at the luxurious furniture—all in shades of white and gray and dotted with perfectly positioned throw pillows in embroidered linen—the gas fireplace between a thin wall of glass that divided the dining and kitchen area, and the long waterfall marble counter that ran the length of the kitchen and overlooked the units' high transparent balconies. It was clear that this was no place for children. Not that they were really interested, she knew—the way their own baby wrapped her fingers around her mother's as she finally slept on her chest was more rewarding than anything the condo could offer.

The other tour had been for Rishi, who took the opportunity to quiz Clementine on everything she knew. A test she passed with ease if not quite enough enthusiasm, given that he wasn't a real buyer.

It was after Arianna scooped up the ninth potential buyer in a row (yes, she was counting) that Clementine finally spoke up.

"Look, the next one that comes in is mine. I can't just sit here all day." It came out more harshly than she intended.

"You showed that couple with the baby around," Arianna said, not bothering to look up from her phone, where she was busy Instagramming her smoothie bowl in a ray of sunlight that beamed in through the window, the Manhattan skyline as her backdrop.

"Right, the couple with the baby who were never going to live here."

"Seriously. Sorry they were such time wasters. Who'd live in a building like this with a baby?"

"Look, I'm not blaming them for wanting to have a peek around, but I think we need to divide it up a bit more fairly. Besides, I need to leave in an hour anyways to get my son, so you'll get everyone after that. If I could just take the next two people that come in I'd really appreciate it." Clementine reached into her pocket for her lipstick and reapplied it as Arianna studied her.

"How old is your kid?" she asked.

"Six, almost seven." She still remembered answering the same question in weeks, then months, then years. Soon it would be "He's in middle school," then high school, a freshman in college. It all went by too fast.

"I didn't know you were married," Arianna said, walking over to where she sat and taking off her sky-high leopard-print heels to rub her feet over the soft shag carpet.

Clementine looked at her bare left hand. She'd stopped wearing the small gold wedding band when she was pregnant with Jonah and her hands swelled, and hadn't put it back on. The fact that Steve had never worn a wedding band and that she should be the only one to do so had never sat right with her.

"I'm not. I mean I am, but we've just separated. It's only been a few days." Would it now be the same thing with Steve? Weeks, months, years, my ex-husband? The thought saddened Clementine.

"Why'd you split?"

Clementine would never think of asking this of someone she'd just met. But Arianna had asked it as if she wanted to know what her favorite color was or what she'd eaten for lunch. She supposed it wasn't going to be the last time someone pried, so she tried out an answer.

"He betrayed me—not in the way you might think, but he lied to me and it was a big lie and I can't forgive him."

"Liars are the worst." It was obvious by the way she said it that she'd had personal experience. "I'd rather have someone tell me the truth and break my heart than lie to me."

Clementine was silent for a moment as Arianna stared at the carpet. "What about you, are you married?"

"Not yet. Two more years."

"Oh, you're engaged?"

"No," said Arianna. "I'm single, but I've worked it out. I've got six months to meet someone, and then a year to date before we get engaged, then married six months after that. It'll happen fast, now that I'm focused on it."

"Oh."

"Listen, I'm sorry I hogged everyone, but I thought

you were looking for a husband too. You can take the next one, unless it's a guy who really fits my checklist."

Clementine wasn't sure what surprised her more: that Arianna was husband shopping or that she had a whole list. "You have a list?"

"I have a whole system," Arianna explained. "Well, it's not mine, it's Samantha Love's."

"Who?"

"The influencer? 'Love yourself, Love your life'? You've never heard of her?"

"I'm not on social media."

"Why not?"

Clementine wasn't a Luddite, she just didn't see the point of wasting time staring at pictures of other people's food or the glamorous places they traveled to and their witty one-liners about what they loved or sometimes hated, selling their points of view and themselves to an audience who could scroll through them and hundreds more in a matter of minutes. Steve had eaten it up, though. She'd often accused him of paying more attention to what other successful entrepreneurs did online than to his own family, obsessing over their tweets and trying to befriend them in the hopes that he could become one of them. But Clementine wasn't about to share all of this, so she just shrugged, which Arianna took as a sign that she wanted to hear more.

"She's amazing," Arianna said, her whole face lighting up. "She was just this regular woman working in a department store in Los Angeles, hawking face creams to rich people. She was about to turn thirty on the fifth anniversary of her arrival, five being a very powerful number, and decided that it was now or never. She quit her job, and hiked up Mount Hollywood trail in Griffith Park toward the Hollywood sign like she had so many times before, only this time she told herself if she could figure out a reason to stay by the time she reached the top, she would, and if not, then she would go back to Texas. And as she got to the end of her hike, the sky opened up and this freak rainstorm happened and it was like a balm for her soul washing away all her fears and frustrations. And that's when she knew."

Arianna smiled widely, as if everything she'd just said made perfect sense. The copywriter in Clementine appreciated how neatly this narrative had been packaged, but she also wondered how anyone could even verify such a story.

"She knew what?" Clementine asked, taking the bait.

"Balm. Lip balm. That's what she was going to do. Make the world's best-selling organic lip balm." Arianna reached into her pocket and pulled out the tiny little round baby-pink tin that Clementine knew so well.

"She makes Love's Lip Balm?"

"Yes." Arianna smiled, satisfied.

"I love that stuff. It's ridiculously expensive, but I still buy it." Now it was Clementine's turn to sound like a Love-struck fan. She liked the little inspirational notes that could be found on the underside of the cover's light pink tin. *Love yourself. Love what you do. Love is love. Love to Laugh. Love Life.* There were a ton of them. Clementine knew that they were cheesy, but they made her smile each time she saw them. She reached into her pocket for her own tin and, feeling like a middle grader who had just been invited to sit with the cool girls in the cafeteria, held it up.

"That's a great story, but how do you know it's true?" Clementine asked, the words "Love Yourself" shining up at her.

"She filmed the whole thing. You can find it on her YouTube channel."

"She filmed her epiphany?"

"Well, she did a reenactment. It's amazing, you have to see it." Arianna pulled out her phone and called Clementine over. "Check it out, changed my life," she said, finding the video and fast-forwarding it to show Samantha Love at the end of her hike, standing beneath the Hollywood sign and scanning the city skyline. Suddenly, Samantha throws her arms up in the air and yells, "Just give me a sign!" And the sound of thunder is heard, and the camera tilts up toward the sky as the clouds part and rain falls down against the backbeat of an anthemic pop song.

It felt vaguely like a music video, or one of those melodramatic movie montages that always made Clementine laugh. But Arianna wasn't laughing, her face was full of emotion as she gently rocked back and forth to the music.

"Thank you!" Samantha yelled to the sky as the rain soaked her. In the next second, the rain was gone, Samantha was dry and gorgeous and looking out over the city as the sun was rising on what looked like a new day. She turned slowly to the camera and addressed her viewers directly.

"That wasn't just a sign, it was a *balm*, a balm for my soul," she said, and nodded meaningfully. "I think we could all use a balm, don't you?" With a twinkle in her eyes, and a smile on her lips, she looked off into the distance, where a rainbow cut across the screen as the video faded out.

Clementine thought it wasn't so much an epiphany as a carefully edited and slickly produced teaser for the Samantha Love Brand, and the Love's Lip Balm product launch that would follow, but she didn't see any reason to offer that to Arianna.

"Amazing, right?" Arianna said, standing. Sharing time over, she put away her phone, flipped her hair down her back, and plastered a huge smile on her face. "Hi, welcome to The Point. Let me show you around," Arianna said to a well-dressed man who looked to be in his mid-thirties and had just entered the showroom with an older woman who appeared to be his mother. She turned to Clementine and winked. "Next one is yours, I promise."

Fourteen

S *pace. It means different things to different people. Room to grow and explore, the square footage of a home, the distance between ourselves and someone else. And then there are the spaces deep within ourselves where our memories and dreams exist, stuck in time between what was and what could've been.*

Clementine checked her card to see if there were any more charges from Steve, but so far nothing. She'd texted him five times already, asking him where he'd gone, when would he be back, what should she tell Jonah? But he hadn't responded once. She tucked the phone in her pocket and told herself to focus. Perched on a chair near the entrance, she was determined to hold Arianna to her promise that the next potential buyer who came in was indeed hers. Holding an information package, she scanned the pages as if she were really interested in the copy that she'd written, in an effort not to appear as if she was just waiting to pounce on the next person who walked in, which of course she was. The second she heard footsteps cross the entrance she looked up with a big smile on her face and moved forward to claim the visitor as her own.

"Welcome to The Point," Clementine said, as she came face-to-face with Dominic Provato, who strolled into The Point like he owned the place, which he kind of did.

"Why, thank you," he said, and leafed through the sign-in sheets.

"I thought that you were a customer . . . ," Clementine mumbled, feeling stupid. She could smell his cologne, a mixture of salt and lemons that made her think of lemonade stands and how she'd promised Jonah she'd pick up ingredients on the way home so they could hold one this weekend. It always cost her more than they made, as Jonah inevitably spent more time talking than selling, telling people about the origin of lemons, the fact that they were actually first grown in Asia and were really a hybrid between a citron, and a bitter orange. Most people just moved on after that.

"How's it going today?" Dominic asked.

"It's good," Clementine said. She stood up, suddenly feeling awkward, not knowing if she should hug him or shake his hand or apologize for bleeding all over his handkerchief the last time she saw him. So she folded her arms in front of her body instead.

"Arianna showing you the ropes? She's my best sales associate."

"I can tell."

Dominic tapped the sign-in sheets and smiled. "Just don't let her hog all the commissions. While it's great for sales, it hasn't made it easy to find anyone who can work with her."

"I heard that," Arianna said, walking up behind him and punching him in the arm.

"Good. You need to make sure Clementine gets to work with some real potential buyers, not just the ones you don't want. Just because you're family, doesn't mean you can get away with not sharing."

"Wait, you're related?" Clementine said.

"Arianna's my niece," Dominic answered.

"Why didn't you say anything?" Clementine asked Arianna.

"Same reason you didn't tell me that you're Barb's sister. You would have thought I got this job just because I'm related to someone. Although in your case it's kind of obvious."

"I will need to actually show some people around in order to get better."

Arianna smiled. "Fair enough."

Clementine looked at the clock on the wall and jumped. "I'm sorry, I have to get going or I'll be late picking Jonah up from camp again. Maybe I can call Barb. Shit, I'll figure this all out soon, I'm just not used to . . ." She trailed off, stuffing her folders into her tote bag and rummaging in her purse for her phone.

"Don't apologize," Dominic said. "Family comes first. I actually have a meeting with Barb at her office in an hour, so why don't I give you a lift? That way you can get Jonah, and Barb won't have a reason to cancel on me."

"But you'd be going to Long Island City, just to turn around and come back to Greenpoint for your meeting. Are you sure?"

"I'm sure. I have the time, it's fine. I'll see you tomorrow," Dominic said to Arianna, who was already on her phone and didn't bother looking up as she waved.

Dominic held the door open for Clementine and led her onto the street where his car, a brand-new Porsche SUV, was double-parked.

"Thanks again," Clementine said. She carefully climbed into the car, aware that it cost more than she'd make in a year, and quickly checked the bottom of her shoes to make sure they were clean before placing them on the floor mats. She always wondered who drove a car like this; it was the midlife crisis of a rich family man. Sporty, yet sensible.

Clementine and Dominic kept their gaze at the road up ahead, but Clementine *was* remembering the night they first met. Barb was in her final year of her five-year Bachelor of Architecture program at RISD, and had invited Clementine up to Providence for the weekend. It had been a long train ride from New York and by the time Clementine arrived a snowstorm had kicked up and was threatening to shut everything down. They'd just made it back to Barb's apartment from the supermarket, their faces frozen and their lashes covered in tiny icicles, when the phone started ringing. As they unpacked wine, cheese, olives, and bread, the answering machine played a steady stream of cancellations for Barb's dinner party, from friends who were too nervous to make the trip for fear of getting stranded.

It was no surprise to Clementine that Barb was the most frequent hostess in her friend group. Her sister had a grown-up place with real furniture, floor models of sofas and chairs from design stores along with pieces that she'd bought from student artists, a coffee table she'd made herself from a tree trunk cut in half, and her own photographs on the walls. She'd moved out of residence the moment she could to create a real home for herself. Barb had been a grown-up to Clementine for as long as she could remember.

"Looks like it's just us," Barb said, uncorking a bottle of wine and pouring them each a glass. "Next time you come up, I'll have everyone over."

Although she was disappointed that there wouldn't be a party, Clementine could hardly blame her sister for the storm that now immobilized the city, hiding it beneath a thick frosting of white that sparkled under the streetlights. She took the half-glass of red wine her sister handed her, making eye contact to avoid bad luck, or seven years of bad sex, as Barb had once warned her, and took a sip.

"So why don't you tell me what's bothering you? And don't say nothing, because you haven't stopped chewing the inside of your mouth since you arrived, which you only do when you're nervous, and it's a disgusting habit, so please stop it."

Clementine released the inside of her cheek from her teeth and exhaled. "I got into the marketing program at UCBerkeley, which means I could do an internship at an agency over the summer in San Francisco and get real experience, and seeing as you'll already be there after you graduate, I thought I could come out and stay with you and we could get a place together." Clementine had hoped to play it cool, but she couldn't keep the eagerness from her voice.

"Wow. That's huge. What does Wendy say about all this?"

"You know Mom, she thinks New York is the greatest place in the world, and as I also got into NYU, she thinks I should stay, live at home, and save the money for grad school. But who says I'm even going to go to grad school?"

"She probably just wants you to keep your options open."

"But I know what I want to do, is that so hard to believe? You know what you want to do."

"Yeah, but it is expensive to live away from home." Barb took a sip of her wine and looked outside as the snow continued to fall.

"I get it, you don't want me around."

"It's not that. It's that I don't know how long I'm going to stay in San Francisco. It might be a year, it might be a month. I'm thinking of buying a van and fixing it up and traveling around the country," Barb said.

"Wow," Clementine said.

"I wasn't sure if I was going to do it, but I've saved up enough for the first few months, and I've never spent the money that Dad left us. . . ."

Her voice got quiet, and for a moment the two of them sat in that shared silence of missing him that they'd known ever since they were girls.

"I thought I'd go north to Woodstock, where a visiting professor of mine is designing tiny houses that I want to check out. Then I'll head up to Toronto while the weather is good. . . ." She paused for a moment—they hadn't been back since their dad died. "I want to see our old place, then head west to Chicago, maybe stay awhile. I could get a van and drive down to Bellingham and Portland, then to Los Angeles to see the Case Study Houses. After all that, I was thinking I could go to San Francisco," she said.

"Wow, that's a lot of driving."

"I know, but there's a lot I want to see. Like how are all these cities staying vital using space in innovative ways as they grow. They can't just demolish everything and start over every fifty years, so what about all those old abandoned buildings and warehouses? What about all those unused little patches of land? We need to figure it out, because after a while we're gonna run out of space."

Clementine had never seen Barb so excited. With a sinking heart, she understood that this was something her sister had to do—and she had to do it without Clementine tagging along.

"It sounds amazing. Are you actually going to live anywhere? You can't just drive forever."

"No, of course not. I already have a couple of offers to intern at firms in Chicago and San Francisco, and they both sound good, so who knows how long I'll be gone."

"A long time, it looks like," Clementine said, trying to take in all the places where her sister wanted to go. These last few years were the longest they'd ever been apart, and until this year Barb had come home at least once a month to visit. Wendy had been traveling more than ever to promote her books and as a guest speaker at book fairs, and Clementine had convinced herself that her days of feeling alone were coming to an end with Barb's graduation.

"You're going to be okay," Barb said. "We'll still talk and I'll send you postcards from all the places I go."

"I know," Clementine said, trying not to feel sorry for herself. "It's just not the same without you."

"You're not going to be alone," Barb said. She sat next to Clementine on the bed and put her arm around her. "You'll live on campus and you'll meet so many new people and who knows, maybe you'll do your own big trip after you graduate. This is your time to find out."

"Maybe," Clementine said. She'd spent so much

time in the shadows of her mother's and sister's dreams that her own seemed less important.

"Look at me," Barb said, looking her in the eye. "Have fun, play the field, live a little. This is your time now."

And Clementine nodded like she understood what that meant, as if "her time" was something she'd just been waiting for her whole life, and not a terrifying prospect that came with the expectation that she should do something important with it.

Before either of them could say any more, there was a knock on the door and Barb jumped up to answer it.

"Sorry we're late. Are we the last to arrive?" Dominic asked, stomping his boots on the mat outside and shaking the snow from his mop of dark curls. He reminded Clementine of a Roman statue, his limbs almost too long for his body, the bones in his face strong and serious. He and Barb's friend Gwen had been around the corner at the library; thanks to Dominic's new truck, they had been able to drive through the snow.

"You're the only ones to arrive," Barb said. "Everyone else bailed because of the storm."

"Should we go?" Dominic asked, clutching his brown paper bag closer as they stood in the hall.

"I'm not going right back out in that," Gwen said, coming inside. She was all coat and scarf at first glance, but as she undressed a tiny woman with pale-pink hair emerged from the center and gave Barb a quick kiss on the cheek, making her blush. Clementine had met her sister's other girlfriends before, not that Barb would necessarily call them that, given that she wasn't big on labels. Nor was she big on personal displays of affection, which made seeing her sister caught off guard by Gwen's kiss a nice surprise.

"Come in," Barb said as she hung up Gwen's coat. "Gwen, Dominic, this is my sister, Clementine." They exchanged hellos and then Barb continued, "I hope there's food in that bag, because I was in charge of drinks and appetizers, so all I have is olives, cheese, and wine."

"I have pasta, parsley, and clams," Dominic said.

"Clams?" Gwen asked.

"Yeah, I was told to bring something."

"And you brought clams?"

"What did you bring?" Dominic asked.

"I brought the fun," Gwen said. She grabbed the bottle of wine and filled a glass for herself and for Barb. "Who brings clams?" she said laughing, taking Barb's hand and crossing the room to look at her record collection, leaving Clementine and Dominic alone.

"I love clams," Clementine said, forcing herself to speak. She took the bag from Dominic, her heart beating faster than normal, the way it always did when she was around a good-looking guy. Clementine had very little experience with guys her age, let alone handsome older ones who looked at her the way Dominic was looking at her now.

"Do you like to cook?" he asked as he wiped the kitchen island down with a cloth and grabbed a colander off the wall.

"I like to eat. I'm just not much of a cook," she said, resting on a stool that Barb had made out of two chairs salvaged from a thrift store. In truth the only meal that she knew how to make was a Crock-Pot chili that she could eat for the week when she was on her own. When Wendy returned from her travels, the first thing she would do is take Clementine out for dinner at a restaurant of her choosing and they'd catch up. The rest of the time they'd pick up falafel sandwiches or pizza and make a green salad. Wendy didn't see the point in cooking for just two people, but Clementine knew it was also that her mother had never really been much of a cook.

"Neither is Barb. Hence the clams. Let's cook them before the power goes out again," Dominic said.

"What can I do?"

"How about a glass of white wine? Gwen seems to have forgotten us," Dominic said, looking over at

Gwen and Barb at the other side of the apartment in the living room.

"That I can do," she said, pouring them each a glass and wondering if he thought that she was twenty-one. She passed him the wine as he filled a pot of water on the stove, and spread slices of French bread drizzled in olive oil on a baking sheet for the oven. Clearly he knew Barb's kitchen better than she did. "Not your first dinner party here, I take it?"

"No. But I love to cook, so it's okay. And this apartment . . . ," he said appreciatively. "I mean, who has a place like this at school?"

Clementine sipped her wine, her cheeks warming. Her sister had always been a woman who knew what she wanted, which at that moment must be Gwen, or else she wouldn't be letting her take one of her records out of its sleeve so clumsily. Clementine saw Barb cringe as Gwen carried the record with her thumbs on its surface and put it down on the turntable, making them all wince at the sound of the needle's hard landing before the melodies of Fleetwood Mac filled the apartment.

"I bet you're not on campus," Clementine said. Not with that brand-new coat and those boots by the door, or the bag of groceries from the fine food store, or the ease with which he carried himself. Having had and not had money growing up, Clementine was aware of what the difference looked like. Before her mother married Ed, Clementine could remember her polishing her one good pair of dress shoes after she wore them, and wrapping them in paper before storing them back in their box, or tucking a lavender sachet in her coat pocket after brushing it. It wasn't that they were poor, but they were careful, her dad a big believer in not wasting and making things last. *You only get one chance to make a first impression,* Wendy was fond of saying, and she wanted hers to be that she was doing well. It was only later, when they lived with Ed, who would come home and toss his cashmere coat on the bench by the front door and kick off his leather loafers, that Clementine understood that these were just things to him, easy to replace.

"No. I have a condo downtown. It's new and it's boring, but my parents don't believe in wasting money on rent, so . . ."

"They bought it for you?"

"Well, yes, in a way. They built it. My dad's a developer," he said, dropping the clams into the boiling water with a palmful of salt.

"And is that what you're going to be?"

"Well, it's a family business, so . . . what about you?"

"I'm going to go into marketing, or advertising. I thought maybe I'd be a writer like my mom, but I think it's hard to make money doing that."

"And money's important to you?"

Clementine had never known a time when money wasn't important. After her father died and her mother had remarried so quickly, Clementine remembered her mother arguing on the phone with a contentious friend, saying that people could call her whatever they wanted but she needed to take care of her two girls. After Ed, Wendy had fought for a settlement large enough to buy their Midtown apartment and insisted that the reason she worked so hard afterward was *so they wouldn't lose it,* property taxes and maintenance costs eating a big chunk of her earnings every month. Until Wendy really started making money from her column and books, Clementine would find the backs of envelopes tucked around the apartment covered in calculations, her mother regularly juggling their finances as she tried to find a way to pay for piano lessons and swim classes and trips to see their grandparents in Montréal when they were still alive. "Money's important to everyone except those who've never had to worry about it."

Dominic nodded in agreement as he chopped parsley and lemon and set them aside. "True enough."

"My mother taught me that, and to always have my own."

"An independent woman, just like your sister."

Clementine looked over at Barb, who was reading the back of the album cover and trying to talk to Gwen, who was more interested in nuzzling her neck.

"Well, not just like her." She hadn't meant to sound flirty, but by the way Dominic stopped chopping the parsley and raised his eyebrows, she guessed she had.

"Good to know." He placed his hands on the counter to lean forward and really look at her. His voice was deep and low and it made Clementine glow inside; the idea of being the center of attention to anyone, especially someone as attractive as Dominic, was intoxicating.

"What else should I know about you?"

It was a good question, and if she was better at flirting she'd say something like, *I don't know, why don't you tell me* or *Why don't you find out*, like a character in a movie, but it would sound stupid coming from her, and he'd probably just laugh, so she thought for a moment and answered. "I'm kind of good at a lot of things, but not exceptional at one thing. Not like Barb. Or my mother." Clementine had always felt that her mother was disappointed that she wasn't more ambitious, that she couldn't say that she wanted to have her own agency that would change the face of advertising, the way that Barb wanted to change the world of architecture or the way Wendy claimed to change women's lives with her advice.

"Somehow I doubt that." If he was flirting back she couldn't tell.

"It's true, and that's okay. You can't light a sky with only North Stars." It was something her mother had said to Clementine when she didn't get a solo in the school choir and had to be a member of the chorus. She'd meant to cheer Clementine up, but she'd always wondered if maybe her mom had been trying to tell her something, soften the blow for what she believed were inevitable future disappointments based on Clementine's shortcomings.

"Don't sell yourself short," Dominic said. "There'll be enough people that will do that for you." The seriousness with which he said it made Clementine self-conscious and she reached for the wine to top up her glass, reminding herself to take it slow so that she didn't end up drunk and embarrass herself. The most she'd had to drink to date had been two glasses at a wedding.

There were cheese and crackers and more wine and more nuzzling on Barb by Gwen and by the time Stevie Nicks was singing about dreams, everyone was humming along, happy to be in each other's company and inside where it was warm, eating dinner by candlelight. As Clementine listened to Barb and Dominic debate each other, she could see why they were friends.

"Not only is it unrealistic to only focus on new builds, it's irresponsible," Barb said.

"I'm not saying tear everything down, but it's impossible to think that you can meet the needs of a growing city by just rehabbing old buildings," Dominic shot back. "First of all, the retrofitting is expensive and not always feasible, and second, you need to increase density in order to accommodate a growing population."

"What happens when you run out of space?" Clementine asked, then felt proud when Dominic looked at her appreciatively and held his glass up to her in salutation.

"What do you think happens?" he asked.

"Well, if you can't go out, you go up."

"Ugh, high-rises," Gwen said. "All those energy-sucking glass towers, stacking people on top of one another, that's not a community, that's not a neighborhood. Nobody wants to buy air, they want land."

"Well, actually," Clementine said, "if you position it right you can get anyone to buy anything. Our mother works at a magazine and she's always saying that if somebody wants something enough, they'll find a way to justify it. I mean isn't that what the entire advertising industry is based on?"

They all looked at her, and she stared down at the table.

"Go on," Barb encouraged her.

"Well," said Clementine, finding her voice. "You sell them the sky, way above everyone else. It's"—she searched for the right word and found it at the last second—"Aspirational."

Clementine caught the look of surprise on her sister's and Dominic's faces, and liked the way it made her feel, like maybe she was smart too.

"All I know is that I'm not going to waste my time building another large dick like the CN Tower, or the Space Needle," Gwen piped up, slightly drunk, and for a moment things lightened up before Dominic and Barb got into it once more.

"We're running out of wine," Gwen slurred when at last there was a break in the conversation. "We need to go out and get more."

"Nobody's going anywhere in that," Barb said. They followed her gaze out the window, where the wind whipped the branches of barren trees. "And I think that maybe you've had enough wine."

"Bullshit. But I might need a nap. Care to join me?"

She smiled slyly, and Barb followed her into the bedroom.

"Don't mind us, we'll just clean everything up!" Clementine called out as the two of them left the room. Her stomach somersaulted at the idea of being alone with Dominic, who had only grown more attractive to her during dinner.

"Thanks!" Barb yelled back.

Clementine rolled her eyes and started clearing the dishes, Dominic close behind her. "She's unbelievable," she said, with equal parts exasperation and affection.

"That she is," Dominic agreed. "Requests?" he asked crossing the room to Barb's record collection.

"You pick," she said and was surprised when she heard Billie Holiday's voice traveling across the apartment and wrapping around her. As she rinsed the dishes and stacked them on the side of the sink, she was aware that Dominic was watching her. She turned to find him standing on the other side of the island, his hand on a bottle of wine. "I thought we were all out."

"I may have tucked this one out of Gwen's sight. It's more for sipping and less for chugging. I was going to share it with you and Barb, I swear. Although now that I think about it, are you even old enough to drink?"

"I'm old enough to know that I've had enough. But seeing we've been ditched, I say go ahead and enjoy it."

"I like your thinking," Dominic replied. He opened the bottle, poured himself a glass, and swirled it on the counter slowly as he watched her.

"What?" Clementine asked, her heart beating quickly at the way he was looking at her.

"You're really something, you know that?"

Clementine shook her head, her cheeks burning.

"But you're also my friend's little sister, so maybe I shouldn't have said that."

"Do you always do what you should?" she asked, emboldened by the alcohol.

Dominic sipped his wine. "Yes. I'm afraid so. Son of Italian immigrants, all builders. My grandfather was a laborer, my dad a developer, and I'm the first to go to college, so there are a lot of expectations. A lot of *shoulds*."

"Like?"

"Like I *should* join the family business, marry a nice traditional girl from a good family that my parents know, and have kids. And then one day, when my dad is no longer able to run things, I *should* take over and eventually inherit the business."

"I see," Clementine said. The spark in the air that she'd felt between them was snuffed out by his honesty.

She didn't know anyone who talked about their future this way.

"I'm sorry, we were having fun and I just totally killed it."

"That's okay."

Dominic smiled and moved closer to her. He took the dish towel out of her hand, and set it aside.

"What about you? Any *shoulds*?" Dominic asked.

"Well, if you ask Barb, I *should* be excited about going to college, and having a lot of adventures, but to be honest I'm not that adventurous. Having a family with lots of people around sounds kind of great actually. It would be nice to have my own place and someone to share it with, someone who was always there. I know, it's boring."

"I don't think it's boring."

Dominic looked at Clementine for a long moment and then closed the distance between them and kissed her, tenderly at first and then more passionately, before stopping himself. He pulled back and looked at her.

"I'm sorry, I shouldn't . . ."

"It's okay," Clementine whispered, and leaned in to kiss him again.

"Are you sure?" he asked, holding her face in his hands.

"Yes," she said, and placed her hands up under

his sweater. Until now the only guys she'd kissed had been her age. They were sloppy, eager kisses that she'd wrangle her way out of. But it was nothing like this. He hoisted her up on the counter and kissed her again, pausing as she lifted his sweater up over his head, and dropped it onto the kitchen floor. She ran her hands over his chest, and then undid the buttons of her shirt and pressed herself closer to him, the feel of his skin against hers and his mouth on hers exciting her in a way that she hadn't experienced before. She was just about to slip out of her shirt when she heard the sound of Barb's bedroom door opening. Quickly she pulled her shirt closed and buttoned it as Dominic ducked out of sight and pulled on his sweater.

"Gwen's passed right out. And wow, can she snore. Who knew?" Barb said as she walked into the kitchen and stopped at the sight of them so close together. "What's going on?"

"Well," Clementine said, hopping down from the counter.

"Barb, I'm sorry, but . . ."

"Don't be mad at Dominic," Clementine interrupted, "but he had another bottle of wine that he was actually hiding from Gwen, and he opened it."

"Is that so?" Barb asked. "I thought maybe you'd had enough wine."

"I have," Clementine said, "which is why this bottle is just for you two." She grabbed a glass out of the cabinet behind her and passed it to her sister.

"I see," Barb said, slowly taking the glass, and looking back and forth at each of them, then filling her glass to the top. "Well, then how can I be mad?"

Sometime in the middle of the night or early morning it stopped snowing and in the midst of a conversation between Barb and Dominic about whether design dictates a city's personality or the other way around, Clementine had fallen asleep. She woke up on the couch sometime before noon to find that Dominic had left, and she felt silly for being disappointed. It wasn't as if she actually knew him, and yet there was something about him that made it feel like she did—it had been like picking up with an old friend with whom you left things off years earlier.

Clementine waited that day at Barb's to see if he'd call, and when he didn't, that's when Barb told her that he had a nice Italian girlfriend that his family expected him to marry eventually, and besides he was too old for her anyway. After all, her life was just beginning to take shape and his was already so clearly outlined, each chapter written and just waiting for him to step into it.

His next chapter, Clementine would later learn, began just as he said it would, when he proposed to his girlfriend that spring after graduating. And Clementine, left behind by Barb and her mother, stayed in New York for school and kept living at home as Wendy thought she should, and tried to have adventures as Barb suggested. She attended first-year parties and joined a film club, where they watched old movies and then talked about them over coffee at a local diner afterward. Almost everyone she met came from somewhere else and couldn't believe how lucky they were to be in New York. And while she loved the city, for Clementine it was just home.

It was this confession that she made to Steve one night over a slice of lemon meringue pie after having watched *On the Waterfront* with her film club. Steve had come to New York from the Boston suburbs after taking a year off to backpack around Europe, and had declared that out of all the cities he'd been in, Manhattan was still his favorite. And when he suggested that maybe Clementine just needed to see it with new eyes, like he was, she agreed to accompany him around the city as a tourist, then as a friend, and finally as lovers, Steve's sense of adventure just big enough for both of them. As for Dominic, he became a memory, softening over time from painful to wistful and finally finding a fond place in Clementine's brief romantic history.

"You know," Clementine said, breaking the loud silence between them as Dominic drove, "I was pretty sure that I was the thing you regretted about the night we met."

"Why?" Dominic asked, looking over at her.

"Because of Ella. I didn't know that you two were . . ."

"On a break. A long break, actually. I wasn't sure that she was the one."

"And kissing me made you sure. Well, I'm glad I could help," she said, teasing, and squeezed his shoulder as they pulled up to the YMCA.

Dominic put the car in park, undid his seat belt, and turned to face her.

"Kissing you made me realize that I wanted all the same things that you did. I was boring too. It's why I asked Barb to give you my number. I was hoping that you would call. And when I didn't hear from you, I figured you weren't interested. And Ella had been there all along, so . . ."

"Barb never gave me your number," Clementine said before she could stop herself, her mind reeling.

"She told me she did."

Of course she did, Clementine thought. "I had no idea you were actually interested," she said. "We'd only just met, and I was finishing high school."

"I know, and I know it sounds crazy, but I just had this feeling with you that I hadn't had before. And I thought that you felt it too. Did you?"

"It was so long ago. What does it matter?" Clementine said, when what she was thinking was *Yes, I did, and what would my life look like now if it had been you?* What if Dominic had been Jonah's doting dad instead of self-absorbed Steve? She didn't want to think about the answer, let alone have the question to begin with. It was one thing to live with a decision she'd made and another to know that choices had been made for her. She looked at Dominic, unable to speak, and held her breath when he gently reached out and put his hand on hers.

"Don't get me wrong, I'm grateful for everything I have. But there are no surprises."

Clementine looked at his hand and wondered when was the last time she'd held hands with any man besides Steve. Then again, when was the last time she and Steve had held hands? The only person whose palm she'd had in hers was Jonah's, and she was startled to see a grown man's fingers intertwined with her own as he gently pulled her closer to him, his forehead touching hers and making her heart beat wildly.

"You were a surprise that night," he whispered, "and sometimes I regret not finding out if there were more. Don't you?" He leaned in and kissed her on the lips, and for a moment she was eighteen again and in Barb's Providence apartment and now she wished that she'd been able to decide for herself if there was more. But before she could answer, she heard the sound of kids coming outside and pulled back from Dominic as fast as she could, just in time to see Jonah walking out with Seth.

"Clementine, I'm sorry, I . . ."

"I have to go . . ." Clementine whipped off her seat belt and hurried out of the car.

"Wait, I'll drive you both home."

"No, we're good," Clementine said, slamming the door shut and running toward Jonah.

There are always more surprises to discover, she thought, *but not all of them are good.*

Fifteen

A Wise Woman doesn't ask for answers,
she finds them.
—WENDY WISE, *WISE UP*

Wendy was frustrated over the way her arrival had played out, and the coffee-stained Formica counter was proving a worthy outlet for her anger. It astonished her how anyone could make so much mess over one pot of coffee and two bowls of cereal and a glass of juice. As Clementine and Jonah had raced around eating breakfast, Wendy had sat in shock at the kitchen table, nursing her cup of coffee and reading the news on her iPad. She'd checked her new Instagram account and saw the pictures of Samantha, the only person she followed, in another great outfit, another plane, with another clever caption (Love is in the air!) and allowed herself to feel better that someone had appreciated her advice recently. She told herself not to give up, to pivot, to try and take control of the situation. But there'd been no time to clear the air with Clementine as she raced around the house, and Wendy hated that her daughter believed she thought less of her.

Wendy sprayed the counter with soap, giving it one final scrub in the hopes that her physical exertion along with the NPR food show that she'd been listening to about how to make perfect croissants (the right amount of flake on the outside and the right amount of soft on the inside) and the best time to eat them (no more than an hour out of the oven) would drown out her internal replay of the conversation from the night before. But unfortunately her conversation with Clementine kept replaying itself over and over in her head until she finally shouted out loud, "I didn't mean it like that!" and Betsy looked at her suspiciously and got up from her cool spot on the floor near the fridge and moved to the back door for her to open it. Wendy let the pug out to bark at squirrels and stuck her head outside for some fresh air. It would've been easier if this terrible mess had happened to Barb—not that she wanted it for either of her children, but Barb could take care of herself, she was tougher than Clementine and more resilient.

The now clean kitchen made her briefly feel better

about herself, but its rewards were short-lived. As she snooped through the stack of unpaid bills on the kitchen table, her anger toward herself for not being around for the debacle shifted toward Steve, a more comfortable and deserving target. She needed to find him and make him pay for what he had done. For Jonah, and if she was being honest, for herself. The moment she heard that Steve had taken all of Clementine's money, a conversation that she'd had with him a few years earlier had surfaced in her memory, bringing with it a sick feeling that she had somehow emboldened him. It was just after she'd told Clementine that she wouldn't be able to loan them money for a down payment. Steve had driven Wendy back to her apartment, and Wendy had told him that she was sure that he and Clementine would still be able to buy the house, because when something is really important to you, you will do whatever it takes to make it happen. Whatever it takes. At the time she'd been thinking about Steve getting a job so that he could actually contribute financially, not about him stealing all her daughter's money and betraying her and Jonah, of course. Did he really think what he did was okay?

There were so many questions Wendy had and if she wanted answers she was going to have to look for them herself. And what better place than right here? Steve still hadn't been back to collect his things, and Wendy doubted that Clementine had touched anything, whereas Wendy would've taken all of his belongings out to the backyard and lit them on fire. Samantha Love would've done one better, lighting them on fire and posting the whole thing on Instagram.

Wendy climbed the stairs to the master bedroom and opened the closet, finding only shelves of T-shirts, jeans, rows of Converse sneakers, and a variety of base-ball caps. There wasn't a suit or tie in sight, or any of the other uniforms that Wendy associated with men who were in business, an outdated idea, she knew, but still liked. She'd always loved getting dressed up for work, loved the distinction between weekday and weekend wear, and had never really gotten used to seeing her colleagues looking so casual, even though she knew that their jeans and tops could cost just as much, if not more, than her own tailored outfits. She looked around the bedroom. There were stacks of books piled up on the bedside tables and she spotted a couple of her own books piled under a scented candle on Clementine's side. It always gave her a thrill to see her books out in the world, and this was no exception. She picked up *Marry Wisely* and read the inscription.

Dearest Clementine,

I have no doubt that you will make a very Wise Wife.

Wishing you a lifetime of happiness.

xoxo Mom

For a moment, Wendy was happy to see that Clementine valued her advice, but as she flipped through the book, a wave of embarrassment came over her. Had she really highlighted sections of the book for her daughter, and made notes in the margins? She cringed at how pushy it seemed. She'd only meant to be helpful, and judging by the number of pages she saw Clementine must have dog-eared—Wendy would never dog-ear a book herself—maybe she had been.

On Steve's side of the bed she found a stack of business books—*Dare to Disrupt, Paving Your Own Way, Million Dollar Ideas, From Start-Up to Stay Up*—and autobiographies of successful entrepreneurs, all bookmarked somewhere near the middle, making her think that Steve never actually finished them. On his bedside table was a Father's Day picture frame Jonah had made from painted Popsicle sticks, and in it a picture of Jonah at the park, his arms thrown around his parents, all three smiling for the camera. In the background you could see Manhattan, and Wendy could tell that it was taken near Barb's, probably by Barb, on a special occasion when they were all together. All of them except for her.

She carefully put the picture down and opened the drawer of Steve's side table. There she found a glass bowl with loose change, a few old MetroCards, and a photo ID for something called Let's Work featuring what looked like a mug shot of Steve. There was also an opened pack of gum, a couple of pens, a stick of deodorant, and a loose photograph of Steve and Clementine when they were still in college, young, happy, in love. At the back of the drawer, she found Steve's Big Ideas journal and opened it to find another picture tucked in the front side pocket—this one of Clementine and a two-year-old Jonah, holding each other tightly, smiling as they stared into each other's eyes. The edges of the photo were well worn from being handled countless times, and she carefully returned it.

An idea crossed her mind, and she held the journal upside down and shook it. Wendy herself had lived with an unfaithful husband and she knew that there was always something that gave them away. But no picture came tumbling out, no photograph of Steve with some unknown woman. Frankly, maybe an affair would've been easier to handle than the long con of embezzling money from his wife and child. Was Clementine completely naive, Wendy wondered, or had she intentionally ignored the signs?

She half expected to find the journal empty, but the pages had almost been filled with notes, bookmarked with a Co-Pilot coffee card full of frequent visit stamps. She turned the card over, locating the address of the café, in Williamsburg. A clue.

"Shoot," Wendy muttered as a perfect layer of croissant left its buttery mark on the journal page she was reading. Oh well, Steve would probably never notice it, given how careless he was. Only a careless man would cover his tracks so poorly, not to mention be so irresponsible with the coffee card full of frequent visit stamps. Out of spite, she'd redeemed the free cup of coffee it afforded Steve.

The coffee shop was on the main floor of a converted warehouse in Williamsburg, and as soon as her taxi dropped her off, she noticed a sign across the street— LET'S WORK. Another mystery solved. A wide open space with a long tufted leather bench on one side and an enormous communal table on the other, Co-Pilot was dotted with small tables and chairs in between, each one occupied by a young person with a laptop, journal, or phone. It was easy to see why Steve had

chosen this place to write in his Big Ideas journal, surrounded by creative types, but Wendy couldn't help
but feel a little bad for her son-in-law as she read. The
journal was littered with inspirational quotes and bio-
graphical details about people he admired. Entire pages
were filled with trivia about entrepreneurs who'd made
a fortune by turning an idea they had into a reality,
everything from Silicon Valley start-ups to massive
food and beverage companies. It was clear that he was
both impressed by and envious of their success and had
decided that the best way to achieve his own was to
replicate an existing idea with a twist.

The middle of the book was filled with list after list,
that read: Coconut water => *Macadamia Nut Water?*
Or Avocado Toast => *premade avocado toast?* Oat milk
=> *oat milk cheese?* The list went on and on for pages
until it arrived at fruit water + carbonation => multi-
billion-dollar industry, so why not *vegetable water +
carbonation?* It was the first truly original idea that
Steve had written, and he'd circled it many times in
red. Wendy shuddered. The idea of carbonated tomato
water made her ill. She couldn't imagine how anyone
could have invested in the idea and then realized that
they likely hadn't—that was why he had used the down
payment money for his company.

As Wendy turned the pages, looking for clues, it

dawned on her that it wasn't so much a journal of big ideas as it was a journal of longing, and for a moment she had another pang of sadness for Steve. She knew what it was like to want more, to strive for something bigger than one's daily reality, but that didn't make what he did right. As she came to the last marked page, there was a list entitled "Potential Investors," all the entries scratched out except for one: Barb. She bookmarked the page so she could go back and check out the other names a little later. She might even circle back later to check out Let's Work. But first, her oldest daughter was going to get a surprise visit, whether she liked it or not.

Sixteen

You can't choose your family, but you can choose your spouse. Best to make sure they get along.
—WENDY WISE, *MARRY WISELY*

"Fuck me," said Barb, hearing the doorbell ring as she was coming out of the shower. "Can you get that?" she called out to Jill. She took a sip of the green juice that Jill had left for her on the bathroom counter and tried not to be sick. Jill didn't really drink enough to get hangovers; if she did, she'd know that what Barb actually needed was a bacon double cheeseburger and fries.

Barb wasn't going anywhere fast today, her night having only ended hours before. When she'd stumbled into her friend Ivan's dive bar after her fight with Jill, he'd suggested that they do a quick shot for old time's sake. That shot led to Ivan's tearful admission that the bar might be closing for good if the city approved a plan to tear the building down and put up condos, which led to a second shot and Ivan sobbing on Barb's shoulder that he had nowhere to go if they forced him out, which led to a third and final shot and a terrible a cappella rendition of "We Are the Champions" and Barb's slurred promise to find and stop the mother-fuckerswhothinktheycanjusttearthewholecitydown. It was only in the middle of the few hours of sleep that Barb got after she went home that she had remembered that she was one of those very motherfuckers.

"Wendy! Hi! What a nice surprise," Jill said, loud enough for Barb to hear.

Shit—so much for a morning of Netflix and hash browns. Barb was going to have to deal with Wendy and the fact that she hadn't told her mother that she'd actually gotten back together with Jill.

She dressed as quickly as the pounding in her head would allow, pulling on a pair of expensive jeans, her best shirt, and the large David Yurman silver and dia-mond ring with matching bracelet that she only wore to meetings where she needed to impress someone. She wasn't so much concerned with impressing her mother as she was showing her that she had her act together, and didn't need any of whatever Wendy was peddling.

Barb ran her hands through her hair and looked

at herself in the mirror. Her face was blotchy, which she knew would lead to a conversation about getting enough rest and taking care of herself, a conversation she had no interest in having, so she slapped on some tinted moisturizer and added in a few drops of Visine for good measure. Much better.

"Stay cool," she told her reflection and headed out.

"I'm so sorry, I didn't expect you to be here." Barb heard Wendy's icy tone and cringed; it was one thing to not have told her mother about Jill, but if Jill found out that she'd kept it a secret, she'd be pissed.

"My first client isn't until eleven," Jill said.

"I see. Well, don't let me distract you from your shows," Wendy said just as Barb entered their living room. Wendy glanced at her watch, as if to confirm that it was indeed morning—a time when only lazy people watched TV.

"Oh, I was just doing research," Jill said and quickly shut the television off.

Upon seeing Barb, Wendy threw her arms up in the air and moved in for a hug. "Surprise, surprise!"

"I didn't know you were coming by," Barb said, her arms stiff at her sides.

"And I didn't know Jill would be here," Wendy whispered in her ear. "Anyways," she said, raising her voice back to a normal volume, "we didn't get a chance to talk last night and I thought that maybe we could all get breakfast before you go to work."

"I'd love to," said Jill, "but I gotta be there to supervise the work we're having done."

"Business must be good if you're renovating," Wendy said, smoothing the front of her patterned shirtdress. Wendy always dressed well, but Barb could tell from her popped collar, color-coordinated handbag, and chic leather sandals that she meant business today.

"It is. Well, I mean, summer's not the busiest, which means it's a great time to make improvements. We're adding a new obstacle to our *Ninja* course."

Barb saw Wendy's confusion and felt compelled to explain. "Jill's obsessed with that show *Ultimate Ninja Warrior*," she said. "Personally, I don't get it."

"You should try watching it," Jill replied, and then turned to Wendy. "It's so inspiring. Regular people from all around the world compete on an obstacle course for the title of 'Ultimate Ninja Warrior' and the chance to win a fifty-thousand-dollar prize. But it's not so much about the money as it is about the community and the idea that anyone can conquer life's obstacles and . . ." She stopped as Wendy raised her hand to cover a small yawn. "My clients are really interested in it, so I'm just adding a few new obstacles," she said, and tugged at one of the multicolored plastic bracelets on her wrists, which the gym gave to clients after every hundred visits.

"I see. Yes, why not. After all, what do you have to lose?" Wendy said, emphasizing the "you" a little more than the other words. "Again, don't let me keep you."

"We should all get together for a barbecue, Clementine and Jonah too," Jill said.

"I'd love to, but I can't imagine Barb has any time to cook, working as much as she does," Wendy said.

"Jill does all the cooking, Mom, she's a great cook," Barb interjected. "If it were up to me, we'd live on takeout."

"Well, if you have the time . . . ," Wendy said to Jill, and then turned to look out the garden. Jill shot Barb a pained expression. For a moment, Barb forgot her anger at her girlfriend; it wasn't easy being on the wrong side of her mother.

"I think it's a great idea. We'll find a time that works for everyone," Barb said. They stood for a moment awkwardly staring at each other, neither of them having had a chance to discuss the night before.

"Okay, well, enjoy your breakfast, you two. Let me know if you're going to be late for dinner, babe, I'm grilling fish," Jill said. She moved to kiss Barb on the lips but Barb turned so Jill caught her cheek instead, and then darted into the bedroom to get ready.

Knowing she was going to have to explain Jill's presence sometime, Barb sighed.

"Walk with me," Barb said, getting on her shoes and grabbing her messenger bag. "We can grab breakfast on the way."

She held the front door open for Wendy, who waited until she was outside to answer.

"I've already eaten," Wendy said archly. "I just didn't want Jill to come, and I know that she doesn't like to eat solid foods in the morning."

"Here it comes. . . ."

"What?" Wendy asked. "That I don't want to spend time with a woman who lives off your hard work and spends all your money and cheats on you? Or that I can't believe that you took her back and didn't tell me?"

"It was one time. . . ."

"That you know of. . . ."

"And we worked it out," Barb said, clenching her jaw.

"Well good for you. I'm glad to hear it, even if you hid it from me," Wendy said.

"I wasn't keeping it a secret. I just wasn't ready to tell you."

Wendy turned her attention to the neighborhood,

stopping to stare into the windows of the new restaurants and trendy boutiques that brightened the streets. "I hardly recognize this neighborhood. It was so run-down when you first moved here, I was convinced I was going to get mugged every time I visited, remember?"

"You told me not to buy here. Said it was a big mistake."

"And you told me to stick to giving relationship advice—not that you listened to any of that either." Wendy stopped in front of a toy store with a blow-up shark in the window diving up out of bright blue tissue-paper waves. She tried the handle, which didn't move. "For crying out loud. Who has a toy store that opens at eleven? That's right when parents are heading home for naps or lunchtime. If you want to sell to parents, open your store at seven A.M. They've already been up for two hours by then."

Barb allowed herself to smile at the fact that her mother was right. "I can go back later and get the shark for Jonah if you want," she said.

Wendy adjusted her belt and started walking. "Thank you," she replied, tucking her hands in her pockets.

They stopped at Barb's tiny local coffee shop, which was like a walk-in closet with a couple of espresso machines and few metal stools. There were lots of other coffee bars that had opened over the years, each one more innovative than the next, offering cold brew, or ghee lattés, but Sip Happens was still the best.

Barb greeted Patty, the owner, and ordered her usual triple Americano. On the counter next to a plate of banana bread samples was a little handwritten sign in a black frame, thanking the neighborhood for years of customer loyalty and announcing that they'd be closing at the end of the month.

"Where are you going?" Barb asked Patty, watching as she pushed down the espresso and twisted the filter into place.

"I don't know yet, but I can't stay here. The rent's already astronomical and they're tripling it when my lease is up."

"Tripling it?" Wendy said.

"It's easier than trying to get rid of us. Raise the rent to a level they know we can't afford, so we have to move and then they can sell it. Fucking developers," Patty said, then added, "no offense."

"None taken," Barb said, her cheeks turning red.

"I mean, where am I supposed to go? I'm too old to start over again somewhere else, and be the first shop on the block. I've done that. And the truth is I probably couldn't even afford that. We're being pushed out, all of us who made this place what it is. As if it's possible to separate the places from the people who made them. All these developers that swear up and down at the beginning that they want to keep the integrity and character, won't go higher than ten stories with their new buildings, and the next thing you know you're walking by some concrete and glass tower and bumping into people who look at you like you're the one who wandered into the wrong neighborhood."

"I'm sorry. You know I've been working really hard to make sure that it's done differently here," Barb said.

"I know," Patty replied, looking defeated as she handed Barb her coffee. "I've been here fifteen years and you're the only one of them who has ever come to all those development meetings instead of sending some junior employee. The only one who actually gave a shit."

Barb winced at being thrust into the "them" side of the them vs. us equation.

"Well, it's my neighborhood too."

"Right." She wiped her hands on her apron, dusting it with espresso grounds. "Ivan tells me you're going to save his place." She looked up at Barb like it was a test.

"He did? When?"

"This morning when he came in for his coffee. I gotta admit, he looked pretty rough, but he said it was worth it. Said you guys closed the place down talking about how you were going to save the strip. I'm just sorry it's too late for us."

"Me too," Barb said, not knowing what else to say. The truth was she couldn't do anything except put pressure on people like Dominic to work with the local businesses as they moved in, arguing how much they needed each other. People built in neighborhoods they were attracted to, and it didn't do anyone any good to gut those neighborhoods and make them cookie-cutter replicas of what they could get in the suburbs. She handed Patty a ten-dollar bill, but she waved it away.

"No, this one's on the house. Good luck."

Barb took the bill and stuffed it in the tip jar instead, feeling worse than she had when she'd woken up, guilt piling on top of her hangover.

"You all right?" Wendy asked as they headed back out into the sunshine. "You look like you're going to be sick."

"Yeah, I just . . . I go to that place every day. I didn't know they were leaving."

Wendy shrugged her shoulders, as if it was inevitable. "It's the same everywhere. People want to be a part of something that's already working, but they want it neater, cleaner, safer . . . younger." She shook her head in irritation and picked up her pace. "Anyway, we need to figure out what to do about your sister.

Did Steve ever say anything to you about another woman?"

"When would he have done that?" Barb asked.

"When he asked you to invest in his business?"

They were only a few blocks away from her office, but Barb didn't want to have this conversation there, so they walked instead to the East River. Finally, after years of delays, the decaying waterfront had begun its transformation into an esplanade with parks along its path. The waterfront with its views of Manhattan had been a draw for Barb when she first moved to Greenpoint. She loved looking across the river at the Chrysler Building and Empire State Building gleaming in the distance as the sun rose and set, the ferry that crossed back and forth between them bridging the old and the new.

"How did you know he'd come to see me?" Barb asked, turning her attention back to her mother.

"I read it in his journal," Wendy said, tapping her purse, where she had stuffed it.

"You what?" Barb asked.

"You heard me, I found it in his bedside table, and in it he had a list of potential investors. You were one of them."

Barb had stopped walking and waited for Wendy to turn around and realize that she wasn't there.

"What? Oh, don't tell me you've never snooped. I bet you have, probably still do. It's what happens when you live with a cheater, I would know."

"Jill's not cheating."

"You don't sound so sure," Wendy said, gently.

"I'm sure that it's none of your business," Barb said, her jaw hardening.

Wendy nodded and after a moment continued, "Okay. Well, I'm sure that a man who hid a secret for two years is probably hiding others. And seeing as everybody else is just waiting to see what happens next, I thought I'd better actually do something. So can you help?"

Barb exhaled slowly. She did want to help. She wanted to find Steve and wring his neck. Just thinking about it made her feel better.

"He came to see me in secret. Said Clementine didn't know. He asked me to invest, and before he could even pitch me on his product, I told him that I didn't invest in friends' businesses as a rule. He seemed pretty desperate, and when he kept at it, I felt bad and said I could give him the names of a few people who could."

Wendy pulled the journal out of her bag and opened it to the page she'd bookmarked. "These people?" she asked, showing Barb the list.

She scanned it quickly. "Just Rishi, who doesn't

really have any money but who I knew would be so flattered that he'd take the meeting. He told me that nothing came of it, though. I don't know the other two people."

Wendy took the notebook back and circled the last two names on the list.

"I don't see how this helps. So you find someone who invested in his business, so what?"

"So maybe they know something. We have to find him. We can't just sit around and wait for him to come back. Who knows what he's doing."

"Racking up her credit card, by the sounds of it."

"What do you mean?"

"Clementine's credit card, Steve charged his trip there, and a car, and a new computer, and a room at a five-star resort in Turks and Caicos."

"Turks and Caicos?"

"I know, the guy's unbelievable," Barb said. She sat down on the nearest park bench and placed her head in her hands. "I never told Clementine that he came to see me. I just decided that it was better she didn't know. But what if it wasn't? Maybe if she knew how desperate he was, she could've been more careful. I should've just invested in his stupid business and written it off as a loss. Then maybe he wouldn't have stolen from her."

"The house money was your money too."

"Clementine told you that? Yeah, well, she needed it and I had it, so I loaned it to her. Isn't that the way it's supposed to work?"

"She's not your responsibility, honey."

Anger straightened her spine. "Oh, really? Since when, Wendy? I may not be a mother, but I know you don't just stop when it suits you."

It was the first time that Barb had said it out loud, and it surprised them both. If there was one person who had no right to give her a lecture on responsibility, it was Wendy.

"You think that's what I did?" Wendy said quietly. "Stopped mothering you?'

"Not entirely. Just when there was something better to do. Something more exciting than taking care of us. A writers' conference, or a book tour, or a party invitation that you couldn't be bothered to turn down even though your daughter was sick."

It was the last one that made Wendy turn and stare. "I never left you alone when you were sick."

"Not me, Clementine. You said it was nothing and you'd be home early from your holiday party, but you weren't. And the only person I could call for help was the 911 operator. Did you know she wanted to send over the police?"

"You never told me that," Wendy said, quietly.

"I tried, but you know what you said? That we're never given more than we can handle. Not 'Thank you,' not 'That must've been so scary for you,' not 'I'm sorry.'"

"I'm sorry I wasn't some perfect single, working mother!"

"You're the only one who expects people to be perfect."

"That's not true!"

"Me, Jill, Clementine. God, poor Clementine. All she's ever done is followed your advice. Get a degree, get married, start a business, make enough money to buy a house on her own, pay for her husband to go to business school, and take care of Jonah while he does. And let's not forget be a perfect daughter, and mother, and the kind of wife who puts her husband first. Why? Because you couldn't?"

"That's not fair. Your father died and Ed was a cheater. And I thought I was putting you first. I was focused on my career, because I was trying to do the right thing and provide for you girls. Why are we arguing like this, I didn't come all this way to argue with you!" Wendy yelled. Just then her phone rang and she looked at the call display, said "Not now, Harvey," and put the phone back in her pocket.

"When did you two break up?" Barb asked.

For once Wendy seemed to have been struck speechless. Her eyes widened and her mouth opened, but nothing came out.

"He answered the phone when I tried to call you in Boca the other day. Said he lived there. So either you've broken up, or you live in Florida." Barb had to admit the idea of her mother living in Boca Raton was ridiculous. Wendy loved Manhattan so much she told the girls she would've moved their family to a studio apartment if she had to, rather than leave the city again. But her mother wasn't laughing.

"It all happened very fast," Wendy said cautiously. "Harvey and I . . . we got married, and we were just waiting for the right time to tell everyone. You see, you're not the only one who's capable of making a rash decision when it comes to relationships."

Barb stood up and stared down at her mother. "My decision to get back together with Jill wasn't rash. We'd been together for years before we briefly broke up. Whereas you got married to some guy you hardly know and decided to hide it from your own children!"

"It's not like that. I was going to tell you, I've just been very busy," Wendy said nervously. She reached for Barb, who stepped out of the way.

"Don't give me that. Here you are judging me and Clementine, accusing us of keeping secrets, and you haven't even told us that you're married and living in Boca."

"It isn't like that."

"It's exactly like that, Wendy. God, why do I think you'll ever change? You think you know better than everyone else how they should live their lives and meanwhile look at yours."

"Can we please just focus on helping Clementine?" Wendy pleaded.

"I've never stopped. But once again, you've obviously been too busy to think about anyone else and how your decisions might affect them. So why don't you just go back to focusing on you and leave this to Clementine and me to sort out on our own. Don't worry, we've had plenty of practice, so we'll be just fine," Barb said, hurrying off before her mother could see her angry tears and just how much she could still hurt her.

Seventeen

A Wise Woman knows, a mother's love is forever, and a child's anger is temporary.
—WENDY WISE, "WISE WORDS"

I f there is one thing that Wendy knew, it was that children could be unfair. As Barb stormed off, Wendy watched a young mother with her pant legs rolled up play with her toddler in the splash pad. They were gently kicking up water at each other and giggling when all of a sudden the child grabbed a plastic bucket and whipped it against the side of her mother's head, shrieking with laughter as water covered her. The mother stopped and stared at her child and began to shake her finger. No, no, no, we don't do that, she was saying and the child burst into tears and plonked herself down in the water, sobbing uncontrollably as the mom rushed to comfort her.

One never knew when the bucket was coming.

It was no secret to Wendy that her older daughter harbored a deep resentment toward her, and in many ways she couldn't blame her. She'd asked a lot of Barb growing up, more than she'd wanted to, and her elder daughter had always come through. She remembered the night Barb was talking about, when she'd left an under-the-weather Clementine at home. She'd been up for a raise, and the editor in chief at the time had been making all these asinine comments about her being a mom, not being able to work late or have any fun, and she'd been determined to prove him wrong. Except that it turned out that his idea of fun was to corner her in his office and try to take her clothes off. Luckily the publisher of the magazine had found them before anything could happen, and after coming home shaken, she'd gone into work the next day and they all had pretended that it had been a big misunderstanding, and she'd gotten her promotion.

Perhaps the price of having Barb take on so much at such a young age had been even steeper than she realized at the time. Still, she was here now, wasn't she? Why couldn't her girls see that? See beyond all the trespasses they'd logged, the ways in which they decided that she'd failed them. So she held them to a different standard than she did the strangers she gave advice to. Why shouldn't she? They were her daughters—smart, beautiful, capable, full of promise that she didn't want to see wasted.

As she walked through the park she thought about how unkind she'd been to her own mother as a young girl, judging her for what she saw as wasting her musical talents to stay home and raise her and her brother when she knew very well that it would've been impossible for her mother to do anything else. Never once did Wendy consider that her father, a doctor who kept long hours at the hospital, should sacrifice time away from his important job to contribute to raising them. Instead, her younger self had decided that her mother had simply given up her dreams to be a career pianist rather than clone herself into two perfect beings who could simultaneously rear children and practice for five hours a day. She grew to hate listening to her mother play the black baby grand in the living room on Saturday mornings, knowing that when she did she was somewhere else in her mind, a different country, a different city, on stage living a different life that she could've had if she hadn't had them. What Wendy was too young to understand was that she wasn't actually angry at her mother, but angry for her mother.

She was lucky, her mother would remind her in the years after her marriage broke up. She had a career she loved, and could do what she wanted without needing anyone's permission. Wendy could hear the longing and loss in her mother's voice, and it made her want to do right by her, by all the women like her who could've done more. Unlike her brother, who had moved to British Columbia after he graduated high school and felt no obligation to anyone but himself, Wendy wanted to make her mother proud. She worked as hard as she could, knowing that it meant time away from her girls but hoping that one day they'd understand that she wasn't abandoning them as much as providing for them in a way that would also fulfill her and allow her to return to them happier and hopefully more inspiring than her own mother had been to her.

Wendy had never wanted them to feel responsible the way she did for her mother's sacrifice, needing to prove that she had been worthy of it. But Wendy knew that children would blame their parents for some part of their lives no matter what they did. There was no winning at mothering. But there was no end to it either. Her children didn't have to heed her advice, but maybe if they could see how much they meant to her, she could make things right.

●●●

"Wendy?" a young woman asked, blocking out the sun as she stood in front of Wendy. The voice was friendly, and even though she hadn't heard it in months, Wendy recognized immediately that it belonged to Parker, her former intern. "I thought you lived in Midtown." She said it like it was two words, Boons-ville, Snooze-ville, Dulls-ville. But Wendy was just happy to see her.

"Parker," Wendy said, standing to hug her before remembering that she'd never actually done that before and one couldn't just assume. Some young people didn't even shake hands, and everyone was very particular about their personal space, even though they practically lived on top of one another in their tiny apartments. "My daughter lives here. Has for years, *she's* very cool. And you?"

"You know I'm cool, Wendy," Parker said, adjusting her wide straw hat just so and making Wendy smile.

"I meant . . ."

"I know what you meant," Parker said, teasing. She was one of the few people at the magazine who had seemed to find Wendy's ineptitude slightly comical rather than frustrating. "Yes, I live here, for now. We'll see. It's getting too expensive. Everywhere's too expensive. I might have to leave the city."

"You've technically already left the city," Wendy said.

"True, but I mean leave-leave. You know go to the woods, buy a little cabin. Or just rent, see if it's a good fit, work on my book. That kind of thing."

"What about your job? What about *WMN*?"

"Careful, I think I heard a vowel in there," Parker said, and they both laughed out loud. "Wendy, did I teach you nothing about technology? I'll work remotely. It's not like I have an office anyway. At least I used to be able to take a corner of yours, but it's gone now. Not just yours, a third of them, they let a bunch of people go, and got rid of a whole floor of office space. I wrote you all about it after our last staff meeting. Another one of those *we're all in this together*, and by *we*, we mean you, and by *this* we mean short-term contracts, and by *together* we mean everyone way below our pay grade. So now after interning for free, I'm getting paid, barely, to do the work of three people, running our social media, writing blog posts, and editing the online content. And no more free food, which really sucks, cause it was one of the only ways I was getting by on my puny salary."

"I had no idea," Wendy said.

"Yeah, it's the new leaner, meaner model. Emphasis on meaner. You'd know all this if you bothered to read my emails! Which reminds me, they're going to disable your email address at the end of this month, so you might want to take one last look."

"I'm so sorry, I never checked it after I left. Honestly. But I will."

Parker crossed her arms in front of her, and looked away. "I was worried that you didn't answer me cause you were mad at me," she said, and Wendy could see that she'd hurt the younger woman's feelings.

"No, no, I've just had a lot going on . . . but that's no excuse." She'd been so focused on Parker's cohort edging her out that she hadn't stopped to consider how her absence might affect them. Fewer columns meant fewer writers, researchers, and editors, not to mention that a shrinking print edition and stronger online offering would reduce staff and costs, and lessen the amount of square footage they needed. Wendy knew that the articles for the online publication were shorter and didn't pay nearly as well. They were turned out quickly to meet the needs of an audience used to having access to a vast amount of content on demand.

It dawned on her that it wasn't that young people like Parker were trying to take her place; they were looking *for* a place when the ones they'd been led to believe they were working toward kept being taken away from them. She thought about what Barb had said about her being so wrapped up in her own world that she didn't notice what was going on around her, and felt badly that she hadn't considered how the changes at the magazine had affected the one person who had done her best to keep Wendy up to speed.

"I better get going or else I won't get a good desk," Parker said. Wendy gave her a puzzled look, and she explained, "At Let's Work. It's a coworking space, I'm remote today."

"Oh, Let's Work!" Wendy said, brightening. She opened her bag and proudly pulled out Steve's ID card.

"Wendy Wise, you are just full of surprises, hanging out in Greenpoint, working in Williamsburg! I'm starting to think that your Midtown address is just a decoy for some secret CIA operation."

"I'll never tell," Wendy said with a smile. She'd missed these little exchanges. "I never properly thanked you for all your help, Parker. But I should have. So . . . thank you."

"Anytime," Parker said and tipped her hat.

"Really?" Wendy asked hopefully.

"Let me guess, you forgot how to log in to your email?" Parker said, smiling at Wendy.

"How did you know?" Wendy replied, feeling slightly better that even though it wasn't one of her daughters, there was someone willing to accept her apology and give her another chance.

Parker sat down on the bench and held her hand out to Wendy, who quickly reached into her bag for her iPad.

● ● ●

After Parker had shown Wendy how to restore her password, she discovered that there were 150 emails sitting in her inbox. One hundred and fifty people all wondering where she had gone, Wendy thought. But as she started to go through them she realized that a lot of them were junk mails, promotional offers, phishing messages asking her to update her credit card information for cards she didn't own, plus a few dozen legitimate notes from readers seeking advice.

Parker had offered to help her craft and send a group email saying that she had moved on to the next chapter, but Wendy had insisted that the right thing to do was to read and write everyone back personally, and had stayed behind at the park to do so while Parker went to hunt down a desk. What she couldn't explain to the younger woman was that she also needed to read and respond to each email personally. She needed her readers' kind words about how they had leaned on her in the past, how they valued her advice, how she had always been there for them. She needed to feel appreciated, useful, and loved. She didn't want to judge, as Barb had accused her, but to help, and if she could do that for these remaining strangers, then she would.

The first few were easy; a woman was invited to

an ex-friend's baby shower and didn't want to go, as she felt she'd been invited just so she'd give a gift. *Stay home if you like, but purchase something, even something modest, from the registry,* Wendy had advised. Maybe her friend was really reaching out, and even if not, a small gift for a new mom and, more important, a new baby was always a nice thing to do. A bride-to-be was stung over her mother-in-law's assertion that she couldn't wear white to the wedding, as it was her second wedding and white was inappropriate. *Wear whatever color you want, it's your wedding, and it's unlikely you were a virgin the first time you wore white for that matter, so do what makes you happy. If she still pushes, tell her it's not white, it's Chantilly, that way you both win. She is going to be your mother-in-law, so it wouldn't hurt to try and find a compromise,* Wendy counseled.

Wendy breezed along, reading and answering faster than normal, because the stakes were lower, because they would never be printed, because it made her so damn happy. And then there were a few from a familiar name that Wendy recognized from years before, Tangerine. She remembered the name of the young woman because it had been so similar to Clementine's, and because she'd been thrilled that a young person was seeking her counsel. The first time she'd mentioned it to her girls had been at the dinner table and she could still see how Barb had snickered, while Clementine, always supportive, told her it was great that she had young fans. Tangerine had written to Wendy at many pivotal moments in her life, when she'd wanted to go away to school, when she'd been deciding to move in with her boyfriend who became her husband, when struggling with how to share new responsibilities of parenthood—the things her own daughter had grappled with.

The things her own daughter had grappled with. Wendy nearly dropped her iPad as she stared at the name again. It was as if someone had turned a light on, and for a moment it was so blinding that she was disoriented and dizzy. She felt sick that she hadn't seen what had been staring her in the face all this time. Tangerine. Oh God, no, please don't let it be, it couldn't be, but yes, of course it was—Clementine.

Wendy quickly opened the new emails from her daughter's alter ego, feeling stupid that she hadn't made the connection before, but it was all right there. She did a search in her email history with the name Tangerine and a string of answered emails smacked her in the face. Tangerine was struggling with a husband who was always searching for the perfect job and she was so tired of waiting for him to find one. How long should one person wait? *Better to know who you're waiting for than to start looking all over again.* Tangerine's husband resented her making all the money, even though he was the one who refused to get a job. *Why not let him take care of the finances? It's okay to be the breadwinner as long as your husband feels like he's the bread baker.* Wendy's cheeks burned bright with embarrassment. This was the response that Barb had been referring to when she first arrived.

Wendy shook her head in disbelief. Her own daughter had been writing to her for years, afraid to speak to her directly. Had she really been so unavailable? She exhaled deeply, realizing that her well-meaning responses might have actually hampered Clementine, made her play it safe, encouraged her to stay in situations that held her back. She'd encouraged her to compromise—she'd encouraged a whole generation of women to compromise. But as Wendy sat in her truth, just as that damn yoga instructor at La Vida Boca had suggested, she knew that it was also because she had grown to believe that something was better than nothing. In fact, for a lot of women of her generation it was almost as good as everything. It was more than what they'd had before, more than what her mother had had. It was good enough, Clementine said. Well, good enough wasn't what Wendy wanted for either of her girls, or for her grandson, she wanted what was best.

Eighteen

*A Wise Woman knows never to start a fight
she isn't willing to finish.*
—WENDY WISE, *WISE UP*

Barb was in no mood for bullshit. Her assistant, Yukiko, had called as she was leaving the park to say that it would be better if she used the back entrance when she arrived at the office. Just as she was about to text back and ask why, she saw a small group of picketers in front of Mission Statement.

Barb knew who they were. She and Dominic had been to their local neighborhood association meetings in the early stages and listened to their concerns about building height, sidewalk infringement, and main-floor retail spaces, and had taken their concerns seriously. She got it. They wanted the old run-down and abandoned buildings restored and repurposed, but not replaced. They didn't want their neighborhood to lose its eclectic personality. They also wanted it to be affordable, but not so affordable that their own increased property values would diminish. If there could be cool retail space on the main floor that would be great, but no big-box stores, or chain grocery stores. A bookstore might be nice, or a food hall, but the lease rates needed to be reasonable, because they wanted to make sure that the existing residents who had moved in decades before could still shop there. And Barb wanted to give them all of this, because if she could she'd feel a lot better about putting up another tall glass tower.

It was sometime during the third town hall that Dominic had thrown his hands up in the air and asked, "Oh, is that all? What about ponies for everyone?" to which someone pushed back in all sincerity that his suggestion seemed excessive, and besides they weren't in favor of animal captivity, and with that Dominic walked off the stage, with Barb following close behind. She'd told him to relax, that people just wanted to be heard and to make sure that their neighborhood still felt like a neighborhood. With time, people would come around to the changes they saw in the neighborhood. But she stressed it was in his best interest to actually try and make all these things happen.

At the fourth meeting Barb came alone and shared her plans for the art space and community kitchen. She did it for her neighbors and selfishly for herself, hoping her good deed could go toward offsetting the impact that another luxury high-rise would have. She also knew that if she couldn't find a way to give them what they wanted, they would make her life hell.

Much like they were trying to do now.

She watched them walk back and forth in front of her Mission Statement offices, raising and lowering their handmade cardboard signs and chanting "No Point in Greenpoint! Mission Statement is Mission Sellout!" Barb rubbed the center of her forehead, where a massive headache was brewing, then angrily crossed the street, narrowly missing a cyclist.

"Watch where the fuck you're going!" he shouted and gave her the finger.

"Learn how to ride!" Barb shouted back as she mounted the sidewalk and came face-to-face with Ivan, who was trying to quiet the small group of protestors.

"Here she is, let's just ask her."

"What's going on?" Barb asked Ivan.

"Why don't you tell us?" asked an older gentleman in khakis, a SIP HAPPENS T-shirt, and shoes with toes in them.

"Ivan?" Barb said.

"We've heard a rumor that The Point is going back on its promise about the ground-floor art space and is going to lease it to a Whole Foods instead."

"That's ridiculous," Barb said. She turned to the others. "We talked about this. For months, ad nauseam, and we bent over backward to give you . . . to give the neighborhood, everything it wanted."

"Everything but affordable prices."

"Somebody has to pay for the building, and that's what it costs to live here now. I can't control the real estate market."

"So it's just a rumor then?" Ivan asked hopefully.

"I haven't heard a thing. And I think I would know."

"Yeah, well, until you can guarantee us that it's not happening, we're not going anywhere."

"Well, I am, so get out of my way," Barb barked, pushing past Ivan and his cronies, opening the front door to find Yukiko hiding off to one side behind a tall potted plant. "Have you really been there the whole time?" Barb said as she passed.

"I'm sorry, I didn't know what to tell them," she replied, handing Barb a coffee, "and I wanted to give you a heads-up that Dominic's here and waiting in your office."

"Shit," Barb said, her headache now trying to pound its way out of her forehead. "Advil. Now. Please."

She took a moment to collect herself and then walked into her office and greeted Dominic. "Hey, I thought we were going to meet on-site."

"Something unexpected came up and I thought it was better we talk about it here. You okay?"

"I'm hungover," Barb said just as Yukiko appeared with a glass of water and an Advil and quickly left. "I spent all night trying to talk the owner of Ivan's off the ledge. Someone is spreading a rumor that the owner of his building is going to sell to another developer and then today there's this bullshit about a Whole Foods taking over our art space and community kitchen. That's what all the fuss out front is about. I take it you missed all that."

"I have. I've been here awhile."

"Well, lucky you. So tell me, who do you think is starting these rumors and trying to cause trouble? Northern Construction? Are they still sore over losing the bid?"

"It's not them."

"Well, then who? Because I didn't spend six months trying to make this thing happen only to have some asshole try to blow it up with a bunch of lies."

"They're not lies," Dominic said, his voice calm and steady. "I've been approached by Whole Foods to take the entire main floor, and I think I'm going to do it."

Barb stared at him in disbelief. "What do you mean you think you're going to do it? We had an agreement.

You made a commitment. I made a commitment. All those meetings, all that time we spent planning, do you have any idea how hard it was to get everyone on board and agree?"

"Of course I do, I was there."

"So what am I missing?" Barb's stomach was turning over on itself, the ramifications of Dominic's actions overpowering the nausea of her hangover.

"Nothing. That's just it. You're not going to miss a thing. I'm the one who has to take the financial hit, not you. And why should I, when Whole Foods is willing to pay me five times what the art space and kitchen are going to pay?"

"Why? Because it's not about making a profit, it's about building goodwill in the neighborhood, and that's priceless."

"Yeah, well, goodwill isn't going to pay for all my cost increases, and you aren't prepared to take a bigger cut, so what do you expect?"

"So this is my fault? Because I can't come down any further on my fees? I'm not the one getting rich over here."

"Don't give me that. We're both rich."

"Apparently not enough." Barb took in Dominic, his arms crossed in front of his chest, his jaw clenched.

For a man about to sign a lucrative deal, he didn't seem all that happy. "Dominic, if you do this it's going to be a PR and community relations nightmare. You're going to be just another evil developer and I'm going to be painted as your asshole architect. I'm not trying to cost you money, I'm only trying to do what is best for everyone."

"Is that why you never gave my number to Clementine?"

Barb stared at him in disbelief. That was twenty-five years ago, when they were all just kids. He couldn't be serious. "What did you say?"

"My phone number, I asked you to give it to her after that night, but she says you never did."

"You asked her?"

Dominic just stared at Barb silently.

"You're kidding me, right? You'd blow all this up over some make-out session you had with my *kid* sister when you were in college?"

"We had chemistry! What if we'd had a chance to try it out? Things might have worked out totally differently for me."

Barb couldn't believe what she was hearing. "Then you wouldn't have Ella and the kids."

"Sometimes I think Ella and I are only still together

for the kids. I love my kids, but who's to say that Clementine and I wouldn't have been the ones to adopt them, maybe I would've been Jonah's dad, maybe she wouldn't have married that asshole and be in this terrible situation if you hadn't decided what was best for everyone. Did you ever think about that?"

"Dominic, that was a million years ago."

"I felt something between us, today. A connection."

"What you felt was nostalgia. Don't throw your life away over some midlife crisis. It's crazy."

"You don't get to tell me what I can and can't do, nobody does." He stood to leave, and Barb stopped him.

"You're right, I didn't tell her. You weren't right for her, and she was just a kid. It never would've worked."

Dominic's face hardened. "Did you ever ask her what she wanted?"

Barb was silent. They both knew that the answer was no.

"If you had, maybe her life wouldn't be such a mess right now."

"If she was really so important to you," Barb spit out, "then you should've tried harder. But you didn't, because you've never really had to try hard for anything. It's all been handed to you, by your family, by me. If it weren't for me, you never would've even considered this neighborhood. So don't start blaming me for your life not working out exactly like you hoped it would. That's on you."

Barb was aware that Yukiko and a few of her associates had come out of their offices and were lingering in the hall, eavesdropping. She was out of breath, her body flushing with heat. She wiped her forehead on her sleeve.

Dominic stood and slowly walked toward her, his tall frame towering over her. "All right then, let me start with fixing my bloated budget for the next building by taking you and Rishi off it. Then I'll sign the lease for Whole Foods, and then maybe I'll buy your friend's bar and turn it into somewhere that people who live at The Point will actually want to go. You know what, while we're at it, tell Clementine we won't be needing her services anymore."

Fuck, Barb thought, she'd never be able to cover her costs now; this building, her employees, Jill's gym, the mortgage, her legal fees for those damn brownstones. And Clementine needed money, and without Rishi on the project, she wouldn't have her job. But she couldn't apologize for what she'd said, when she knew that she'd meant every word. "Sounds like the easy way out, perfect choice for you." She marched toward the front door and opened it wide. "And seeing as some of those folks you lied to are here, you can tell them your big plans yourself!"

Her whole body was shaking as she watched Dominic walk out into the chanting crowd, taking with him the only way she knew how to fix her problems.

Nineteen

*If you're going to speak your mind, you
better make sure that you're heard.*
—WENDY WISE, "WISE WORDS"

"I don't want to stay long," Clementine said, balancing a boxed pie in one hand as she rang the doorbell with the other. The doorbell had one of those security cameras, and Clementine, aware that maybe she was being watched, spoke through clenched teeth and with a smile that made her look slightly maniacal.

"We just got here," Jonah said, holding his shark. "I want to see the house and Ethan's room. I heard he has bunk beds and a PlayStation and a trampoline out back and I've never been invited before. Mom, please."

Clementine looked at Jonah working himself into a sweat, his little body starting to vibrate with anxiety, and squeezed his clammy hand. It irritated her to no end that Jonah wanted anything to do with a spoiled brat like Ethan. She hated how much Ethan mattered to her son and didn't have the heart to tell him that if she'd been able to get ahold of her mother, who wasn't answering her phone, she would never have brought him. But now that she was here, standing at the doorway of this renovated, magazine-feature-worthy house, she had to admit she wanted to see the inside too.

"It's okay. Don't worry, I'll check in with you before I say we have to go, all right?"

Jonah nodded and then jumped as Kimberly opened the door.

"You made it!" She leaned forward and gave Clementine a hug she hadn't been expecting and then leaned down to talk to Jonah. "Why don't you go outside?" she said, pointing to an open door that led to the backyard. "Ethan's there, and I know he will be so happy to see you."

"This is for you," Clementine said, handing Kimberly the pie they'd picked up from the little mother-daughter bakery around the corner.

"Oh, I *love* pie," Kimberly exclaimed in that way that Clementine knew meant she probably never ate it. She was all wheatgrass and raw foods and keto and whatever other dietary trend was going around, and looked terrific, but as far as Clementine was concerned, life was too short to skip pie.

"You have a beautiful home," Clementine said, of

the handsome house on the corner whose living room and stunning kitchen-dining area were flooded with light.

"Thank you. I'm glad you like it. Charles hates it, thinks I went too modern with the reno. Not that he's ever really here, so what does it matter. If he's in charge of the work, I get to be in charge of the home. That's the thing about being a real estate agent—I spend so much time looking at other people's places, it gives me so many ideas for my own. If you're not passionate about something, why bother doing it?"

"Because you need a paycheck?" The moment she said it, Clementine realized that it hadn't actually been a real question.

"Right, of course," Kimberly said, her face serious. "I mean everyone has to, even Sunnyside is so much more expensive now. What choice do we have?"

Clementine needed wine. She was used to Kimberly's faux folksy act, but it had been a long week and her filter wasn't working properly.

"Could I trouble you for a drink?" Clementine asked, looking around, her eyes landing on the bar set up outside.

"Oh my gosh, yes. I'm a terrible hostess. Follow me," Kimberly replied, leading Clementine outside where the side and back gardens merged into one enviably large landscaped retreat, empty of other people besides the kids.

Clementine made herself a barely spritzed wine spritzer in one of the palm tree–festooned acrylic goblets that Kimberly had set out on a rolling bar cart full of cocktail fixings for the grown-ups and flavored sparkling water drinks for the kids. She took a long sip. When Kimberly wasn't looking, she refilled her glass and joined her on the luxurious woven cabana furniture set beneath a shade pergola.

"Am I the first one here?" Clementine asked, relaxing her body into the cushions of the chaise and checking in on Jonah, who so far was still in one piece and jumping up and down with Ethan on the trampoline.

"I was hoping we could have some time to talk before the others arrived, so I asked you to come a little early."

"Oh, is something wrong?"

"Well, it's a delicate matter and I didn't want you to be embarrassed."

Clementine took a sip of her drink and racked her brain to see if there was anything that Jonah had mentioned lately about Ethan, but other than their brief encounter in the Uber, she was sure that this was the first time that the boys had actually been together since the end of the school year.

"Okay . . ."

"Well, some of the other parents at the last PTA meeting were saying that they didn't really think it was fair that Jonah and some of the other children"—she paused, thought for a moment—"Children like him, are going to be in their own special class next year."

Clementine couldn't believe what she was hearing. "Nobody said anything to me."

"Well, it was after you left. They were quite upset."

"I don't understand. Why would they care if Jonah was going to be a part of a pilot program?" Her cheeks suddenly felt hot, and she lifted the wineglass to her face to cool them.

"They just feel like it isn't fair to the rest of the students."

"But he isn't like the rest of the students. He can't be in a regular class, he gets too anxious. He has stomachaches and headaches and wants to stay home from school. So in many ways, his having to be in a regular class, where he can't learn properly, hasn't been fair to him."

"I understand," Kimberly said as she leaned forward. Placing her hand on top of Clementine's, she began to speak to her like she was a toddler. "But you can see how, from their point of view, it might upset the other kids, Jonah and his friends getting to learn with Mr. Nettler while they're stuck sitting at desks all day."

"No, actually, I can't. Maybe their parents should take the time to tell them that not everyone is the same, that some kids need to learn differently than they do, and there's nothing wrong with that. Jonah is going to be in a different *class*, not all-day recess, Kimberly. He's going to be learning just like they are." She slid her hand out from underneath Kimberly's and resisted the urge to wipe it clean on her linen pants. "I don't see what the problem is." Clementine gulped her wine, making Kimberly raise her eyebrows and sit up straighter in her chair.

"The problem, is that it only makes things worse. He's going to be singled out and then everyone will *know* that he has issues. You know how people talk. Is that what you really want for him? Wouldn't you rather he just blend in?"

Out of the corner of her eye, Clementine saw Ethan pelting Jonah with his shark, Samuel, as Jonah bounced around struggling to get it back. She stood to get her son's attention. Jonah saw her and swatted his hand in her direction, as if to say, get away.

"Jonah, everything okay?"

"I'm fine, Mom," he answered, his face furious as Ethan sucked his thumb and laughed. Jonah laughed too, in spite of the fact that he was the object of Ethan's ridicule. Clementine wanted to scream and cry all at once, wishing that Samuel would magically transform into a real shark and take a bite out of Ethan. But she knew it wasn't just the kid's fault, so she turned to Kimberly.

"Let me tell you something—there was no blending in for Jonah last year. And there certainly wasn't anything fair or special about the way he was treated either, taunted and bullied by kids like Ethan and then called out by the teacher for being disruptive when he got upset."

"I'm glad you brought that up, actually. Ethan's not a bully, but now everyone thinks he is. The truth is that kids like Jonah make him feel uncomfortable, and when he's uncomfortable he snaps. It's not right that he gets into trouble for that. Jonah's just so serious about everything, always going on about sharks, and pollution, and global warming when the other kids are just trying to be kids and have fun," Kimberly said.

Clementine tried to hide the sting she felt. "Jonah's a kid too, Kimberly. He can have fun just like everyone else. But he has anxiety, and even though we're doing our best to manage it, sometimes he needs an adult to help get out of a loop. Mr. Nettler really knows how to reach him." She felt her eyes fill with tears.

"I didn't mean to upset you, I'm just trying to be helpful."

"Have you spoken to any of the other parents whose kids are part of the pilot class? I mean, Jonah's not the only one."

"No . . . but from what I hear, he was the catalyst. I thought that maybe you could speak to them, explain the merits of how important it is to be able to fit in and get along with everyone else."

"I don't believe this."

"Clementine, believe me, I'm just trying to help. Have you considered private school? It might be what's best for him."

Clementine stared at Kimberly, wondering how she could really be this clueless. "The thing is, Kimberly, public school isn't just an experience for us, it's a necessity. It's the only option we have." Out of the corner of her eye she could see Ethan whispering in Jonah's ear.

"Well, you know, if my petition goes through, and you move out of the area, you might *have* to explore other options."

"Who said anything about moving?" Clementine shot back.

"I know your house is going on the market. Mr. Gregoris has given me the listing. To be honest, I was shocked to learn that you didn't actually own it."

Clementine slammed her wineglass down on the side table, sending Kimberly deep into the safety of her overstuffed lounge chair. "I doubt that. I bet you were delighted, a chance to get rid of another lowly renter. Well, now you can sell it to someone just like you who is gonna pretend to be all folksy and take advantage of an affordable neighborhood and a great public school all while claiming that you're just *keeping it real*. That is until you send your own kids to private school when public school no longer works out, because you *can*. Just like you can have them escape the city every summer for your vacation home and private clubs. Because you have options. So how dare you sit there and tell the rest of us who can't afford to be anywhere else what our options are!" Finished, Clementine gasped for air while Kimberly stared at her, her mouth opening and closing like a fish. It was the only time Clementine had ever seen her at a loss for words.

"Jonah, we're leaving." She walked over and grabbed Samuel away from Ethan and took her son's hand.

"But, Mom—"

"*Now*," she said. "And we're taking our pie with us."

Twenty

*A smart woman always has an extra card
up her sleeve. A Wise Woman knows when
to play it.*
—WENDY WISE, *WISE UP*

I t was shortly after noon when Wendy swiped Steve's
entrance card to get into Let's Work. She quickly
made her way past the receptionist sitting at her glossy
white desk, who seemed confused as she looked back
and forth between Wendy and Steve's face, which
popped up on the screen in front of her.

"Afternoon!" Wendy said as cheerfully as she could,
and rushed inside. If there was one thing Wendy had
learned about getting older, it was that there were
things she could get away with that a younger woman
couldn't—such as cutting to the front of a line for the
bathroom, asking someone to hold her place at a grocery checkout, and pretending not to hear receptionists

call her out for using an entrance card that clearly didn't belong to her.

As Wendy hustled through the common space, she could see why Parker had been concerned about getting a good spot. Freelancers and their laptops had claimed every available surface: a communal table, a booth, low leather couches and modern armchairs accompanied by side tables and cheerful potted plants. Overhead, bright bubble lights lit up the space, as did the glow of candy-colored neon signs that said things like HELLO, LIKE A BOSS, and LET'S DO THIS.

The Let's Work-ers looked just like Parker and the rest of the young staffers who had increasingly populated the magazine in her final years. They were independent contractors who arrived with their backpacks and laptops and reusable coffee cups and water bottles, only to pack their little offices back into their bags as the day ended, leaving Wendy to wonder if they would return. She feared Parker was right about there being no turning back this trend; companies were all too happy to attract the best talent there was without having to commit to paying benefits or payroll taxes, an unbalanced open relationship where only one of the parties is really interested in keeping their options open and the other is just saying they do, because admitting otherwise might terminate their gig. There was something so impermanent and noncommittal about the whole arrangement, and as she stood in the open space surrounded by all those people focused on their screens, Wendy suddenly felt very lonely. For the first time since she arrived, she wanted to talk to Harvey.

She slipped down the hall to the private phone booths, which were meant to feel retro and cool but only reminded Wendy once more what a dinosaur she was, and called Harvey.

"I'm sorry I can't come to the phone right now, but I'll get back to you. Not right away, because I don't do that anymore. I'm retired, not rushing. Have a wonderful day."

Wendy sighed and waited for the beep. "Harv, it's me. The girls really do need me, and I . . ." There was more to say, but those words were not quite ready to be spoken, so she told him to call her and then hung up. She left the booth and walked the halls, looking for something that would betray any recent visits from Steve.

And then she saw it—a huge billboard advertising AquaVeg hanging on the wall of a private glass-walled office, one that was empty of people. Seizing an opportunity, she used the entry card once again to let herself in. The billboard looked professional, as did the booklets that were fanned out in a row on the wooden conference desk in the middle of the room. She picked one up and opened it.

AquaVeg takes the saturated fruit water craze and turns it on its head by being the first carbonated vegetable water with CBD on the market. Flavored with the essence of nutrient-rich vegetables and hints of citrus, and infused with relaxing CBD, it not only hydrates the body, it calms it as well. Hydrate and Veg Out with AquaVeg.

The booklet featured pictures of Steve all around the world. There he was standing on top of a mountain that overlooked a farm in Costa Rica where acai berries grew. In another he was pulling up kale alongside some smiling workers in California. And there he was again, inspecting hemp plants in a greenhouse in Colorado.

The message was clear; he was willing to travel anywhere to bring you the finest ingredients from people and places he actually knew. Even more impressive, Wendy had to admit, were the colorful charts and all the information that explained the differences between hemp and marijuana. She had never even known that there were different classifications of cannabis plants but learned that the term "marijuana" referred to the viable seeds, flowers, and leaves of the plant, whereas "hemp" indicated the sterilized seeds, stems, stalks, and roots. There was a quote from one of the leading growers in Colorado that read, "Finally everyone knows that it's Marijuana and THC that gets you high, and it's Hemp and CBD that gets you chill."

Steve predicted that AquaVeg was poised to be the biggest disruptor the beverage industry had ever seen. Wendy read on with interest about the health claims of CBD: reducing inflammation, decreasing anxiety and depression, and relieving migraines, amazed not only that Steve had done so much research and development but that he also might actually be on the forefront of something major.

At the back of the book was the investor sheet that broke down the kind of money one needed to become a stakeholder in the company, along with projected revenue and the amount of capital the company had raised so far.

Wendy couldn't believe it, but apparently AquaVeg was on its way to being fully funded, boasting interest from leading venture capitalists. It was all much more professional than Wendy had expected, and she grudgingly admitted to herself that while she still wanted to throttle Steve, a part of her was impressed that he'd actually done something and had gotten this far. She even liked the logo design, a cresting wave that circled an *A* and *V* made up of green vines. Along a console on one wall sat a row of bottles with prototypes of the different flavored waters they had in development. Was it possible that Steve really did intend to pay Clementine back and buy a better place for her and Jonah? And if so, why hadn't he ever shown Clementine what he was working on? No matter what his reasons, she reminded herself, they didn't excuse his lying to her.

None of it made sense. If she could just find Steve, she'd ask him herself. Maybe if she left a message for him at reception he'd know what she'd seen and he'd get back to her. It was worth a try. As she tucked an investor booklet in her bag and walked back to the front desk, she noticed the young woman who'd let her slip by on the way in was staring in her direction.

"That's her," she said.

Wendy started to turn around, pretending that she hadn't realized that the receptionist was talking about her, but had barely taken two steps when she was stopped.

"Just a minute, ma'am," a man in a suit who looked to be about her age said as he caught up to her. "Want to tell me how you got in here?"

Wendy looked down at the card she was holding, confused. Yes, she'd taken Steve's card without his permission, but surely that wasn't a crime. "I borrowed my son-in-law's ID card."

"Steve Jenkins?" the man asked.

"That's right."

"Is there somewhere private we can talk?" he said. "I have a few questions."

You're not the only one, thought Wendy as she led him back to Steve's office.

Wendy insisted that there had been some terrible mistake. She wasn't connected to AquaVeg, she didn't know where Steve was, and she wasn't an accomplice to some pyramid scheme. She'd tried to tell all of this to Rodney James, the retired police officer who told her he was doing investigative work for some big law firm in Manhattan.

"So why were you in this office?" Rodney asked.

"I've already told you this," Wendy said. She placed her hands on the conference table, connecting with something sticky, and quickly pulled them back and folded them in her lap. She hated when people didn't listen; what was the point of asking a question if you weren't going to listen to the answer? He was wasting her time. She'd missed three calls from Clementine and one from Barb, although she didn't know what she'd tell either of them, even if she could pick up.

"For the one hundredth time, I was trying to find out where he was," Wendy said.

"For personal reasons."

"Yes."

"So you went into his office and stole his files to go with the journal you had stolen earlier."

"I wasn't stealing. I was borrowing."

"And impersonating him with his passcode because you were hoping to destroy incriminating evidence."

"What? No! So that I could find him and ask him why he . . ."

"Why he what?"

"Nothing," Wendy said.

"Why he's trying to get people to give him money for a product that doesn't exist?"

"It obviously exists," Wendy said, fanning her hands out before her. "Take a look around."

"Yes, the bottles exist. That doesn't mean that there's an actual product to go into them."

"Yet," Wendy said.

"Right, I suppose that there is a small chance that this is all some huge misunderstanding and that he's actually not trying to scam my client into investing in some cannabis carbonated vegetable water drink."

"AquaVeg."

"Terrible name."

"I know," Wendy said with a sigh, and slumped in her chair. "I want to help, I do. I wish I knew where he was, but I don't. Is he really in a lot of trouble?"

"Depends," Mr. James said softening. "Look, we just want to talk to him. Get some answers."

"Me too," Wendy said as her phone beeped. She pulled it out of her purse and saw that she had been tagged in an Instagram post from Samantha Love, #Tingles, #WendyWise, #GreatAdvice. "I need to use the bathroom."

"Go ahead."

Once she was sure that she was alone in the ladies' room, Wendy checked in on her Instagram to find Samantha Love sharing her trip, just as promised. "Well, we made it. We're here in beautiful Turks and Caicos." A quick pan of the camera revealed her stunning hotel suite with its gray and white marble floors, sleek teak furniture, and a large rattan swinging chair on the balcony with a view of the ocean behind it.

Turks and Caicos. Wasn't that where Barb said Steve had gone? Wendy watched as Samantha settled into the chair, champagne glass in hand, and addressed her followers.

"We did it. Our first ever Made with Love Movers and Makers conference. After months of planning I'm looking forward to meeting all you Lovers out there and hearing your pitches for your fabulous ideas and innovations. As you know, the Lover with the best pitch gets the chance to bring their product to life, with me. I'm so excited."

"Hold on," Wendy said out loud, as if Samantha could hear her, which of course she couldn't. Is this conference why Steve was in Turks and Caicos? It would make sense, a last-ditch effort to launch Aqua-Veg, but it seemed too coincidental.

Samantha held up a pink binder and waved it. "I have the list of potential new partners right here, and I want you to be with me, when I find the one. But first, a toast." Samantha lifted her glass of champagne and said, "Cheers to all of you, for helping me pass one million followers today. I cannot tell you what an honor that is. To me that's over a million of you who care, who also believe in pursuing your passion and making your own dreams come true. Who know that the only way to do something right, is to do it with *love*." She smiled warmly, sipped her drink, set it down, and opened her folder.

"Let's see what we have here, lots of beauty products, who doesn't love those, some clothing, some cookbooks, a meditation app, socks. . . ." Samantha's eyes moved down the page, her smile faltering. "So . . . many . . . great ideas . . . friends . . ."

It was clear to Wendy, who had seen that look of disappointment on Samantha's face before, that whatever Samantha was hoping to find, it wasn't there. She watched as Samantha turned the page over, and after a moment her eyes got wide and a smile that Wendy recognized as genuine covered her face. "I think I just found it." She shivered a little. "Tingles. A Wise Woman once told me to always listen to that little voice inside you; it's your truth teller. And my little voice is telling me that we have a winner."

Wendy was touched that Samantha would reference her, and for a moment forgot that she was hiding from a private investigator in a bathroom.

"And I can't wait to share it with you soon. See you after the conference. Bye for now!"

Her mind reeling, Wendy returned to Steve's office, where Rodney was standing off to one side and talking to someone on the phone. What if Steve had gone to Samantha's Movers and Makers conference? What if he really was trying to do the right thing? It didn't change the fact he'd stolen from her daughter and possibly tried to kidnap her grandchild, but it was marginally better. Should she reach out, or would that only make him run? This time it was Wendy who needed good advice, and she thought of the one person she knew who'd give it to her.

"I need to make a phone call," Wendy said.

Mr. James waved for her to go ahead and turned away from her as he kept talking.

Oh, please pick up, she thought. *Please, for once, have your ringer on.* When he did, her whole body sighed with relief.

"Harvey, it's me." She could hear Latin music in the background and remembered it was during their afternoon Zumba class. Harvey never missed it. "I've been falsely accused of aiding and abetting a criminal and as the best criminal attorney I know, I need your help." She hoped that Mr. James heard her and was intimidated.

"Wendy? What are you talking about? Hang on," he said, moving away from the music. "You do know that I was in intellectual property law, right?"

"Yes, but he doesn't," Wendy whispered into the phone and then told him everything she knew.

Twenty-One

A Wise Woman knows it's easy to make a promise. It's keeping it that's hard.
—WENDY WISE, *WISE UP*

"Why did we have to go? I told you, he wasn't being mean. He's my friend!" Jonah wailed as he tried to keep up with Clementine, holding on to her hand as she practically jogged up the street, her feet slipping off the edges of her sandals and making her stumble.

"A real friend doesn't throw things at you and make you cry. If he acts like a bully and talks like a bully . . ."

"That's not nice."

"He's not nice," she said, squeezing his hand a little too tightly.

"Why are we running? Are we in trouble?" Jonah yelled. Clementine stopped and looked to find Jonah's face wet with tears and his whole body trembling. She immediately felt terrible.

"Oh, honey, no, no," she said, crouching down so they were face-to-face. "Of course not. I just, I didn't like the way Ethan was treating you and I had a disagreement with Kimberly, so I wanted to leave."

"Was it about me?"

"Why would you ask that?" She placed her hand on his chest and felt his heart beating quickly.

"Because Ethan said that his mom was going to make sure that I couldn't go back to PS 150 in September, and that I'd have to go to a school for morons and when I called him a liar, he said it didn't matter anyway because I was probably going to have to move really far away, because we couldn't afford to stay in the area. Is that true?"

Some friend, thought Clementine. She sat on the edge of a small stone wall that outlined one of the neighborhood's many beautiful gardens and brought Jonah to sit next to her. Tucking him into the side of her body, she looked up at the canopy of green overhead and sighed. She'd walked these streets countless times over the years, admiring the old houses and their proud little postage-stamp front yards, which came to life every spring. Every April, folks would roll up their sleeves and make the most of the first warm weekend planting and weeding and creating a continuous cycle of blooms that followed one after the other until the cold weather returned. She knew the streets by their gardens: the one that had the fountain and the hydrangeas, the one that was all green hostas and rosebushes, the house on the corner that was edged with a wall of lilac trees that swayed as they walked past, beckoning her and Jonah to stop and smell the heady blooms that filled the air with their sweet scent. This neighborhood was home, and she couldn't imagine being anywhere else.

"Oh, Jonah."

"I don't want to go to a school for morons, I want to go back to Mr. Nettler and my friend Turner."

"Sweetie, look at me. Deep breaths."

She held Jonah's hand in hers and they inhaled and exhaled together. "First of all, there's no such thing as a school for morons, that's a terrible thing to say. And I want you to go back to PS 150 too."

"So why would Ethan say that?"

"Maybe he's jealous. Maybe he wishes he could be in a cool new class. But, Jonah, someone who treats you badly isn't a real friend, even if they say they are. Their actions have to match their words, otherwise they don't mean anything."

"I know. Like a promise. It only matters if you keep it."

"Yes, that's really wise of you, buddy," she said, her fingers brushing the hair off his forehead.

"It's what Dad said. He said you were fighting because he broke a promise, but he was going to make it right on his trip." Jonah looked up at Clementine, his sweet face and red-rimmed eyes searching her own.

"He said that? Did he tell you *why* he went?" She forced her voice to stay light and calm.

"To meet the lip balm lady, on the island."

Samantha Love? Clementine's mind filled with images of Steve spending all that time on social media, the money he spent on expensive webinars, Arianna espousing the merits of Samantha's Love Your Life system. Steve wasn't on the run; he was at a conference with Samantha Love. It was the kind of thing that would normally make her furious, but instead she felt like she was going to laugh and cry with relief at the same time.

"Mom," Jonah said, interrupting her thoughts, "can you fix a broken promise?"

"I don't know, honey," she said, pulling back to look him in the eye, "but you can always do your best not to break one."

She held Jonah's face in her hands and kissed him, wanting more than ever not to break the promise she'd made to him about where they'd live, when her phone rang with a call from Wendy.

"Mom, are you okay? I've been trying to get ahold of you."

"I need to tell you something," Wendy said.

"Me first," Clementine said, standing and turning and taking a few steps away from Jonah as she spoke. "I know where Steve is."

"You do?"

"He's at some conference with some Instagram star who makes lip balms."

"Samantha Love," Wendy said.

"You know her?"

"I sat next to her on the plane."

"Anyway, maybe he wasn't trying to kidnap Jonah, maybe he just went by the YMCA to say goodbye before his trip," she said, lowering her voice, and turned back to see Jonah lifting the entire slice of pie and biting into it like it was a piece of pizza. Her heart melted.

"That is good news."

"I'm just thinking, what if Steve really did plan on paying me back? Not that what he did was right, but maybe it's not as bad as I thought—"

"Clementine," Wendy interrupted. "There's something I have to tell you."

Twenty-Two

*We may not all be mothers, but we could
all use some mothering.*
—WENDY WISE, "WISE WORDS"

Barb's day was going from bad to worse.
"I'm here for Wendy Wise," she said, approaching the receptionist at Let's Work and resting her elbows on the shiny counter. She couldn't get rid of her headache, in spite of the cheeseburger she'd had for lunch, and was about to set the record for the world's longest hot flash. She inhaled and exhaled slowly in a futile attempt at calming her breath, but she still felt like she'd just run around the block. The fight with Jill the night before, her mother, the protestors, and then Dominic, no wonder she was winded.

"Oh, *Wendy . . .* ," the receptionist said, picking up the phone and making a call, the orange and blue elastic bracelets of Jill's gym peeking out as she did so.

"That's my girlfriend's gym," Barb said, her mind

drifting to Jill, and the fact that they still hadn't talked since their fight the night before. "You must be a regular."

"Ten more visits till my next one," she said, and gave Barb the once-over. "Have we met?"

"I doubt it, but I'm Barb," she said. Barb couldn't remember the last time she'd been to the gym, even just stopping by to say hi to Jill. "I don't get to the gym very often. I work a lot."

The receptionist glanced at Barb but didn't offer her name in return and continued to wait for the person on the other end to pick up the phone. What? It was true. She did work a lot, she had to, how else could she help everyone out and pay all the bills? It's not like she was on salary or part of a union or getting a pension when she retired. Barb felt judged, even though it was possible that the judgment was her own.

"There's a Barb here for Wendy," the receptionist said, then hung up and turned to Barb. "Well, maybe we'll see you in Daytona. If you can get the time off."

Barb snapped to attention. "Daytona? What about Daytona?" But before she could get an answer Wendy rushed out.

"Thanks for coming," Wendy said, her eyes avoiding Barb's as she walked unsteadily past her, toward the elevator, looking slightly worse for wear. Her hair frizzed out in all directions, and there were dark circles under her eyes.

"Don't seem so surprised, Wendy. It's not the first time I've cleaned up one of your messes," she said, following her mother out of the building.

"Don't worry, I've contacted my lawyer," Wendy said, once they were on the street.

"Why would I be worried? Because you're living some kind of double life as a married Floridian private investigator who was almost arrested for breaking and entering the offices of your delinquent son-in-law?"

"I wasn't arrested. I was just speaking to an actual private investigator for some law firm looking into Steve on behalf of one of their clients. "

"Oh well then, that's good, no need to worry," Barb said sarcastically. She took her keys out of her pocket and clicked the fob to unlock the door of her Range Rover. "Did you want to drive? Never mind."

Wendy hadn't driven in over thirty years, not since she left Long Island and moved to Manhattan. Just like Clementine, she didn't see the point, meaning that driving had been left to Barb and today it was just another thing to add to her list of grievances.

"After everything I've just been through, I suppose you would've preferred if I had just called an Uber!"

"Oh, spare me the drama."

"An angry woman is never an attractive one," Wendy said, getting into the passenger's seat.

"And a Wise Woman knows that being attractive to her husband is more important than being right." Barb closed her door and fastened her seat belt.

"I never said that."

"Yeah, you did. It's in *Wise Wife*. Don't worry, not being attractive or having a husband, I chose not to follow your advice."

"Then why bother reading it?" Wendy said.

"To know exactly what not to do. I only wish the same could be said for Clementine."

"Don't you mean Tangerine?"

Barb's surprise quickly turned to contempt.

"Took you long enough."

"I suppose you think it's funny that she was writing to me? That my own daughter wasn't able to ask me for advice?"

"I don't think there is anything funny about it."

"How could you know all this time and not tell me?" Wendy said, her voice cracking.

"I didn't know she was still doing it. If I had, I would've told her to stop. It's idiotic and immature and she's better off without your meddling anyway."

"Oh please, I only ever wanted to help!" Wendy cried out. "It wasn't easy being on my own. I did the best I could. I thought you of all people, Barb, would grow to understand how hard it was."

"Why me?"

"Because you know how hard you have to work to be successful and you don't have children. It's just you and Jill, and how much time do the two of you even spend together?"

"Not enough, apparently! And it isn't just me and Jill, Wendy, it's me and Clementine, and Jonah, and Rishi, and Dominic, and Yukiko, and all of my other employees, and the Greenpoint Neighborhood Association, and let's not forget you. It's everybody, all the fucking time, constantly needing me. So I have to work hard, whether what I'm doing even makes sense to me anymore, because everyone is depending on me!"

Barb set the air-conditioning at full blast and angled the vent toward herself, hoping it would cool the sweat that was dripping down the sides of her face, and started to drive, her breathing fast and shallow.

"I didn't realize, I . . . ," Wendy said, her face full of worry. "Barb, are you feeling okay?"

"I'm fine!" Barb snapped. But she was feeling anything but fine as a sharp pain gripped her chest. She leaned forward over the steering wheel, thinking she might be sick, tingles going up and down her arm, her whole body shaking and her breath feeling heavy. "And yeah, I like to be needed, it feels good. . . ."

"Of course it does," Wendy said slowly. "There's nothing wrong with that, but, Barb, you need to pull over, now okay? Please, pull over."

Barb pulled alongside a fire hydrant, her hands still gripping the steering wheel, her breathing labored.

"Barb, look at me, deep breaths," Wendy said gently.

"I think I'm having a heart attack," Barb said, her face twisted in fear.

"You're going to be okay. I'm going to call an ambulance. We need to get you to the hospital."

"No, it's just around the corner, I can get us there."

"I'll drive," Wendy said, jumping out of the car and coming over to Barb's side.

"What?" Barb wailed.

"It's okay, I know how, and it'll be faster than waiting for an ambulance. Now move over, you can do it, there you go," she said, carefully putting the seat belt around her daughter and locking it in place.

Wendy sat up as straight as she could and leaned forward over the steering wheel to watch the road. She followed Barb's directions to the hospital and drove the two minutes with her hazards on, her knuckles white as she clutched the wheel. She pulled into a parking spot right outside the entrance and rushed inside, quickly returning with a wheelchair and a nurse who helped Barb into it and brought her back through the front doors.

"I need you to stay back in the waiting area, ma'am, and fill in her admitting forms," the nurse said, wheeling Barb down the hall.

"Don't worry, she has insurance!" Wendy snapped, spotting a doctor and waving frantically. "And I'm not waiting anywhere, I'm going in with her. I'm her mother."

"Ma'am, please," the nurse said, gently directing her to the waiting room. "I need you to wait out there and I'll come get you as soon as we know anything."

"Mom?" Barb called out to Wendy, her voice full of worry. Mom. Barb couldn't remember the last time she had called her that, and by the look on Wendy's face, neither could she.

"I'll be right here, love, don't worry, it's going to be fine, you're going to be fine, I know it," Wendy said. For once Barb didn't ask how Wendy could be so sure, or accuse her of doling out platitudes, because more than ever, she desperately wanted to believe that what she said was true.

Twenty-Three

A Wise Woman knows that if you get a
second chance, you take it.
—WENDY WISE

Wendy hated hospitals. She hated the antiseptic way they smelled, their fluorescent lighting, the color they all seemed to be, sea foam or beige or some other kind of insipid shade chosen because it offended the least number of people but pleased no one at all. She hated that within these walls time was suspended, interminably long and not long enough, a bubble from the outside world, that some, like her beloved first husband, would never get to leave. The final moments void of anything that felt like home, strangers witnessing their last breaths as they slipped away forever. It still amazed her how much she missed Dan after all these years. She shifted in the uncomfortable plastic seat with its stuffing coming out of one side, closed her eyes, and swallowed hard.

There was so much of Dan in Barb—the confidence, the strong sense of self and capacity to handle so much, the willingness to help others simply because they could. Anger was the only trait that separated them, but even that had in a way been an inheritance from Dan, his dying while Barb was so young changing her in ways that Wendy would never be able to undo. She couldn't sit still but she didn't dare move either, she didn't want to be anywhere other than right where the nurse left her in case she was needed. It didn't matter how old Barb was, she was still Wendy's baby, her first-born, and the thought of anything being wrong with her was terrifying.

"Mom, is she okay?" Clementine asked, bringing a blast of heat from the outside world as she ran toward her mother and hugged her tightly.

"I don't know, they're doing some tests on her, but no one has told me anything. Where's Jonah?"

"With his camp director. I managed to catch him before he left the Y. Seth's taking him to the park so he doesn't miss his bocce ball game with the seniors' group. What happened?"

Wendy burst into tears, and let Clementine hold her. Where to start? She gathered herself as best as she could and told Clementine about the journal and seeing Steve's

Let's Work space and AquaVeg and getting questioned and her fight with Barb that she was sure had caused her daughter's heart attack. They were right, she was a terrible mother, and it was no wonder that her children wanted nothing to do with her.

"Oh, Mom," Clementine said when Wendy had finally finished and was blotting her eyes with her tear-soaked ball of Kleenex. "You're not a terrible mother, and nobody wants you out of our lives. We love you, even if you make us crazy sometimes."

"Wendy Wise? You can see your daughter now," the nurse said, holding the door open for Wendy and Clementine to follow.

"Hey," Clementine said as they entered Barb's room, Wendy rushing past her to sit next to Barb.

"Oh, Clem, you didn't have to come."

"Are you kidding me? After Mom told me she drove you here, I had to make sure that you made it in one piece," Clementine said, making Barb smile. "Seriously, how are you feeling?"

"Like an idiot," Barb answered, brushing her damp hair off her forehead. "It was a panic attack."

"That's great!" Wendy said, momentarily holding Barb's face in her hands. "Well, not great, but you know, better than the alternative."

"The alternative is less humiliating."

"The alternative could've killed you," Clementine said, taking a seat opposite the bed.

"Turns out it wasn't my first one, that I've actually had small ones before, and just didn't know it. I just chalked it up to stress and perimenopause and high blood pressure, and being generally overworked, but this, this was . . ."

"Scary," Wendy said, holding Barb's hand as she nodded. "I thought I gave you a heart attack."

"Not yet," Barb said, making them laugh. "Although I still don't know what happened with you today."

"Now's not the time," Wendy said, waving her hand to dismiss the subject.

"I'm fine, Mom. You can still tell me what you were doing."

"Well, I wanted to see if AquaVeg was real. And not only is it real, but it's got CBD in it."

"What?!" Clementine said.

"You didn't know?" Wendy asked.

"That Steve's making stoner water now? No, I didn't!"

"It's not stoner water. That would be THC, tetrahydrocannabinol, the chemical responsible for marijuana's psychological effects. CBD comes from hemp, it's therapeutic, not trippy. It's a good idea, actually," Barb said, begrudgingly.

Wendy and Clementine stared at Barb in surprise.

"It's supposed to be good for inflammation, Jill's all over it. It's a huge growth industry," Barb said, then shrugged, as if everyone knew this.

"Well, the private investigator I talked to thinks AquaVeg is some kind of scam, so he's been trying to track Steve down, but I'm not convinced. I saw the bottles and the marketing materials for investors and I have to admit, I was impressed. It's real. It's why he went to Turks and Caicos, to attend Samantha Love's conference."

"Whose conference?" Barb asked.

"Samantha Love, she's an influencer with a huge social media following. Arianna, Dominic's niece, told me about her. She's the one with the lip balms," Clementine explained.

"Oh," Barb said, clearly not knowing who they were talking about.

"Very bright girl. I sat next to her on the plane. She set up my Instagram for me and ever since I've been getting notifications from her account, which is surprisingly often. She's having some contest where people pitch her ideas and she invests in the one that she likes the best. It's her something new." Wendy paused and stared at her hands. "I was her something old."

Barb and Clementine looked at Wendy in confusion.

"My books," Wendy explained. "She's getting married and someone gave them to her. She's actually quite nice, if a bit self-absorbed. But then again, I suppose people thought the same thing of me."

"Mom . . . ," Clementine said gently.

"It's okay. They weren't entirely wrong. I did want something for myself, a career, and a way to provide for you girls. I thought I was doing it all and that you'd be better for it." She took Barb's hand in between hers and stared down at them. "You've always been so strong and so organized, Barb, much more together than I was. It didn't seem hard for you, but of course it was. I shouldn't have expected so much from you, and for that, I really am sorry."

"Thank you, Wendy. I'm not sure I've ever heard you apologize before," Barb told her.

"Well, that's because I'm not very good at it," Wendy replied. "And because one apology doesn't solve everything. But it's a start." She stood, helped Barb up, and extended her other hand to Clementine, who took it. "Come, let's see about taking you home."

"You're not driving me again," Barb said as the three of them made their way down the hall.

"No, Jill's coming to get you."

"You called her?"

"I did. She's going to meet us out front. She really loves you, you know," Wendy said, hooking her arm through Barb's.

"You don't say?" Barb said, raising an eyebrow.

"Clementine told me that she takes good care of you too, and I'm glad. But you also need to take care of yourself. You're no good to anyone if you don't."

"Why didn't you ever give me advice like that before?"

"I don't know," Wendy said, pausing to consider it. She stood on her tiptoes and gently kissed Barb on her cheek. "You know, maybe Jill could give Harvey and me a personal training session on her *Ninja* course. He's always up for something new."

"Okay, way too much information," Barb said, making Clementine laugh. "Are you *trying* to give me a heart attack?"

Twenty-Four

It takes a Wise Woman to know one.
—CLEMENTINE WISE

lementine's feet were killing her. She had forgotten how terrible high heels felt and seriously regretted thinking she needed to wear them at work, like Arianna did. Hobbling down the street with Wendy to get Jonah, she knew that now was the time to talk about their argument the night before, but she was worried about giving her mother any more to deal with. For the first time since she could remember, Clementine was seeing her differently. Unlike Barb, she'd always resisted criticizing their mother, finding Wendy's prescriptions for life comforting and uplifting. It hadn't been until recently, when she'd discovered that Steve had lied to her and taken all their money, that she had started to question whether Wendy's advice was really good for her. Perhaps she'd been foolish to expect that someone else—even her mother—could solve her problems. But before she could get a word out and talk about any of this, Wendy spoke.

"Why did you do it?"

"Excuse me?" Clementine said, caught off guard.

"Use a pseudonym to write to me? For all those years. I mean, it wasn't like it was just the one time. I've been trying to remember all the other times, and asked myself what was going on that you couldn't ask me directly?"

"Mom . . ."

"Was I traveling? Was I on tour?"

"No, I just couldn't."

"Why not?" Wendy said, stopping in the middle of the sidewalk with her hands on her hips, drawing the attention of others, and making Clementine worry that one of them would be a neighbor or a parent from Jonah's school. She didn't want to do this here, but she didn't want to do it at the park in front of Jonah either, so she walked ahead to the end of the street, away from all the activity.

"Was I really so intimidating that you couldn't just ask me in person?" Wendy asked as she caught up to Clementine, slightly out of breath.

"It's not that."

"Well, what then?" she said, catching Clementine's arm and making her stop.

"I didn't want you to know that I was having problems. I didn't want you to think less of me."

"Why would I think less of you?"

"Because you've had so many challenges: Dad dying, moving us here, divorcing Ed, having a career, and you always figured it out on your own. You always knew what to say and what to do, and here I am, unable to handle my own small life and making all these mistakes."

Clementine watched Wendy's face turn hard as she took her by the shoulders, causing her to rock back on her heels.

"Don't say that. Don't you dare say that. Your life is not small. You're a wonderful wife and a wonderful mother and a talented writer and the kindest daughter anyone could ever ask for. I don't know how you do it. I couldn't handle half as much as you do, let alone support someone else's dreams and my family at the same time."

"But I messed it all up, so what does that say about me?"

"It says you're human. For goodness' sake, we all mess up. I messed up. I was let go from the magazine for being too old and too outdated, for crying out loud."

"What? When did that happen?"

"A few months ago."

"That's terrible," Clementine said. She reached her arm out to comfort her mother, but Wendy put her hand up to stop her and took a deep breath to collect herself.

"What's terrible is that it's true." Wendy sat down on a wooden bench outside of a vintage shop and folded her hands in her lap. "My advice *is* outdated, or retro, as Samantha Love called it, but for years it's what people wanted to hear. Do you know when I was first hired at the magazine, it was because they wanted something new, something for the real modern woman, and I was so excited. I had a career, I could leave Ed, and we could have our own place, in the city," she said, throwing her hands up in amazement. "I wouldn't just be giving advice, I'd be an inspiration to others, and one day hopefully to you and your sister. The column was going to talk about all kinds of things: dating, marriage, being single, sex, what it was like to work and have a family, all the things that women like me were dealing with."

"So what happened?" Clementine asked, taking a seat next to her.

"Money happened. The magazine got purchased and *Women* became part of a portfolio of magazines. There was already a magazine for single women, and another for upper-middle-class homemakers, and another one of those grocery store circulars with the recipes that they kept near the cash registers. There was a magazine tackling themes of the new working-career mother, not to mention other magazines that cornered the *Sex and the Single Girl* audience, and feminism. The company decided that we needed to reach out to what they called *real women,* not *Cosmo* girls, not women who read *Ms.* magazine, but women who needed advice for the lives they were actually living. As if all women could only belong in one box or another. Our magazine was aimed at the women who didn't necessarily live in cities and didn't get to put their careers first, who felt that the world was maybe changing too fast, who wanted to be reassured that their roles as homemakers were valued and appreciated and not something to be dismissed or frowned upon. I was told that if I wanted to keep my job that's who I needed to write for, and if I didn't like it they could find someone else."

Wendy was quiet for a moment, seemingly lost in her memories.

"What did you do?" Clementine asked.

"I called my mother. I told her how I'd lost Dan and I'd lost Ed and now I was going to lose my job and way of supporting my girls too. She was living in a home by then and wasn't well, and I immediately regretted burdening her with my problems, but I honestly had no one else to call. And she took a deep breath and said, 'Wendy, do you know how lucky you are? You had one husband who adored you, another who financed your new life through a divorce, two beautiful girls, and a career that very few women get. So it's not everything you wanted, but it's likely so much more than the women who are writing you have, women who are just looking for ways to make their situations better. Can't you help them with that? Shouldn't they be allowed to feel good about the lives that they are living, even if it's not everything they wanted, even if they wished for more, knowing that they may never get it?'"

"Wow, she wasn't messing around," Clementine said.

"I knew right then that she was talking about herself. She'd given up her musical career to be our mother and she never held it against me and my brother, or our dad, as far as we could tell. I had a responsibility to help, to give those women the kind of advice they could really use. So the next month we changed the title of the column from 'Ask Her Anything' to 'Wendy's Wise Words,' and my 'brand,' although we didn't really call it that back then, was born."

"I had no idea."

"I never talked about it. What was the point? Readers loved the column, my editors were happy, the board was happy, and I got to keep my job. It felt good to be recognized and rewarded and I loved giving out advice that people could use, even if it was a bit outdated. I knew these women. I'd been one and my mother was one and so the idea that I'd have to change anything, when this latest overhaul at the magazine happened, seemed not only exhausting, but also . . . unfair. They wanted things to be different now? I couldn't do it, so they let me go."

"Why didn't you say anything?" Clementine asked.

"Because who am I if not Wendy Wise, the advice columnist?" she said, her eyes filling with tears.

"You're my mom," Clementine said. She wrapped her arms around Wendy and hugged her. "And that doesn't change, no matter what happens." They were both quiet for a moment and then Clementine teased, "Wow, you've been really busy. Now I know why you didn't reply to Tangerine's email."

"That and I was marrying my boyfriend of three months, and moving to a retirement facility in Boca that I can't stand, all because I was scared and lonely. Not exactly a *wise* move."

"Really?" Clementine asked, pulling back, her eyes wide with surprise.

"Really, and I know I should've told you, but Barb

already yelled at me once today when I told her, so if you don't mind, I can't handle being yelled at again," Wendy said wearily, and Clementine was struck by how old and frail she looked.

Clementine had always thought of her mother as perpetually young, her life busy and full with all those strangers who needed her. She hadn't considered that she'd kept them around not as much for her ego as for their companionship. She thought of how scary it must be for her mom now, at this stage of her life, to have her whole identity questioned, her purpose taken away from her. It was scary for Clementine to think of starting over, and she was so much younger.

"I wasn't going to yell at you," Clementine said softly, looking her mother in the eye. "I was going to thank you, for being honest, and telling me the truth. You've never told me any of that before."

"It was easier not to think about it and just carry on as usual, but it's all over now, so it doesn't matter anymore."

"Who says it's all over?"

"Well, I mean the magazine let me go. . . ."

"So what? You don't need them."

"No one is going to hire me at this age, Clementine."

"All I'm saying is, it sounds like you have a lot more to say, and I think you should find a way to say it if you want to, the way you want to. After all, there's nothing holding you back anymore."

Wendy looked at Clementine, her head tilted to one side, a smile tugging at the corner of her eyes and lighting up her face. Clementine stood and offered her hand to her mom, who took it. "You know, it doesn't sound like you need me to tell you what to do, Tangerine. That's some pretty great advice, right there." And Clementine had to agree, and think that maybe if she was brave enough, she'd find some good advice to give herself.

Twenty-Five

*A Wise Woman knows it takes more than
will to find a way, it takes love.*
—WENDY WISE

Wendy stood on the steps of the New York Public Library. She'd brought her girls here often when she first moved to the city, and marveled at the majestic stone lions, Patience and Fortitude, that guarded its entrance. She was in need of both of these qualities right now. There were so many answers in this building, so many great ideas and perspectives that could be found both in the pages of the books that lined its shelves and in the people searching for knowledge.

She climbed the steps with her pen and notebook in hand, just like she had when she first moved to Manhattan. Sometimes when she'd gotten a letter that she had a particularly hard time answering, she'd walk among the desks or in the halls, looking for someone who seemed like the kind of person who might have written the question she was trying to answer, letting herself imagine who they were and what the rest of their story was. It had always been important for her to remember that these were real people with real problems and she was there to help.

Things changed once she got her office and the column grew in popularity. There were more letters to answer, longer articles to write, the people whose problems she chose to feature supporting whichever topic she was highlighting that month: the importance of celebrating anniversaries, how not to alienate your in-laws, and how to make family time the best time. She'd learned how to sum up complicated questions with pithy answers that made for excellent pull quotes, and aphorisms that could be repeated over again. The more general the answer was, the greater the number of women it could be applied to. She put women into categories: ready to marry, married with children, and married after children, and wrote books for them, *Marry Wisely*, *Wise Wife*, and *Wise Up*. Listening and arguing with her daughters the last few days had reawakened a desire in her to really help. She wanted to do more than just offer advice that could work for anyone or no one at all. This time, Wendy wanted to do what was best for her children individually, women so different from herself but who she not only adored, but admired.

Wendy was passing through the doors of the library when her cell phone beeped.

"Ma'am, you have to turn your phone off," a security guard said.

"Yes, yes, I'm sorry," Wendy replied, rushing outside as her Instagram alerts started coming fast and furious. There was another video of Samantha, standing on the stage of the hotel's ballroom under a wall of flowers that spelled out the word *LOVE*. Staring out at a sea of fans clad in pink and white, Samantha clapped along with her audience, her arms outstretched as she applauded them in return. "Thank you. I've loved listening to all your great ideas today in the Innovation Lounge, and I feel honored that you chose to share them with me. I know it's not easy to put a big idea out there and take a leap of faith. But you did it, and I'm grateful. And now, the moment of truth." She reached her hand out to Todd as he walked onstage and handed her a pale pink envelope, then stood off to one side. Samantha looked at the envelope in her hands, her smile faltering for a moment, and then rallied. "We had a lot of discussion about which idea to go with, there were so many to choose from, but you all know how much I love beauty products, so it should come as no surprise . . ." Samantha stopped, and turned the envelope over in her hands. "No surprise . . . but isn't that what life is all about? Surprises? There are the surprises that catch us off guard and force us to rally and be resilient. And then there are the surprises we give ourselves when we do something new and unexpected that challenges us to go further and be more than we are."

From the side of the stage Todd could be seen waving his hands to get Samantha's attention and mouthing, "Open the envelope."

Samantha looked at Todd, and shook her head. She put the envelope down and extended her hand to Todd, who warily stepped onto the stage. "Babe, I know this isn't what we planned, but I gotta listen to my inner truth teller. Which is why I'm going with the idea that surprised me the most in the best way, AquaVeg, the world's first carbonated vegetable water, infused with . . ."

"No wait, you can't—" Todd said.

"What are you talking about?" Samantha interrupted, turning away from the audience.

"We can't do that idea, I promised it to someone else," Todd whispered.

"You promised someone else an idea from my conference?" Samantha said at full volume. "Are you kidding me? Who?"

Todd swung around to face whomever was filming all of this and yelled, "Turn that thing off!"

But the camera holder must have ducked out of Todd's reach, and they captured the audience turning away from the stage toward the entrance of the conference room where Sunny Day appeared with two large security guards on either side of her. She raised her arm and pointed at Todd angrily, "Liar!" And then the video cut out, just at the one-minute mark.

Wendy's heart was racing as she phoned Harvey's number, praying that he'd pick up.

"Wendy?"

"Harvey, you need to see something. Do you have Instagram? I think I have an idea, but first you need to get Instagram. I can talk you through it."

"Why don't you just show me?"

"Show you?"

"Wendy, I'm here in the city."

Wendy paused and looked around. "In New York? Why?"

"Because you're in New York, honey," Harvey said gently.

"Harvey . . ."

"I know your girls need you, but I thought maybe you could use someone too."

Wendy was quiet on the other end of the phone. She did need someone, but she couldn't imagine living the rest of her life in the retirement community. As if reading her mind Harvey continued, "I know that things aren't entirely working out for you in Boca, but I believe we can find a solution. What do you say? Can we try and figure this out together?"

It was what he'd said to her when he proposed, that life was complicated and it was too short, but maybe they could figure it out together.

This time when she said yes, it wasn't because of fear, it was because of love.

"I'm a lucky man, Wendy Wiseman," Harvey said, rolling onto his side after they'd just finished making love.

"Yes, you are, Harvey Feldman," Wendy replied, getting out of bed and putting on her hotel robe.

Harvey had gone all out, splurging on a fancy hotel room and greeting Wendy at the door with a glass of champagne, roses, and an earnest declaration that there were no expectations, that he just wanted them to talk and share their feelings. Wendy, overwhelmed by Harvey's romantic display, told him she'd rather show him how she was feeling. And so they made their way over to the bed, knowing that at their age, they really did need a good mattress, and let's face it, the mattresses at the Four Seasons were the best.

"Harvey, I know you want to talk and I know we need to, but . . ."

"You need to check your phone," Harvey said, handing it to her while he looked at Instagram on his. Had he always had Instagram, or had he downloaded it after their call? *Impressive*, she thought, right before she saw that the story about Samantha's conference was garnering a steady stream of new comments.

"Do you think Steve really is in a lot of trouble?" Wendy asked.

"Hard to say. We don't know what he's actually done, whether he was scamming people besides Clementine. . . . We need to talk to him to find out," Harvey said, staring at his phone. "But just look at how many people are following the story and have now heard of AquaVeg! Terrible name, by the way."

Wendy paced the room, thinking aloud. "I know Samantha. I mean, I spent a few hours with her, and we hit it off, and she liked his idea. Is there any way it could still work?"

"Wendy . . ."

"Just hear me out. Samantha wanted a big idea to

champion, and she loves Steve's idea. If I—we—could find a way to work this out and then maybe AquaVeg can become a reality and maybe Clementine can get some of her money back and maybe she could start to repay Barb. . . ."

"And *maybe* your girls would appreciate you?" he asked softly.

Wendy sighed. "See how much they mean to me. See that I can offer more than just outdated advice, I can really help."

"Oh, Wendy . . ."

Now it was her turn to ask a question. "Come on, Harvey, what do you say we figure this out together?"

Thanks to her recent tutorial from Parker, Wendy knew how to message Samantha, who called her as soon as she learned that Aqua-Veg-Steve was actually Wendy's-son-in-law-Steve, and holy tingles, talk about synchronicity. At the same time Harvey left messages for Steve, who finally called Wendy back in a panic.

"Wendy, what's wrong? Did something happen to Clementine and Jonah?"

"No, nothing happened," she said. She was touched by his concern but also wanted to reach through the phone and shake him, and yell *you mean something other than what you've done to them?* But she took a deep breath instead.

"Well, is everything okay?"

"Not yet, Steve, but it will be," Wendy said. "Now listen carefully."

Twenty-Six

There comes a time in every woman's life
when she has to learn to trust herself.
—CLEMENTINE WISE

B y the time Arianna arrived at the office the next morning, Clementine was already nursing her third cup of coffee. She'd been up half the night worrying. She'd texted Steve three times asking him to call her, that she wanted to talk, that she wanted to know what he was doing in Turks and Caicos, and finally did he know that a law firm had hired a private investigator to look for him? She knew the moment that she pressed send on that last text that she'd made a mistake. What if she had scared him into actually going on the run? Either Jonah would grow up without a father, or the police would find him, prove he really was part of some pyramid scheme, and put him in jail.

Clementine was good at worrying, a skill she'd culti-vated for most of her life, ever since her father's death when she was five. She'd never really known him, but she remembered how he used to pick her up under the arms and swing her until the two of them were so dizzy they'd fall down laughing, only to do it all over again. He was cheerful and patient, reading to her for as long as it took her to fall asleep. And then one day out of the blue he just got sick and died. She used to worry that Wendy would suddenly get sick and die too, or not come home, because Clementine talked too much, or Barb was acting out. She'd done her best as a child to make her mother's life easy, do as she was told, listen to all her stories, and let her know how important she was. Over the years she had shifted the focus of her worrying from Wendy to Steve and Jonah. Clementine had just assumed that Wendy was fine. She was as busy as she'd ever been with work and book club appearances and a healthy social calendar. But that was before she knew that her mother had gotten fired, remarried, and nearly arrested, and had just opened up some sort of truth valve in herself that Clementine welcomed, but now made her worry what else about Wendy she'd discover.

Still unable to sleep as dawn arrived, she'd let her mind turn to Dominic and how they were going to work together and what else she could do for money, and the fact that she was indeed going to have to find a new place to live and a new school if Kimberly really could get her petition pushed through, and then there was Barb's health and how much Clementine had contributed to her sister's stress and panic attacks and why she hadn't seen any of it before and maybe Jill really was cheating again and above this carousel of never-ending worries that robbed her of sleep was a flashing neon sign that screamed JONAH!

"Wow, are you okay?" Arianna asked as she took in Clementine's appearance.

"That bad?"

"Not great. No offense, but you look like you pulled an all-nighter and then did your makeup in the dark."

"I did. Pull an all-nighter, that is, and the makeup I did in the bathroom here, but it's entirely possible I got carried away. My eyes aren't really focusing yet." She took another swig of her coffee.

"May I?" Arianna said, tracing her finger in the air in a circle around Clementine's face.

"Go for it," Clementine replied, too tired to object. She reached in her purse and handed Arianna her makeup bag.

Arianna squirted some sanitizer in her hands, grabbed a handful of Kleenex, and gave Clementine's face a quick once-over. Using a makeup brush, she started smoothing and blending while Clementine closed her eyes, cursing the fact that only now she felt sleepy.

"Why the late night?" Arianna asked.

"I had a lot of worrying to do and everyone knows it's best done in the middle of the night."

"Your husband?"

"Among other things. I think he's at that conference," Clementine said, yawning, "with what's-her-name the lip balm lady."

"Samantha Love?" Arianna said, stopping suddenly. She handed Clementine her lipstick and held up a compact mirror for her. "Lightly," she said, and Clementine did as she was told before smiling at her reflection.

"Wow."

"I used to work at a cosmetics counter, and I'd get a lot of tired moms looking to take a break."

"Yes, Samantha Love. He's at her . . ."

"Movers and Makers conference. I've been following it. Samantha was supposed to announce the idea she was going to champion and lend her star power to, and then at the last minute she changed her mind and didn't read the envelope Todd passed her and instead said something about some water thing and then it was just mayhem. I haven't had a chance to find out the latest." She whipped out her phone and checked her Instagram, updating Clementine as she read the comments. "Apparently some guy from New York came to the conference to pitch an idea and Todd tried to steal it for his new client, Sunny. Samantha's followers couldn't believe that Todd would choose Sunny over Samantha. And Sunny's lawyers aren't even sure that this whole thing is legit anyway, so they've been trying to find the guy whose idea it was."

"Steve. His name is Steve Jenkins. He's my husband."

"Damn, no wonder you couldn't sleep," Arianna said, finally looking up from her phone.

Clementine's mind was reeling. Wendy had said that AquaVeg was real, so what had gone wrong? She needed to get a hold of Steve and tell him to come back before things got worse. And if they couldn't find him, would they come after her?

Just as she was reaching for her phone, Dominic walked in. He looked like he'd already put in a full day of work, with a five o'clock shadow on his face, even though it was only ten in the morning. Apparently no one had gotten any sleep last night. The sleeves of his rumpled shirt were rolled up and he carried a stack of papers in his hands. He stopped when he saw Clementine.

"I didn't expect you to be here today," he said, setting his papers down on Arianna's desk.

"Why not?"

"I just thought that after what happened yesterday with Barb . . ."

"Oh no, she's fine, or she will be. Jill's taking care of her. I'm just glad it wasn't an actual heart attack."

A wave of confusion washed over Dominic's face as he walked toward her. "What are you talking about?"

"Her trip to the hospital."

"Is she okay?"

"Yeah, it was a panic attack, not a heart attack. What are you talking about?"

"I, we . . . had a disagreement. I've decided to take things in a different direction, with the retail spaces of the building . . . and the marketing team."

"I don't understand," Clementine said, then turned to Arianna to see if she had any idea what Dominic was talking about, but she wouldn't even look in his direction.

"The main floor, it's going to be a Whole Foods now. I've run the numbers and the other option is just way too expensive. This makes more sense, and besides it's what people really want."

"Unbelievable," Arianna said, rising out of her chair.

"This has nothing to do with you, Arianna."

"Really? A whole part of my pitch, which you said you liked by the way, was how this building was going to be different, how this company was different, 'cause you're different. I've been telling that to everyone who comes in, and they believed me, so I guess now I'm supposed to call everyone up and tell them I was lying. Sorry, I know we promised you one thing, but now we think it's going to be too hard, so we're going to backtrack and call it an option, because we're not going to do it after all."

Clementine's eyes were wide as she listened to Arianna. She hadn't seen this side of her new friend before.

"People change their minds all the time," Dominic said evenly.

"Do they now? They just decide they're going to try something new? Something easy. Because staying and working things out with someone who they've been with for decades is no longer an option?"

Clementine's mouth dropped open as she made the connection. Arianna wasn't just his niece, she remembered; she was his niece on his wife's side.

"It's more complicated than that," Dominic said, looking at Clementine nervously. "You don't understand."

"I understand that you didn't go home last night, and that my mom and I spent the night with Ella and the kids because she didn't know where you were."

"That's enough. And that's personal, this is business."

Arianna glared at him and then went to her desk,

picked up her purse, and coolly walked toward Dominic, flicking her long hair over her shoulder.

"You're right. It is business, your business. So why don't you take care of it and sell your own condos today. Come on, Clementine, he obviously thought he'd fired you already." She walked out of the office. Clementine, realizing that Arianna was right, that she had been fired without realizing it, walked over to Dominic. He looked terrible, his usual demeanor of calm control nowhere to be seen as he fidgeted uncomfortably before her.

"Tell me your disagreement with Barb didn't have anything to do with what happened all those years ago," she said quietly.

"What if it did? What if I'm tired of everybody telling me what I should do?"

"Then I'd say before you make any more decisions, ask yourself why you're really running away from Barb and this project and your wife. Why, when you have everything, is it not enough?" she asked, then strode out of the building.

"Hold up, are you really going to quit?" she said, catching up to Arianna on the sidewalk outside.

"You can't quit your family," Arianna replied, putting on her sunglasses. "I'm just pissed. Let him suffer a bit, he can see what it feels like."

"Okay . . ."

"I told you, I hate liars. And I won't be made into one. And if that's not enough," Arianna continued, gesturing to where she'd left Dominic, "I've been following every step of Samantha Love's six months to find the love of your life plan and now this? Todd just pulls this stunt with Sunny Day? I thought I'd log on and see that they'd made up and that the wedding was still on. I don't get it. She has it all—looks, a huge brand, a massive following. Was he only pretending all this time? Was any of it even real?" Arianna threw her hands up in the air and then plonked herself down on one of the benches outside of the fake park at the entrance to The Point offices.

For a moment Clementine felt dismissive. Arianna didn't even know Samantha, and she was basing her life plan on her? But then again, people who didn't know Wendy had written to her wanting to know what to do with their lives and often reported back that they'd taken her advice. Wasn't it the same thing, wanting someone to tell us what to do so we didn't do the wrong thing and irrevocably take our lives off track? Samantha Love was an inspiration to Arianna, a kind of role model for young women like her who wanted to manifest their own success stories and happy endings.

Clementine sat down next to Arianna and stared out over the perfectly green synthetic grass, the plastic lawn giving off an unpleasant smell as it heated up in the sun. "What if it was all those things? Real and fake and perfect and flawed and ideal and doomed all at once? Nothing is ever exactly as it seems and there are no guarantees in life, but that doesn't mean that you give up striving for what you want. Nor does it mean that there is only one way to get it."

Arianna sighed and picked at her manicured nails. "I just wanted a plan to follow."

"I know, but sometimes you have to follow your own lead."

Arianna leaned back and raised her eyebrows at Clementine. "Follow your own lead. Wow, stick that inside a tin and sell it."

Clementine laughed. "I wish. I mean, I am suddenly unemployed." She paused for a moment, realizing that on top of everything else, she was now going to have to find a way to pay for health insurance for her and Jonah. "No, I'll leave the notes in a tin to Samantha Love. But it might look good on a business card."

Twenty-Seven

We can never really start over, but if we're lucky we can start again.

—WENDY WISE

"Sorry we're late," Wendy said, walking out onto the back deck of Clementine's house, where the smells of woodsmoke filled the air.

Barb was barbecuing and Clementine was setting the table, while Jill attached the slack line she'd brought for Jonah to the tree and the fence. The makeshift obstacle course was both delighting and confounding Jonah as he tried to navigate it, all while quizzing Jill on everything she knew about the previous season of *New World Ninjas*' competitors.

Wendy walked Harvey over to meet Jonah and Jill, making good on her promise to herself to keep an open mind about Jill and show Barb she supported her no matter what.

"Harvey? What a surprise!" Clementine said.

"Good to see you, Clementine," Harvey said, leaning in to give Clementine a warm sandalwood-scented hug.

"Harvey?" Barb asked, coming over and sticking out her hand for a shake before Harvey could hug her. "I didn't know you were coming."

"Neither did I, but I had to see your mother," Harvey said, looking at Wendy adoringly.

Wendy blushed and then turned to her girls. "Why don't I help you bring the food out?" she said, motioning them to follow her.

"Mom, what's going on?" Clementine asked when they were all in the kitchen.

"Right, well, after I got to the library the story broke about Todd stealing the idea Samantha wanted to back and giving it to Sunny, so I called Harvey because I had an idea, but he was in New York, to see me, and we decided that we would try and find a solution together."

"I don't understand," Barb said.

"I've been texting Steve to find out what he's going to do, but so far he hasn't gotten back to me," Clementine said.

"That's because he didn't want to say anything until Harvey and I were sure that we could find a solution."

"What do you mean? Did you talk to him?" Clementine asked.

"Look at this," Wendy said. She pulled out her phone

and opened it to Samantha Love's Instagram page and a fifteen-second video telling her fans to head to her YouTube channel for some big news. Wendy found the link, and there were Samantha and Steve on a beach in Turks and Caicos, carrying their shoes as they walked along the sand, the sun starting to set behind them.

"I really loved your idea," Samantha said, looking wistfully out at the water.

"Really?" Steve asked, accidentally looking into the camera, before Samantha directed his attention back to her.

"Yeah. CBD-infused water. Water that quenches and calms. It's revolutionary. I mean you'd have to work on the vegetable part of it, use something mild and inoffensive like cucumber and add fruit. Nobody wants to just drink kale."

"Okay," Steve said, nodding as if he could get his head around the idea.

"Anyways, I would've done it. That is, if my fiancé Todd hadn't taken it for Sunny."

"I had no idea that he was going to do that," Steve said, sounding a little stilted. "It was always meant for you."

Samantha paused, letting that sink in. "But was it even real?" She stopped and faced him.

"It was real," Steve said, looking hurt. "It just wasn't

as ready as I made it out to be. I've visited all those places in the brochure and did all that research, and I really believe that there is a whole untapped market out there for CBD products. I just needed a spokesperson who believed it too, so that I could get the funding I needed to actually start production. I had it all lined up and was ready to go, but nobody wanted to be the first, so . . ."

"So you were hoping that if I said yes, then you could leverage my involvement, and actually get the money you were hoping others thought you already had, when you said you were well on your way to being fully invested."

"Yes. Are you going to turn me in? Because if you are, I'd really like to call my wife first, that is if she's still speaking to me."

"Why wouldn't she be?" Samantha asked.

"Because I lied."

"About AquaVeg?"

"No, about the money I used to start the company. It was our money," Steve stopped and paused for a moment as he stared out at the water. "No, it was her money, and it was supposed to be used to buy the house we were renting, but I needed it for AquaVeg, and so I spent it on the business without telling her." He said it all in one breath, as if he had to get it out before he lost his nerve, and inhaled sharply at the end. "I thought I'd be able to pay her back without her ever knowing and we'd be able to buy an even bigger house. I thought if I could actually make one of my ideas happen, then she'd see me differently. I'd see me differently, and maybe that would be enough to make me a better husband and father." He sat down in the sand, and rested his arms on his upright knees.

"But she found out before you could pull it off."

"Right. So now I'm not only a failure, I'm also a liar and a thief." He stated it without self-pity, as if it was a relief to say the words. "What I did was wrong, I know that. I just . . ." He turned to look Samantha in the eye. "Have you ever just gone all in, convinced you can make your luck change?"

Samantha sat next to him and dug her feet into the sand.

"Of course I have. It's how I started Love's Lip Balm. Maybe next time, you should try to change your luck by telling the truth."

For a moment the two of them were quiet as they watched the sun start to dip down and kiss the water pink.

"I know it's not going to happen now, but would you mind if I told you about my campaign idea?" Steve said.

"Sure."

Steve ran his hands through his hair and took a deep breath before launching into his pitch.

"Well, it always starts with an aerial shot of a surf-board floating in the middle of the ocean, different oceans for different flavors, but always the ocean, a board, and you on it. . . ."

The video ended with the two of them finishing each other's sentences, showing that they had the same shared vision.

It was another reenactment of a pivotal moment in the story of Samantha Love's life, and it was strange to watch Steve playing the part of himself. After that there were pictures of Samantha boarding a plane with Steve, telling her followers that every dream is just an empty bottle floating out at sea until someone finds it and fills it with love and dedication. An interesting if odd analogy, Clementine thought, getting distracted by the messaging and knowing that she could've done better.

"Is she saying what I think she's saying?" Clementine asked.

"I don't understand what anyone is saying, someone please just tell me," Barb said, exasperated.

"Samantha is going to fill his bottles of water," Wendy said.

"What?" Clementine and Barb asked at the same time.

"She's going to be his spokesperson," Wendy continued. "We weren't sure if she would, or if we could get Steve out of this mess, but thankfully he didn't actually commit fraud or break any other laws."

"He didn't?" Barb asked.

"No, with Clementine, it was technically their money that he took, because they're married. And with Aqua-Veg, he never said that others actually had invested, though he was certainly hoping it came across that way. He was misleading, no doubt about that. But if Samantha signed on, it might be enough to salvage his idea and get real investors on board. So I messaged her and told her that I was Steve's mother-in-law and that I was furious with him for what he did to my daughter, but I had seen AquaVeg and that it was real, and what are the chances of our worlds colliding like this. Synchronicity. Samantha's a big believer in it. And the terms that Harvey came up with are certainly way more favorable for her now."

"Why would Harvey want to help Steve?" Barb asked.

"Because if Steve can get this off the ground, then he'll have a better chance of paying Clementine back," Wendy said.

"Wow. And what about Sunny Day, and her lawyers?" Clementine asked.

"Well, she hadn't signed anything, so she had no claims to AquaVeg, and because Samantha wants to make sure that there's no bad blood with Sunny and her followers, she's going to license Sunny's big comeback song for the jingle," Wendy said with admiration.

"I don't even know what to say," Clementine said.

"That Steve's the luckiest jerk on the planet?" Barb offered. "I'm surprised she didn't think you were in on some scam with him."

"I know. I was worried about that," Wendy said. "But Harvey offered to do the deal for free, and her lawyers approved everything."

"You're right, Steve really is the luckiest jerk," Clementine said.

"He was lucky to get twenty percent, though it's not like he can complain. Harvey's colleagues are drawing up the paperwork now," Wendy said.

"Thank you. To you and your husband," Clementine said.

"That still sounds strange."

"So do you live in Florida now?" Clementine asked, heading back outside with Barb and Wendy.

"I have been. But I can't live in Boca full-time. It's too far from you both and Jonah. I'm sorry I wasn't honest. I was just so embarrassed about being let go from the magazine. Harvey seemed to be the only person in the world who didn't think I was some bumbling idiot giving out bad advice. So when he asked if I'd marry him, I said yes. It was impulsive, and we both know it. But he's a good man and I do love him."

"You know, Clementine was right, you don't need the magazine. You can still give out advice," Barb said.

"And you can still ignore it," Wendy said, reaching for Barb's hand.

"Well, you can't blame us right now if we do. I mean, you're a bit of a hot mess. But it's actually kind of endearing."

"Now, we still have to figure out how to keep your house," Wendy said, wiping her damp eyes and standing taller. She then turned to Barb and whispered, "And I know that you'll figure out what's best for you."

"Mom, enough. You've done enough. Let's just . . . let's just enjoy tonight, together," Clementine said.

Outside a breeze had picked up, lifting the worst of the heat away and leaving the best of the late-day sun, which would lure people out into their gardens to dine outside. Clementine thought of all the times she and Jonah had wandered after dinner for ice cream and taken Betsy to the park, where she could play and splash with other dogs in the little plastic wading pools that were just for pets. All those faces that she knew well enough to say hello and make small talk about the weather or how nice it was that summer was finally here. Not friends, exactly, but neighbors that made this her home. She'd hate to leave it.

"There's something I need to tell you," Barb said as soon as Wendy left to check in on the others. "Dominic and I had a falling-out the other day." She lifted the salmon off the barbecue and plated it for Clementine.

"About you not giving me his message?" Clementine asked, not looking her sister in the eye. She took the salmon and brought it to the picnic table, already full of salads and baked sweet potatoes and Jonah's homemade lemonade. She made sure that Wendy and Harvey were focused on Jonah and Jill, and out of earshot, before she continued. "He told me, right before he kissed me."

"He what? That shit, I'm going to—"

"No, you're not. You're not going to do anything. Nothing is going to come of it, because I don't want it to."

"I'm sorry. I shouldn't have kept his feelings from you. . . ."

"No, you shouldn't have. But I understand. You've been looking out for me and making decisions on my behalf for so long, it's hard to know when to stop."

"I was just . . ."

"Meddling. Like Mom," Clementine said and laughed.

"I really don't want to be a meddler."

"It's okay. You both mean well, I know that. And it's not like Dominic couldn't have found another way to contact me all those years ago, if he'd really wanted to," she said. "He'll get over it."

Barb shook her head. "I'm not so sure about that. He's scrapping the art space and community kitchen and cooking school we planned and talking about leasing it to a Whole Foods, and I think just out of spite he's going to buy Ivan's and turn it into some expensive hipster bar."

"So I heard," Clementine said, filling everyone's glasses with lemonade. "Apparently he's changing direction on the whole sales and marketing team too. He was surprised to see me at work yesterday."

"Shit. I'm sorry."

"Don't be, I'm working on something. I've got a kid to support and a new home to find and pay for if I'm going to do this on my own."

"So you're not going to take Steve back?"

"No. I'm glad he's not in trouble, but it doesn't change things with us."

Barb looked at Clementine. "It's really over then."

"Or maybe it's just the beginning of something else," Wendy said, startling them from behind.

"You've got to stop surprising people like that. Give us some warning, will you?" Barb said.

"Jonah, Harvey, come inside and wash your hands. Jill, you too."

Jill, who seemed only too happy to be included, did as Wendy said.

"Wendy's never better than in a crisis," Barb said, but Clementine was still thinking that what her mother said was right. That if this really was just the beginning, there needed to be some changes. And she needed to make them herself.

Twenty-Eight

It doesn't matter how fast you can run,
the truth always finds you.

—BARB WISE

The first thing that Barb noticed when she and Jill swung by the office on her way home from Clementine's barbecue was the ugly green spray paint covering her beautiful glass door so that the sign now read MISSION GREED.

"What the hell?" Jill asked, jumping out of the car to stare at the graffiti, which was still dripping wet. Catching sight of the vandals, Jill turned to Barb. "Want me to go after them? They're not exactly fast," she said.

"It's okay, I'm pretty sure it's Ivan and one of his cronies from the neighborhood association. They're pissed about Dominic leasing to a Whole Foods."

"I thought you guys had a deal?"

"We did, but not everyone keeps their promises,"

Barb said, taking her keys from her bag and opening the front door. She flicked the lights on, relieved to see that there had been no other damage done, and checked the security footage on her laptop. Ivan's face stared straight at the camera in surprise just before he sprayed the paint.

"I'm calling the cops," Jill said, pulling out her phone.

"Don't. I'll talk to him. He's pissed, I get it. I'd be pissed too if someone came into my neighborhood promising one thing and then doing another."

"Oh please, the value of his place must've tripled since he moved in."

"Yes, and that's great for whoever owns it, but he rents. So do a lot of these other businesses that are being pushed out."

Barb knew that none of the increases in property value mattered if the people who lived here couldn't afford to be a part of any of it. Sure, their apartments and houses were worth more, but only if they sold. In the meantime the neighborhood they lived in was becoming increasingly unavailable to them. Stores and restaurants that they used to frequent were being replaced and rebranded, sending out a clear message that they no longer belonged. The art space and community kitchen had been the one thing that would've tied the old and the new together, and when that had been taken away, they felt cheated. Barb understood, she felt cheated too. She sat on the couch of her office and leaned back into the cool leather.

"What's in Daytona?" She was tired, too tired to wait for any more revelations or surprises. They'd had a nice night at Clementine's, nice enough that Barb wasn't actually angry at Jill anymore for what she suspected, just tired of waiting to be told.

"What do you mean?" Jill said, crossing her arms in front of her body.

"Just tell me, please. The lanyard and badge in your underwear drawer, the boy shorts, the person you've been talking to online. Are you seeing someone else? Because if you are, now would be a good time to tell me. I don't have the energy to fight. And I'm not supposed to, doctor's orders."

"I see you're going to be playing that card for a while."

"I'm serious."

"I'm not seeing anyone else."

"But . . ."

"I'm going to Daytona to try out for *Ultimate Ninja Warrior*. I don't know that I'll even make the cut and I didn't want to bother you with it when you've got so much going on right now."

"Wait a minute . . . are you talking about the TV show?" Barb said, sitting upright.

"Yes. I've been making videos at the gym and sending them in and I finally got a chance to try out in Daytona."

"And do what, be a *Ninja*?" she asked in disbelief.

"See, I knew you would find it stupid."

"I didn't say that. But you're already successful. You don't need a reality TV contest. You're not some kid trying to get enough money to open her own gym. You have your own gym."

"No, you have a gym," Jill said, frustrated, as she paced the office. "And a career and a business, and property and employees, and I don't want to be just another one of your employees."

"You're not," Barb said, stung. "You're my girl-friend."

Jill stopped and looked at Barb. "For how long?"

"What's that supposed to mean?"

"You didn't even tell Wendy that we got back together." When Barb scrambled to figure out how to respond, she continued, "I saw her surprise when she came by the other day. But that's not the big thing. You're not happy. You're so stressed you landed in the hospital, and I'm not even sure I know all the reasons why because you don't share anything with me, and then you're mad when I don't know what's going on. The only time we have sex is when you're angry or drunk. And you've been smoking again—don't pretend you haven't."

"Okay, I won't," she said.

"You're so convinced that I'm going to cheat on you again or leave you that you keep pushing me away." Jill sat down next to Barb and took her hand. "Maybe you're the one who wants to leave. Did you ever think of that?"

Barb looked at Jill's hand in hers, the freckles that covered the surface, the little calluses that rested just beneath her fingers from all her climbing, and thought she might cry. She couldn't remember the last time they'd just held hands and talked. In spite of how hard she'd tried to deny it, she'd missed this intimacy, and the answer to Jill's question terrified her.

"And what if I had thought about leaving . . . everything," Barb said, looking around her office.

"Everything?"

"I don't know, I'm just so tired of taking care of everything and everyone."

"So maybe you just need to take a break."

Barb looked Jill in the eyes and thought she might cry.

"I'll be okay. Your sister will be okay. Jonah, too. Rishi will be okay. Your mother, well, Wendy is Wendy, so she'll always be okay. But maybe you don't need to spend all your time taking care of us. You've done that, and you're really good at it, and we're all grateful. But I really think it's time that you start taking care of yourself. You don't seem to want anyone else to, so maybe you need to give it a try."

"You sound like my mom."

"Your mom? Well, what do you know? That's a first, in more ways than one."

"I know." Barb nodded. "Jill, are you breaking up with me?"

"I hope not. When we got back together, I know you probably thought it was because of the gym, but it wasn't. It was because I missed you and that thing with Karen was stupid. I was sabotaging myself because I felt guilty about you doing so much for me, and that I didn't deserve it."

Barb placed her hand on Jill's cheek, and gently wiped away a tear. "But when we were apart, I didn't miss our house, or the gym, or the fancy dinners or the vacations, I missed you. I still do. But you have to want to be here." She took a breath. "I'm going to do this Ninja thing. I'm good at it, and who knows where it will lead? But I want to do it for me. And I think you should do something for you too."

Twenty-Nine

It takes courage to embrace a future that
looks different from the one we expected.
—CLEMENTINE WISE

It was dawn when Clementine woke up, the sun curling its way under and around her curtains as she heard the sound of Betsy's feet eagerly landing on the hardwood floor. Clementine hopped out of bed, scooping up her pug's chubby little body before she could wake up Jonah, and taking her downstairs.

She'd slept the whole night alone for once, Jonah and Wendy together in his room, Harvey having gone back to Wendy's apartment. Wendy had turned Jonah's room into a makeshift campground, complete with a pop-up tent that squeezed against the wall, a campfire of battery-operated candles, and flashlights they held under their faces as they told scary-but-not-too-scary stories and ate marshmallows from a bag. Clementine had sat outside the door listening to the two of them giggle, both wishing that she could be a part of the fun and grateful that Wendy relished her role as a grandmother. Then she'd quietly cried herself to sleep, her emotions a roller coaster. With no husband and no child, she had tried to sleep in the middle of the bed but immediately retreated to her side, the extra space feeling like a loss rather than a luxury.

"Where are you going?" she asked Betsy, who didn't run to the back as usual, but to the front door, where she sat up as tall as her little body would allow.

"Later," Clementine said, but Betsy refused to move, a low growl threatening to turn into a bark that would wake everyone else up.

"Oh all right," she said, grabbing the leash. She scrawled a note on the fridge for her mom, pulled a sweatshirt on over her pajamas, slipped on her Birkenstocks, and headed out the front with Betsy, the sun lighting the sky in ripples of pink and orange. The street was quiet, although after school it became a hub for kids riding their bikes or playing basketball, the neighbors' portable hoop wheeled out for everyone. Jonah had finally gotten up the courage this year to join in. The unspoken rule seemed to be if you could dribble a ball you could play, the teams constantly changing as children were called in for dinner or let out to play for a few more minutes before bed. It had given Clementine hope to see Jonah participate, even exchanging a small almost imperceptible nod with some of these same kids when crossing paths on the way to school, the subtle greeting making him walk a little bolder.

The weekend was the only time that people were forced to pause their noisy home renovations, and Clementine was just savoring the quiet when it was interrupted by someone calling her name.

"Clementine!"

Marie, Kimberly's assistant, was rounding the corner. Clementine forced a smile, hoping Marie would leave her alone, but instead the woman rushed forward.

"Look, Kimberly told me what happened and I wanted to say sorry. I don't know where she gets off saying any of that stuff to you about Jonah. The truth is, she's the only one who has a problem with it."

"Because she really thinks Jonah's getting special treatment?"

Marie furrowed her brow. "Because she's worried that if Ethan participates in the pilot program then he'll get labeled."

"Ethan? I don't understand."

"Oh, you didn't know," she said, her eyes widening. "Ethan was asked to be a part of the same program as Jonah. The school counselor believes that he's actually acting out to cover up the fact that he has anxiety and is having trouble keeping up, and Kimberly seems to have an easier time thinking of him as a bully than as having any issues or learning differences. If the whole program went away, then she wouldn't have to address it."

"I had no idea."

"That's the whole point. She doesn't want anyone to think any less of Ethan, or her for that matter."

Clementine didn't know what to say. It had never occurred to her that Kimberly's boasting and bravado were a way to hide her insecurity.

"Thanks for telling me."

They stood awkwardly for a moment, and Clementine took in the camera slung around Marie's neck.

"It's for the listing," Marie said, answering Clementine's unspoken question.

"Right," Clementine said, understanding now that of course Mr. Gregoris was indeed going ahead with the sale, and that Marie was coming to the house to take photographs for the listing.

"I didn't realize you were renting. I'm sorry. If it makes you feel any better, it's happening all over the neighborhood. The prices have gone crazy and landlords just want to cash out. It's a good reason to buy, and I'd be happy to help you find a place," Marie said.

As if the reason Clementine hadn't bought was because she hadn't found the right agent, she thought bitterly, but she knew Marie meant well and she muttered thanks, grateful that Betsy was now tugging on her leash, determined to get her to the main drag where all the good smells were.

Inside her sweatshirt pocket her phone rang, and as soon as she saw the name on the display she answered it.

"Hey, too early to call?" Steve asked on the other end of the phone.

"I've been trying to reach you."

"I know, I know, I'm sorry. Can we meet up?"

"When?"

"Now?" Steve asked.

Clementine looked up, and saw Steve walking toward her, juggling the phone with a coffee cup in each hand. When he reached her, he handed her one.

"I was hoping that I could surprise you and take you guys out for breakfast or something, but then I thought I probably shouldn't just show up at the house."

"Yeah, Mom and Jonah are still sleeping," she said, taking a sip of the vanilla latte he'd brought her, with extra foam, just the way she liked it. "You're never up this early."

"I know. I got in late last night and couldn't sleep. How's Jonah?" he asked.

"Better with my mom around, but worried and sad. He misses you. You could've at least checked in on him."

"I'm sorry. I miss him too," Steve said, his voice breaking. "I miss you both."

There was a silence where Clementine could've said she missed him too, a bridge that might allow him to cross back into their lives, making the events of the past week nothing more than the wild and unbelievable conclusion to an exhausting and painful time in their marriage. It would've been so easy and there was a part of her that would like nothing more than to pretend that Steve's betrayal had really just been a misstep in his plan to do the right thing. It made for a better story, the kind of story Samantha Love would tell, but Clementine didn't want to edit and filter her life to sell her tragedy as a triumph; she wanted to live with the truth. And the truth was, her marriage was broken and it would never be fixed. She would never be able to go back, but she could go forward, for herself and for Jonah.

"I saw your video on YouTube, and Mom told me what happened. It looks like it's all going to work out," she said.

"Thanks to Wendy and Harvey. She told me that twenty percent of something was better than one hundred percent of nothing and the most important thing was staying out of trouble for Jonah."

"That really is good advice."

"I know. I was surprised too."

Clementine fiddled with Betsy's leash as both of them were quiet for a moment.

"She also told me that Jonah would be better off with me being a fully present part-time parent than an always distracted full-time one," he continued, "and I think she's right."

"Really?" So Wendy really had heard Clementine when she said she wasn't going to take Steve back. Knowing her mother had faith in her to figure things out on her own strengthened Clementine's resolve to do so.

"I'm sorry I fucked up with us, and I know you won't forgive me, and I don't blame you. I was a selfish prick . . . am a selfish prick, but I want to try and be different, for Jonah. He's amazing and I owe it to him to be better." Steve started to cry, and pulled his T-shirt up to wipe his face. "And I owe it to you. I never said thank you for supporting me and I should have. I was just so angry. I felt like I wasn't getting anywhere and that I was letting you down, both of which are true, but neither of which are your fault. I hated that you could take on so much, even though you had to, because I wasn't exactly giving you any other choice. But it was wrong to blame you, and you deserve better and I'm sorry," he said, "I really am."

"Me too," Clementine said, and she was. Sorry that she'd ignored who Steve really was, sorry that she'd pushed him where he didn't want to go and then blamed him for not being the man she wanted to love, sorry that she'd spent so much time trying to fix him when she could have spent all that time nurturing herself to be the woman she wanted to be. But she wasn't sorry for what they had created. "Why don't we go surprise Jonah? You can tell him your good news. Make him pancakes, and have breakfast in the tree house, just the two of you."

"Really?"

"Really."

"I wish you'd join us," he said as they walked back toward the house. He reached for her hand that held Betsy's leash, the pug walking between the two of them, and she laced her fingers through his as she had done a million times since they met, an action so comfortable and familiar it made her smile. "Next time," she said, and gave his hand a little squeeze before finally letting go.

Thirty

*C*hange—*it's inevitable. Nothing stays the same, nor should it. With each year, we learn and grow and evolve, embrace the lessons of our past and face the future stronger and better than we were before. That's why The Point isn't just a building, it's a link. A connection between all the things you love about your old neighborhood and all the wonderful things you're about to discover about your new one. An art space, a community garden, a youth-driven culinary school, a seasonal farmers' market, and an innovation hub for new ideas and free monthly events. We're committed to not only creating beautiful spaces for people to live, but also communities for people to love. After all, having your own place in a great neighborhood is exactly The Point.*

Clementine held her breath as Dominic finished reading and looked up at her, his face covered in shock.

"You said you liked surprises," she said.

"This isn't exactly what I meant," Dominic said, taking off his reading glasses and rubbing the dark circles under his eyes.

"No, it's better. Because no one expects some rich developer to actually give a shit about the neighborhood that they're gentrifying."

"This is more than I originally agreed to with Barb. And it will be quite a bit more expensive, by the way."

"For now, but it shows that you heard people's concerns and that you care about the neighborhood. And you'll get great press as the events become more popular. Corporate sponsors will get on board."

Dominic looked at Clementine and shook his head. "I don't know."

"If you want things to be different, then you have to do things differently. But first, don't blow it all up with Barb, you've both worked too hard for that. This could be good for everyone, and you'll get all the credit."

"You really are good at sales," Dominic said.

"Well, actually I'm better at marketing, and if you do this," Clementine said, pointing to her pitch documents, "then you'll need a director of communications and events. I'd be happy to step into that role."

"Oh, you would, would you?"

"Yes, and I already have an idea for your first event," Clementine said. It was a bold move, but now wasn't the time to be playing it safe.

Dominic leaned back in his chair, and exhaled. "If I agree, could you start right away and also run interference for the first little while?"

"Sure . . . ," Clementine replied and waited for Dominic to continue. She could tell by the way he looked at her that there was more he wanted to say, and she held her breath as he got up and walked around and sat on the edge of the desk facing her.

"What is it?" she asked.

"It's about the other day. . . ."

"Dominic, you know we can't . . ."

"No, no, I know, and I'm sorry." He paused and took a deep breath. "When Barb and I fought, she basically accused me of being a spoiled brat, and while you can never tell her that I admitted this, she wasn't entirely wrong."

"What do you mean?"

"I mean she's right, you're right, I've got so much, and yet all I do is work and stress about what I'm going to do next and how I'm going to make more, when there's no reason that I can't just stop and enjoy what I already have."

"Are you retiring?" Clementine asked, her voice going up.

"Oh, God no. But I am taking a vacation, a long one. A chance for me and Ella and the boys to just be together and get back to nature and reconnect. I owe that to them, and to myself."

"Surprises," she said.

"Surprises," Dominic said, looking her in the eyes. For a moment neither of them said anything and then he continued, "I think it's time I made some surprises for myself." Dominic extended his hand to Clementine to shake and she took it. "So, let's do this idea of yours. Who knows, it might work."

"Don't sound so sure," she teased. "But seriously, thank you." She picked up her things to go. "Back to nature, huh? I wouldn't have taken you for a camping kind of guy."

"Who said anything about camping? I've chartered a boat and hired a crew and a chef and we're going to sail around Europe for a month."

"Wow," Clementine said, marveling not just at the idea, but also that she knew anyone who had the means to do something like that, it being so far from what was possible in her own life. She wondered if either of their young selves could have ever predicted that they'd end up where they were. Maybe they could've defied expectations and made a go of it back then, but she was certain that they wouldn't now. "It sounds perfect," Clementine said, and she meant it. A new beginning for them both.

Thirty-One

Open house. It's such a strange phrase. We open our doors and welcome people to come inside and take a look at how we'd like them to think we live. A clutter-free living room, a book positioned just so on a side table by a window, a kitchen counter without any crumbs, as if every meal magically made and cleaned up after itself. But we can never really open up all of the places where we made memories, laughed until we cried, shared meals that marked holidays, held each other in the dark as we whispered our fears, hopes, and dreams, knowing that they'd be safe within the walls of our home.

It was August by the time people started visiting the house. Clementine found it hard to stay away, sitting cross-legged in the tree house. Sipping on her lemonade, the takeout container sweating in her hand, she peeked through the little window at the steady stream of people moving in and out of the house, holding the glossy sales sheets with photographs taken at angles to make the rooms look bigger and better than they were. *Original condition, much loved, prime neighborhood* was splashed across the page, luring buyers to the possibility that they could turn the old house into the home of their dreams while simultaneously warning them that they'd be buying it as is. A home that Clementine loved.

For a brief moment she'd thought that she'd be able to handle everyone coming through her home, telling herself that it was a good chance to say goodbye and that maybe she'd catch a glimpse of the family that was going to buy it. She'd lingered on the back porch, hiding as best she could beneath her sunglasses and hat. But the hardest part was recognizing the people who casually wandered through the kitchen where she and Jonah had covered the floor with flour each time they baked, the tiny bathroom where the three of them crowded over the sink as they brushed their teeth, the bedroom where Clementine had rocked Jonah and sang and read him stories until he fell asleep, and the bedroom where she and Steve had tried countless times to find the connection that had once united them.

Some of these people would remember when she'd moved in, neighbors, parents of PS 150 students, who had listened to her celebrate finally owning a home of her own and share her far-off plans for its improvements, a conversation that she'd been excluded from for so long. These same people must now either think that she'd been lying about owning or, if they were active on social media, which most of them were, had connected the dots that her husband had deceived her. *How couldn't she know? What had she been thinking? Can you imagine? Poor woman.* There would be those who judged her as an idiot and those who felt sorry for her, neither of which she needed right now. Eventually she'd headed out back, carrying the poor dog up the wooden steps and inside the tree house to spy with her.

"You're torturing yourself," Wendy said, startling Clementine as she climbed up the steps and slid inside. "I thought you said you were taking Betsy to the park during the open house."

"I did, I was, I am. Torturing myself, that is." She finished her lemonade, opened the container, and poured the ice onto the lid for Betsy, who happily licked at the cubes from her spot on the floor while still managing to lie down.

"Honey," Wendy began, "I've been talking to my financial advisor, and she says that if I . . ."

"No, Mom, don't. I appreciate it, but I need to figure this out on my own."

"I want to help," Wendy said, stretching out her legs and placing the sole of her foot against Clementine's and slowly rocking it from side to side.

"You are helping. You found Steve, you saved his ass, you got me some of my money back. And ten percent of AquaVeg." Now that Samantha Love was a major investor and spokesperson, Steve had been able to start paying Clementine back, although it would be a while before there was anything else, so Clementine had agreed to take the rest of her payment in shares.

"I'm not sure the shares are really helpful, but you never know." Wendy raised her palms to the sky, as if to say anything could happen. "If Steve's right and this whole CBD-in-drinks thing takes off, and that company actually makes money, you'd better get a percentage of it. After all, it was your money that started it."

"Could you imagine?" Clementine said. It was hard to imagine that AquaVeg could go anywhere, but then again from everything she'd since heard about Samantha Love, she had a hard time believing that she would've invested in the company if she didn't think it was a good idea. Poor Arianna had practically fallen out of her chair when Clementine showed up to work the day after the Samantha and Steve video was released. She was now only two degrees of separation from her idol, and had made Clementine promise to introduce her if she ever got the chance.

"Imagine what?" Barb asked, her breathing labored as she squeezed herself into the little doorframe of the tree house. "Three grown women and a fat dog falling out of a collapsing tree house in the middle of an open house? I can imagine that."

"Where's Jonah?"

"He's still at the park with Jill. She's training him on some new obstacle course. It's some *Ninja* thing."

"Amazing," Clementine said.

"I know, and he's loving it. Every time he starts to talk or worry too much about the probability of falling and whether or not the bars could support his weight, she just cheers 'Don't think it! Move it!' and he does. I tried to get him to leave, but he wouldn't go. He says he has to master phase one."

"Now that part sounds like Jonah," Clementine said.

"Huh," Wendy said, as if trying to make sense of Jill and Jonah playing together. "I wouldn't have picked Jill as someone he'd want to play with. It's such a surprise."

"A good one," Clementine said, smiling at her sister, who looked happier than she had seen her in a long time, if a bit winded. "She's so physical and he's so cerebral, they probably balance each other out."

"Speaking of surprises, I heard from Dominic," Barb said.

"Oh yeah?" Clementine looked out the window to avoid meeting her sister's eyes.

"Yeah, he's had a real change of heart. Mr. Community Outreach all of a sudden, full of great ideas and events."

"That's wonderful," Wendy said. "So you two won't have to part ways. It would've been such a shame after everything you've done together." She patted Barb's hand happily, and then to answer the question on Barb's face added, "What? I know everything."

"Of course you do," Barb replied, although the look on her face clearly said she didn't mind. Clementine was happy to see her mother and sister enjoying each other so much. As if sensing this, Barb reached for Clementine's hand, linking the three of them together. "Thank you."

Across the backyard they saw Marie lock the back door and leave out the front, taking the OPEN HOUSE sign with her. No doubt there would be a ton of offers in the days to follow. Families with kids Jonah's age, and many more with kids on the way, looking for their forever home. Clementine knew the feeling well, and could still see the first time she and Steve and Jonah had stood together, holding hands, staring at the house in wonder before moving in.

"I'm sorry you have to move," Barb said.

"Me too," Clementine replied and ran her hands along the knots in the wooden floor that they'd built together. "To be honest, I think Jonah's going to miss this tree house more than anything. I don't need a big place, now that it's going to be just the two of us, and I have an office to go to. I just wanted something on a little patch of land that I knew was ours."

"It's ridiculous," Barb said. "On the one hand, you've got all these people trying to buy these tiny little condos that we make, living stacked up on top of each other, and then you have people who will come along and take a perfectly good house like this and try and make it bigger. The city has to find a better way to deal with its overcrowding issues. It isn't healthy to have such densely populated areas and it isn't right that some people are wasting space the way they are. And everything is so fucking expensive. It can't last. It's unsustainable."

Clementine tilted her head and looked Barb in the eye. "I haven't heard you talk like this since you were at RISD."

"Me either," Wendy said.

"I've just been thinking. I know that Dominic and I do it better than most of the teams out there, but I'm still more of the problem than the solution. You start out with all these ideas of how you're going to change the world or do things differently, or just even shape your own life. And you take the opportunities that come your way, *because* they come your way, and because you need to work, but before you know it they're the only opportunities you're given. And if you're fortunate enough to be successful, then you can kind of forget what it was that you *really* wanted to do, and tell yourself to be grateful because at least you're getting to do the thing that you're now really good at, and because it supports the life that you have."

In the silence that followed, a wave of recognition washed over the three of them. Barb could've been speaking about any of them, but before Clementine could ask her more, she broke the moment. "But I'll tell you one thing, these tree roots are massive, and it will be a nightmare for someone who wants to do a reno and finish that basement. I wouldn't be surprised if they run the whole way under your house," she said, peeling herself off the floor at the sound of Jonah and Jill coming up the street. "I hope their agents warned them, because someone should."

"Maybe you should," Wendy said to Clementine, heading after Barb.

Clementine looked out at the branches that held the tree house, and thought about just how deep and far those roots must go.

"Yeah," she said, scooping up Betsy in her arms. "Maybe I should."

Thirty-Two

*L*ove. *It's what really matters. Loving ourselves,
loving each other, loving this great big beautiful
planet that's covered in water. In fact, without love and
water we wouldn't be here at all. AquaLove, flavored
with fresh fruits and just a hint of cleansing cucumber
in every sip, is the only water that hydrates your body
and soothes your soul. That's because AquaLove is
infused with pure CBD, for calmer, better days. Take a
sip, and feel the love.*

"I like it," Arianna said. "But I'd indent the last line
and have it stand on its own."

Clementine reread the copy and smiled. "You're
right. Can you format it and send it with the other
materials? I promised Samantha we'd get it to her
today."

"Love to," Arianna said, her indoctrination into the world of Samantha-speak complete after working on the company's brand book, a corporate bible with everything from fonts to colors and mission statements.

They'd been at it for weeks, ever since Samantha had reached out to Clementine at Wendy's urging. Wendy had shown her influencer friend the work Clementine had done for The Point and all the goodwill it had generated. Samantha had really responded to the whole synchronicity and second-chances angle and decided it would be a good thing to do, given what Steve had put Clementine through. After talking to Samantha, Clementine had to admit that the lip balm mogul's optimism was as contagious as it was persuasive.

"I've got to run," Clementine said, checking the clock on the wall as she packed up her laptop and folders and put them into the fashionable new backpack she now carted every day to and from the coworking space she'd rented for her and her associate, Arianna, the title in lieu of the proper salary Clementine couldn't yet afford to pay.

Arianna still did sales at The Point part-time but had jumped at the chance to be a part of Samantha Love's orbit, and in doing so, she had discovered that her talent for connecting with people could take her way beyond selling condos for her uncle. She was still a fan of Samantha's philosophies but was now quick to point out that they only worked if you made them your own. *Follow your own lead,* she reminded Clementine, inscribing the saying onto business card holders that she bought for each of them on her first day at work. Clementine had initially worried how the coworking space would affect Arianna's ability to shop for a husband on the job, but it had opened up a whole new world full of inspiring people for them both. With each day, Clementine heard less about what Arianna was looking for in a man and more about the things she wanted to learn and do herself.

"We should get AquaLove in here," Arianna said, grabbing her LOVE WATER bottle to refill it. "Maybe try out some of the new flavors for free and get feedback."

"Good idea," Clementine replied. Just a tiny part of her felt bad for Steve, whose role in the company had been drastically reduced to silent shareholder after market testing revealed that female customers were less inclined to support a company that had been kickstarted by a husband's betrayal. Although he certainly had fared better than Todd, who'd been dumped by both Samantha and Sunny and had earned the wrath of both of their countless fans. Samantha's decision to downplay Steve's role, and amplify her own, had in many ways worked out for Steve. He still earned money and was developing a series of start-up webinars that he was hoping to sell. But best of all, he was spending the extra time he had with Jonah.

"Sorry I'm late," Clementine said, hopping into the car with Seth.

Jonah had mentioned to Seth that his mother didn't have a driver's license, and told him how worried he was that with his dad no longer living at home, there'd be no one to drive him if he needed it, but she suspected it was really a way for Jonah and Seth to keep hanging out, now that camp was ending. Clementine couldn't believe it when Seth had offered to give her driving lessons once a week while Barb and Jill spent time with Jonah. At the end of every lesson, Jonah would insist Seth stay for a snack or that they all go out for an ice cream. Clementine had a feeling it was a way for Seth to keep seeing Jonah, and her too. A feeling, it turned out, she liked.

She fastened her seat belt and adjusted the mirrors before taking the gearshift out of park and signaling to change lanes.

"You know, at some point you're going to have to take your driver's test, otherwise you'll never be able to drive on your own," Seth said.

"I know, I know. Just . . . not yet."

Out of the corner of her eye she could see Seth smiling. "Fine by me, I'm in no rush."

Clementine felt her cheeks go pink and focused her attention on the road. She still didn't have a car, but she and Barb had planned a big road trip with Jonah to surprise Jill at her next competition in Ohio, and Clementine had agreed to share the driving.

No one had expected Jill to make the qualifying rounds at the *Ultimate Ninja Warrior* trials in Daytona, but once she had, she'd insisted that Barb sell the gym so she could pay for her legal fees and finish her brownstones in time for the fall market and devoted herself to all things *Ninja*, traveling from city to city competing and building her fan club, of which Jonah was the self-appointed president. He'd chosen a shark as her logo, having decided that sharks were the ninjas of the sea, his love affair with the misunderstood marine animal still going strong.

Clementine never would've expected her anxious, hyperintelligent, supersensitive son to have taken such an interest in a competition designed around increasingly challenging obstacles, but he had embraced it, especially the whole idea that anyone could become an athlete. Jonah believed that meant him too. Every week he would drag her to a *Ninja* gym, his anxiety decreasing and his confidence growing with each obstacle he conquered, no matter how small.

"Thanks again for inviting me, I know tonight's a big night."

Tonight was Jill's going-away party for her trip and Clementine had insisted she host it, the weather still warm enough for them to spill outside.

"We're happy you can join us. I know Jonah's excited."

"Yeah, ever since I told him I might not run the YMCA camp next summer, he's been bugging me to start a *Ninja* gym with Jill. He's picked the neighborhood and everything, said I could run the summer program and he'd help me recruit kids."

Clementine laughed out loud. It seemed Jonah had inherited more than just Steve's sense of humor after all.

"Sorry, it's genetic. The advice-giving, the pitching, the start-up making. Steve and I are both to blame. But the relentlessness, that's all his."

"That's okay, it's actually not a bad idea," Seth said and shrugged in a way that told Clementine he might actually consider it.

In the end, they'd only had to move thirty feet, to the back of the property where the old London plane tree and its massive roots had indeed proved an obstacle, for buyers who'd hoped to knock it down and build an extension and finish the basement. The tree's roots not only ran under the length of the house, but they also had pushed their way through its foundation. Anyone who wanted to touch the foundation would have to find a way to do so without damaging the tree, which was protected by conservation authorities. The additional expense, not to mention the bureaucracy involved, was enough for the deal to fall through and to deter other buyers, keeping the house on the market just long enough for Clementine to come up with a plan. The sale of the gym and the brownstones gave Barb enough money to give Clementine a down payment on the house (which she'd managed to get at a slight price reduction due to concerns about the tree) and make her a part owner. Clementine decided if she couldn't buy her sister out in five years they'd sell it, paying Barb back in full while still giving Jonah the chance to finish at his school.

In order to cover the mortgage, Clementine rented out the main house to a nice family with a young daughter who were excited about the neighborhood school, and eccentric enough to be willing to share the backyard with Clementine and Jonah and their new tiny house built around the tree.

It was a crazy idea, their three-hundred-square-foot

tiny home, but it had been just crazy enough to get Barb excited about her work again. She'd thrown herself into the project with more enthusiasm and energy than she'd had in a long time, documenting the entire process on her company's website and writing about it as a better alternative to New York's microapartment movement, which had seen the city lower the minimum square footage so they could squeeze more units into developments and also allow for the construction of super skinny homes between buildings. The city was in the middle of reviewing a plan to ease restrictions on secondary backyard dwellings, as other cities across America had.

It wasn't easy convincing the Landmarks Preservation Commission to allow Barb to build in Sunnyside Gardens, but she had made the case that the first planned community in America could still be protected while being home to another first, a tiny house community that looked to the future. Barb had even donated her firm's services and lobbied for Clementine's tiny house to be used as a case study, and seeing as Clementine was already the owner of the main house and therefore had the land to build the new home on, the city agreed.

Clementine and Jill helped with the building of the tiny home, doing the drywall and paint, while Wendy and Jonah had assembled tall wooden boxes and filled them with miniature cypress trees that formed a natural perimeter and created privacy between the two homes. Even Betsy had done her part, standing guard and greeting the neighbors who came out to see what was going on. It seemed impossible that anyone could make a house so small feel so complete, but Barb had done it. With the help of an arborist Barb managed to get permission to torpedo a small tunnel underneath the main root bed, which allowed her to plumb a tiny kitchen and bathroom without harming the tree. She'd built Clementine a bed that could fold down and be concealed by sliding doors to make a private bedroom, or fold up to make more space in the living room. And in a loft that could be reached only by a ladder, she had created the ultimate bedroom retreat for Jonah, with built in shelves and a skylight to gaze at the stars. It was perfect—a wood and steel sustainable tree house made with love that wrapped around the base of the tree and had a rooftop deck that reached up toward the sky.

Clementine leaned against the house and listened as Barb told Wendy about her meetings with the city and the growing support from homeowners who were excited about the prospect of renting out the additional dwellings for supplemental income, putting their homes on wheels to relocate them out of the city if needed, as well as families who saw the tiny homes as a way to keep their aging parents close and take care of them. Already there was talk in the news that the city was considering adding ten thousand new units over the next decade, and Barb felt sure she could increase that number.

"I'm proud of you both," Wendy said, standing in the middle and hooking arms with each of her daughters.

"What about you? Are you going to move back to Boca?" Clementine asked.

"Not exactly. Harvey and I have decided to take things slow."

"Oh, now that you're married?" Barb asked.

"I see you're never going to let me live that down," Wendy said, smiling. "I know it's unusual, but I told him I'm not ready to leave my girls again, or my grandson, and it's not like we're interested in seeing other people, so I'm going to stay here for the summers and Harvey can visit and then I'll go to Boca with him for the winters."

"Wow. I wonder what a Wise Woman would say about that?" Barb teased.

"That the only way to take care of you husband's needs is to be with your husband," Clementine said.

"Wrong," Wendy said, feigning indignation. "An

Older and Wiser Woman would say . . . that there comes a time when every woman needs to recognize that she has needs of her own, and unless she meets them, she can't expect anyone else to."

Clementine nodded and kissed her mom on the cheek.

"That *is* wise," Clementine said.

"Oh good, I'll use it on tomorrow's episode of *Older and Wiser*," Wendy replied, referring to her daily sixty-second Instagram videos, where she gave out empowering everyday advice for women. Thanks to Samantha's endorsement, Wendy's new venture had rapidly gained a loyal following, and she was thinking at the end of a year she'd have enough for a book of daily inspirations.

Barb noticed that Jill and Jonah were deep in conversation. "What do you think that's about?" she asked.

"Jonah's on a quest for Jill to open her own *Ninja* gym," Clementine said. "He's already recruited Seth if she says yes."

"Who knew she was so great with kids?" Wendy said.

"She's amazing," Barb said, looking on adoringly.

Clementine had noticed how much better things were between Barb and Jill since they'd gotten rid of the gym. They'd stayed in therapy and Barb's panic attacks had eased up, along with, Clementine noticed, her drinking.

It was like a weight had been lifted from them both, and Clementine was glad to see it.

Suddenly Jonah jumped up and banged a spoon against a glass. "Everyone, Jill has an announcement to make!"

"Uh, Jonah, I thought I said I was going to wait . . . ," Jill said nervously.

"No, do it," Jonah pleaded.

"Okay, I just wanted to say, thank you so much for doing this, not just for throwing me this barbecue, but for all your support. It means a lot."

"Not that," Jonah said, "the other thing."

"Jonah, I was going to do that later," Jill said, bending down to him. "In private."

"But why? We're all here now, which means we can all celebrate together when she says yes."

Clementine looked at Barb, who looked at Jill, who dropped to one knee and took a deep breath. No one said anything until Wendy piped up with, "He makes a good point."

Jill exhaled. "Okay, who am I kidding? I suppose if I'm going to marry you, then I really am marrying your whole family, so—"

"Yes," Barb said before Jill could get another word out, and crossed the backyard to kiss her. "Yes, yes, yes."

"I told you!" Jonah yelled, clapping excitedly as the rest of them joined him, and Clementine rushed inside to get the bottle of champagne she'd gotten as a housewarming gift and was saving for a special occasion.

Standing in the doorway of her little home before rejoining the party, she closed her eyes, blinking slowly, as if taking a snapshot of this moment. She wanted to imprint it in her mind and heart forever, her little family all in one place, celebrating. She felt Jonah's arms wrap around her middle, reaching farther across her back than they had at the beginning of the summer, his head coming up higher on her body than it used to, and held him tight.

A Wise Woman knows that the biggest investment she can make is in herself.

—WENDY WISE

When you invest in yourself, you're able to invest in others.

—CLEMENTINE WISE

Some people are very invested in giving other people advice. But we love them anyway.

—BARB WISE

Acknowledgments

My team is made up of the wisest women. To my incredible agent, Mollie Glick—your faith in me and in this book has been an absolute game changer. I am grateful for all your guidance and beyond lucky to have you and all the amazing folks at CAA in my corner. To my wonderful editor, Emily Griffin—thank you for working with me every step of the way to make this book the best it could be. I feel so fortunate to be supported and welcomed by all the talented people at HarperCollins. To my dear friend and mentor Caroline Leavitt—if you had a dollar for every e-mail I wrote you asking, wondering, sharing, laughing, crying, you'd be a millionaire. I hope you'll accept this thanks instead. This book was a haven to me during a challenging but rewarding time of change, and I kept it very close. To

Robert Eversz, who saw the manuscript at the beginning, and Andrea Robinson who saw it near the end, thank you for your insights and encouragement.

I'd like to thank the people of Sunnyside for telling me about their neighborhood—the realtors who shared information about Sunnyside Garden's history, taxi drivers who gave me late-night tours and history lessons, shop owners and restaurateurs and teachers who answered my many questions. And to the city around Sunnyside—New York. My first home away from home.

I am fortunate to have the best friends—kind, smart, generous, and so supportive. I love you all, and wish we lived in the same city. To Gloria for happily roaming and researching all the boroughs in New York with me, and Brianna for giving me advice much better than Wendy's. To Jess for cheering me on and insisting that 2020—the year this book sold—was my year. To my beloved family: my dear Sissy, Lisa, always in my corner, and Stu—I write at the desk you built me. To Marc, Gabriel, Grace, and Martine—your support means so much. To Anya, thank you for answering all my architecture questions, and to Eric, for all the conversations about writing. To Toma, just because. To Olina and Kayla, who are full of love. To Matt, Alex, Jenny, and Margaret—too far, yet always close. And to my dear parents, Leonie and

Denny, who share my love of stories and books, and my obsession with real estate—thank you for everything.

Finally, to Jeff and Grady—a wise woman knows when she has hit the jackpot, and I did that with the two of you—all my love.

About the Author

After two decades of working as an actor, **GINA SORELL** returned to her first love—writing. A graduate with distinction of the UCLA Extension Writers' Program, she is the author of *Mothers and Other Strangers* and balances the solitary hours of fiction writing with work as a creative director and brand storyteller. Originally from Johannesburg, Gina has lived in New York and Los Angeles, and now lives in Toronto with her family.

HARPER LARGE PRINT

We hope you enjoyed reading
our new, comfortable print size and found it
an experience you would like to repeat.

Well – you're in luck!

Harper Large Print offers the finest in
fiction and nonfiction books in this same larger
print size and paperback format. Light and easy to read,
Harper Large Print paperbacks are for the book lovers
who want to see what they are reading without strain.

For a full listing of titles and
new releases to come, please visit our website:
www.hc.com

HARPER LARGE PRINT